To my beloved son.
Even when the darkest times are upon us,
we must never lose hope.

Prologue

Internet and satellite communications were the first to be eliminated.

By the time the mind-fog of social media cleared, it was too late. The government had grown tired of looting and rioting, so they figured out a way to give the people what they screamed for most- equality. But, instead of citizens being afforded the same freedoms and opportunities, the government over-corrected, stripping the masses of basic rights to help maintain order and fairness.

By the year 2032, after several quarantines, the government became adept at manipulating the population. The country's name changed from America to Quadra. Splitting the country into four quadrants made the newly enforced borders easier to monitor, the citizens less difficult to control.

A travel ban followed. Grounding planes and recalling all leased or partially-paid vehicles helped the cause. When gas and oil companies came under government control, fuel could not be obtained- rendering most remaining transportation useless. Sailboats traversed coastlines. They were identified as illegal contraband and sunk in harbors.

Because everyone could not be afforded the same education, schools closed. A less intelligent population is not as challenging to master.

All registered gun-owners had to turn in their weapons before they became eligible for food provisions. Businesses considered non-essential were boarded up, while essential businesses operated strictly under government control.

Every week, the same $50 salary was deposited in a citizen's account. It served as a means to purchase Quadra merchandise or services.

Money was no longer of vast importance. Housing, food, and medical care were now available for free.

All choices were made by Quadra, for the good of the people.

Quadra doled out food based on calorie requirements so no citizen carried extra pounds. Only the bravest citizens made doctor appointments because if a malady was deemed too costly, a person would be marked for euthanasia.

History of any kind became outlawed. Quadra began their own narrative, free from wars and conflict, while bolstering the reputation of their caring, new organization. It guaranteed that all people start off with the same, shared past.

Quadra planned to suffocate all historical truth before 2032.

However, many government intellectuals believed that history could repeat itself if not understood and agreed that, for the time being, they needed to keep a referential link to the past.

A secretive library was built in each Quadrant at an undisclosed location. But, in the event that these libraries could be destroyed, the P.O.L. (Public Opinion League) searched for human historians to work for their cause, counseling government officials. Any coveted historians not willing to bow to Quadra's power were eliminated.

As many of the Quadra historians aged, the loss of their highly regarded counsel became a concern. In 2061, Quadra tasked Dr. Shane, a master historian, to teach an in-depth history course to a group of young students. Seven children, with photographic memories, were found to complete the program.

Until the annals of history would eventually be wiped

clean by time and Quadra's efforts- Quadra secretly needed to have historical knowledge in order to move forward and build upon their own.

A six-year-old, named Jessie Moore, would become Dr. Shane's prized student. His parents had no choice in the matter.

Quadra controlled all.

Jessie not only had a memory that surpassed all the other children, but he grew to revel in historical information. World history, cultural interests, war chronicles, political records…nothing escaped Jessie's thirst for knowledge.

As the children grew, some dropped out of the program, which meant the remaining students were increasingly valuable to the P.O.L. Jessie learned hand-to-hand combat to protect the P.O.L.'s investment. By his sixteenth birthday, he was being pitted against men twice his size, easily defeating them.

Jessie wanted no other life. His memory housed pictures and moments with his parents, but they seemed like strangers. Dr. Shane took on the role of both mother and father, teaching him lessons, prioritizing their importance and scheduling Jessie's days.

On the eve of Jessie's eighteenth birthday, he was startled awake by Dr. Shane.

"Listen to me," Dr. Shane insisted. "You go to the northern exit, near the field and get in the transit that's waiting for you. Run faster than you ever have." He gave Jessie an injection in his arm. "Go!"

Jessie's trust for Dr. Shane was absolute and he did what he was told. His heart pounded faster than ever before as he raced toward the exit. He burst through the doors of the place he had called home for the last twelve years and saw that the outside lights were dark. He could hear nothing except his heartbeat.

The transit's lights were visible and the driver stood by the rear of the van, a space usually reserved for cargo. Jessie followed the hand signals of the driver and fell onto the mattress that lay in the back. Before the vehicle started moving, he passed out from Dr. Shane's injection.

Jessie woke up with a wicked headache in unfamiliar surroundings. He got out of bed to use the adjoining restroom, noticing the closet neatly stocked with shoes and clothing. The bathroom had a couple pictures dotting the walls and fluffy, unused, green towels at the ready. He splashed his face with cool water.

"Hello?" Jessie feebly called.

His greeting hung in the air, unanswered.

Jessie looked briefly through the small apartment. It appeared to be situated on the third floor and in the middle of a highly-populated area. He wasn't accustomed to crowds of people or the noise they generated. The clothes in the closet were all his size. A small amount of food in the kitchen would suffice until the next delivery.

He had a standard issue, 24" TV in the seating area. Leaning against the front of the TV, sat the one clue to hint that he may belong there- a piece of paper, folded, with his name on it. Jessie quickly scooped it up and read the contents.

Dearest Boy,

There is little time to explain, but you are safe now.

You will be known as Simon Handler from this day forward, an editor for a local food-labeling institution. It is where you will be posted for the remainder of your life until you age out. It's not a post indicative of your potential, but one doesn't exist that comes close to your talents.

You've been relocated to a town called Portland in the northwest quadrant.

Find a mate, try to have kids- live the best life you can.

Never speak of your time with Quadra...don't ever talk of the history you learned and forget you ever knew me. To do so would be a death sentence.

Good luck, son. Destroy this letter so it can't be found during Quadra's search month.

Dr. Shane

Simon never found a mate, but utilized the escort hubs to keep his libido in check. He followed all the other instructions Dr. Shane had given him, while becoming increasingly bitter, desperate to do something different with his life.

In 2087, at the age of 32, something different found him.

Chapter 1

Simon's life often revolved around his temper, but he couldn't remember the last time he'd been this angry. His captors removed the cloth bag that had been placed over his head, making him squint as the light invaded his vision. Simon breathed deep, while his eyes adjusted to the scene before him. He wasn't sure how long he'd been tied up. He only knew that he was pissed. Being taken against your will could do that to a person.

A man shoved a bottle of water into his mouth, while Simon attempted to choke down the contents, his mouth dry from the experience. The fluids he couldn't drink fast enough rushed down his front, pooling in the small, wooden chair beneath him and soaking through his pants.

"What's the last thing you remember?" A man asked.

Simon jerked his whole body, trying to fight against the restraints, but his wrists and ankles were strapped firmly to the chair, making an escape impossible. His eyes were now acclimated to his surroundings and he saw that he sat in the middle of a crumbling school gymnasium. Two men stood before him and all four exits were guarded by two men each. Simon felt honored these people had a correct level of fear when dealing with him, but it also summoned the uneasy feeling that they were somehow aware of his background.

The heel beat of boots echoed in the gym as a woman walked closer to the chair. Simon couldn't take his eyes off her as she sashayed toward him. She stood between the two men near the chair, wearing the uniform of a high-officer in the Public Opinion League, or P.O.L. for short.

"It's coming back to me now," Simon finally answered the man's question. He addressed the woman before him.

"Do you mean to tell me that the P.O.L. is infiltrating escort hubs? I much preferred that little red dress you wore in my apartment to this uniform." Simon looked her up and down.

"Yes, well, when we looked at your expenses, the escort hubs seemed the only consistent habit that rendered you alone," the woman said. "I'm sorry we had to bring you here like this."

"No you're not. Why am I here? What do you want?"

The woman excused the two men guarding Simon and moved closer to the chair.

"My name is Bree, officer Denton, to you."

"I don't give a rat's ass who you are. Kill me now and get it over with. I'm not doing anything for the P.O.L."

"Mr. Handler, I'm aware of your poor attitude when it comes to most social policies. However, you're the one leftover that can succeed at this mission. We've done the research."

Simon didn't like being called a leftover because most of his kind were well over sixty or dead by now. His leftover status had to do with the fact that he had pre-Quadra knowledge.

"And, besides, we've gone to all this trouble to find you…Jessie."

Hearing his real name quickened Simon's heart rate, but he stayed calm and responded, "Who's Jessie?"

Bree grinned. "We have no time for games. Dr. Shane relocated you because you were scheduled for euthanasia. The last round of personality testing during your schooling proved you were a wild card with no appreciation for rules or conformity. You were deemed a high risk to the organization. It's all in your file."

"Does my file mention my love of nature or cooking ability…how I love long walks on the beach or prefer brunettes?"

"I don't recall reading about your love for nature, but your file did notate that you are a good cook. Apparently you had a crush on the chef's daughter that was posted at the Quadra school."

Simon shook his head up and down in surrender. "So, how did you find me?" Simon asked, genuinely interested to know.

"Well, I can tell you that torturing and eventually killing the good Dr. Shane didn't help whatsoever. He wouldn't talk." Bree shrugged her shoulders. "But, you can rest assured we're a much more civilized organization now."

Simon huffed, "Clearly." Simon wondered what had come of Dr. Shane. He often thought about the good doctor over the years with fondness.

"Your name is how we found you. There are think tanks at Quadra, filled with highly intelligent posts, working on cases of treason or resistance factions. Your file came through and someone became obsessed. She worked your case for two years and got a break when experimenting with anagrams. It took quite a few attempts, but when she used Dr. L. Shane, one of the hits was S. Handler. And here we are."

"Just for fun, since we're all gathered here anyway, why don't you tell me what it is you want. That way, I can officially tell you to go to hell and we can get back to our mundane lives."

"Like I've said, we've done our research and you're the best fit for this assignment."

"Your organization has sent people in before me and they've failed. Is that what's called research now?" Simon asked, not expecting an answer. "I wouldn't be here if I wasn't a last resort or considered expendable, given my file contents. And you wouldn't have tied me up if you thought I'd go willingly."

Bree ignored his comments. Everything he said was true, but she wouldn't dignify his disrespect with a response. She'd killed men for less.

"First, I'd like you to have your hair cut, as it's out of tolerance. And you will thank me later because it's hot here." Bree ran her hand through a bit of his hair.

Simon was, by most accounts, a handsome specimen of a man and he took Bree's gesture to be flirtatious. His deep blue eyes and smile were attractive, but in a world where masculine things were discouraged, the diagonal facial scar on his left cheek was his most alluring feature.

Bree continued to circle Simon's chair like a cat. "There's a group of historical societies that have gone rogue. They've been sharing history scenarios that will affect the current P.O.L. negatively."

"You mean they've gotten ahold of some truth that contradicts your propaganda?"

To this statement, Bree's eyes squinted, giving away her anger. It played into Simon's plan perfectly because if he couldn't act on his anger, making someone else's temper flare would be a close second. One of Simon's many talents included high-level manipulation, but his training didn't serve much of a purpose in the middle of a deserted school gym.

"You, Mr. Handler, have a knowledge of history unprecedented in the world we live in today. You'd easily be able to infiltrate these museum underground groups and possibly become one of the key players. Even though the 500-mile travel rule is in effect, they are somehow able to bleed information into other areas...even other quadrants."

She wasn't wrong. Simon could easily identify artifacts

or anything outside Quadra's statutes.

"Refer to my earlier, rat's ass comment." Simon glared. "Because I know so much history is exactly why I loathe the P.O.L. agenda. Do you even know why your organization is called the P.O.L.!?"

"It stands for Public Opinion League, Mr. Handler. We help citizens keep the right perspective in society."

Simon ignored her ignorance. "Over a hundred years ago, in 1975, a man named Pol Pot killed almost two million of his own people that contradicted his regime. Your department is a nod to Pol Pot himself."

"You're wrong."

"Really? What's the head of the P.O.L. called?"

"The Khmer."

Simon laughed, which Officer Denton didn't understand or appreciate.

"Let's get down to business, shall we? We couldn't find any living relatives to threaten. Money and power are not at our disposal. Other than bi-monthly orders to the escort hub, you don't have many interests. But," Bree paused to make sure she had Simon's attention, "we think we found your daughter."

Bree pulled out a small metal disk in her hand and a video illuminated above it. A girl of four or five ran in the grass, holding her mother's hand. Simon recognized the mother as one of his favorite escorts from years past. He always wondered what became of her. The little girl ran up to the camera that was filming her. The resemblance to Simon was uncanny.

A gun behind the little girl's head appeared. She continued to smile and wave at the camera, clueless to the danger. Bree spoke into her watch, telling the gunman to hold for an answer.

"What's it going to be, Simon? Will you cooperate? If you do, the little girl lives. Your daughter lives in the northeast quadrant and, right now, we're in the southeast quadrant. You have no way of leaving without our help. Freedom and a legacy seem a good deal for one small favor."

Simon knew he was making a deal with the devil. Children were a rare and precious thing. He knew the woman in the picture was an escort that serviced him regularly, but he didn't believe for a second that was his child. He wanted to save the young girl, if she was truly in danger. But, even more than that, he needed an adventure…a purpose…to once again feel like a man.

Bree spoke into her watch and informed the gunman to eliminate the target in 5 seconds.

"I'll do it," he said in a whisper, feeling defeated.

"Stand down." The gun slowly disappeared from the video and Bree pressed a button that sucked the picture back into the disk. "You've made the right choice, Mr. Handler. We'll start your briefing early tomorrow morning and touch base with you every couple of months at the museum to monitor your progress."

Bree motioned for the two men that were previously guarding the chair to return. They untied Simon to which he immediately launched into a martial arts frenzy, leaving the two men groaning on the floor. Bree put her hands up for the rest of the guards to hold their position.

"Feel better now?"

"Ya. I do," Simon said, nodding.

Bree tossed Simon the small disk. "I've left a picture of her on there. You should look at it when you need a reminder to stay the course."

"You know damn well that's not my daughter. Quadra

doesn't post fertile women in the escort hubs. They are married and practically bred with their marriage matches."

Bree shrugged, not that interested in the cover story now that she got her way. They started walking across the gymnasium.

"One thing that bothers me…" Simon said.

"What is that, Mr. Handler?"

"Well, I never did get what I paid for the other night from the escort hub. I bet there are plenty of empty rooms in this school. Maybe you'd like to join me?"

"We'll look into getting you a refund," Bree smiled. "I use the hubs myself, as they serve an important public service, but I assure you that my job isn't to sleep with men."

"You say that like being an escort isn't an important, valid occupation. I have the utmost respect for the profession. You, on the other hand, Officer Denton, have proven yourself to be quite the whore."

Chapter 2

After a restless night of sleep in an old faculty lounge, Simon reported to the designated classroom for his first and only day of briefings. There was a light breakfast buffet laid out for him and he filled the plate to overflowing, but stood there, still looking for something.

"Can I help you, Mr. Handler?" asked the guard at the door.

"Ya, I'm just looking for the coffee."

The instructor spun around, smiling. "That's one of the things I'm here to brief you on, Mr. Handler. In the southeast or SE there is no coffee. In an effort to be self-sustaining, each quadrant eats and drinks only those items grown in that quadrant."

"To my knowledge, we don't grow coffee beans in the northwest."

"No, that's true, but the northwest area had the foresight to purchase a good 50-60 years of supply before the quadrant split. They were afraid that people from that area wouldn't know what to do with themselves. The supply will soon be depleted and then you'll drink your sustainable liquid."

The instructor and the guard tried to keep their composure because the look on Simon's face was that of abject horror.

"Wh-what's our liquid going to be when the coffee runs out?"

"Apple juice," the instructor announced. "All those apples will be pressed into juice."

"You gotta be shittin' me! And what's this liquid, here…on the buffet table?" Simon asked.

"That's something called iced tea. The southeast had to

decide between that and orange juice and the South loves their tea!"

Simon poured a glass, watching the light brown beverage flow into the cup. The act didn't satisfy like when he would inhale the coffee aroma or watch the steam coming off his preferred liquid. He smelled it, but it was fairly odorless compared to his beloved cup of coffee. He sipped the cool beverage, deeming it OK, especially for the warm temperatures of the classroom.

"What does the NE and SW drink?" Simon wondered.

"Both quadrants have the base fluids of water and milk, like all the quadrants. The NE has apple juice and the SW orange juice."

"There's going to be chaos in the streets when the coffee cut-off is announced."

"Everything is under control. Now, would you like to take a seat, so we can get started?" The instructor looked at the guard. "You can wait outside. You've already heard information above your security clearance."

The instructor sat on the corner of an old desk. "So let's face it, Mr. Handler, if we were talking about history prior to the installation of Quadra, you'd be up here teaching this class. Truth is, I know nothing of our world prior to 2032. I'm here to explain a little about how Quadra came to be, the SE, your pending task and also review your co-posts at the museum."

The instructor placed a disk on the desk beside him, which illuminated pictures and videos to support the lessons he'd be teaching during the day. Simon's personal file would include that he had a rare, photographic memory. Some people learned by hearing or touching, but Simon could see something and store it away in his memory. The P.O.L. recognized that about him when he was a young boy and filed away information in his head in the event they needed it.

"Fifty-seven years ago, in 2030, the world practically shut down," the instructor started. "There was a virus that spread across the world and killed a fair amount of people. The government closed businesses, banned gatherings, stopped sporting events…in an effort to protect their people."

"It was during this virus that the government discovered the masses would listen to them if they believed it was for their own benefit. Summits were held over the next couple of years by key government officials and they came to a unanimous decision, deciding to change the country for the good of all people. It's amazing, really."

The instructor put a good spin on the story, but Simon knew that the outcome of those summits stripped people of basic rights. A snapshot of the long-forgotten Bill of Rights flashed across Simon's memory. Quadra probably still made use of the list, but only as a reference of what not to allow the citizens.

Knowing prior history made it hard for Simon to swallow everything. Problems infested America before Quadra's massive changes, but at least people *had* choices.

Government leaders had been terrible for decades before the virus, squandering opportunities to unite the country. And the government that came after the virus literally divided the country into four areas.

Simon vaguely listened; sipping on a lot of iced tea as the temperature in the room quickly rose. The air sat heavy in his lungs. Beads of sweat emerged. He began to fan himself with a plate from the buffet table. The instructor noticed his discomfort and explained humidity, so Simon would know what to expect during the warmer summer months.

He longed for the aromatic trees from Portland. How the rivers and rain made the moss smell wet, but still clean, like a freshly hung sheet on a clothesline. Simon had never experienced humidity and he felt suffocated.

It wasn't long before the guard needed to escort Simon to the bathroom to empty his bladder. Simon had read in his history sessions, when he was young, about people who escaped the "law" a hundred years ago. Alcatraz emerged from his memory…he saw Bonnie and Clyde smiling in pictures while they were on the run…the mystery of Jimmy Hoffa. His mind housed more interesting topics than what the instructor had to offer.

Once Simon returned to the classroom, the instructor asked if he had any questions. Simon shook his head and took his seat. Questions were pointless. The instructor would not veer from his assigned curriculum even if Simon asked hundreds of questions, but he tested the theory anyway.

"So, where are we right now? What was this state called?"

"I'm not sure what you mean by state, but we are in the SE quadrant, on the outskirts of a town called Baton Rouge."

A picture of the city came out of the disk. Simon remembered poring over maps in his spare time at school. Baton Rouge used to be the capitol of a state called Louisiana. He could see the map clear as day in the recesses of his memory.

The fact that the government retained the old names of cities comforted Simon because he could pull up maps in his mind. No one really knew where they were located in relation to other cities. People were allotted 500 miles a year to minimize the carbon footprint, so any maps available in larger towns only covered a 250-mile radius.

"Getting back to the lesson, Mr. Handler. All you need to know is that the virus of 2030 had people in power thinking about a quarantine being a good method to correct the wrongs of the country. In 2032, everyone was told that another virus began spreading through the country…worse than the illness from 2030- two, short years before. The country shut down for two months and that's when everything started changing for the better."

It was difficult for Simon to reconcile how the country became accustomed to the current way of life when it was vastly different from prior history.

"Quadra was split into four sections and any boundary lines other than quadrants were stripped away. The quadrants survive in a sustainable way that is good for the environment and the people."

Simon barely listened to the instructor as he spewed propaganda, still picturing the map.

"I think I'd like to visit New Orleans while I'm down here. When I was a kid, studying cities, they asked me to pick five cities I'd like to visit, if I could. The history books painted New Orleans as a pretty amazing city, rich with musical legacies and down-home cooking. It was on my list," Simon said.

"New Orleans is a LIL town now," the instructor shared.

Simon knew about LIL and GIL towns ("Love is love" and "God is love" towns). Both factions were problematic to the government so they were each given two towns per quadrant and told they could govern themselves as long as they didn't step outside Quadra's basic laws.

The idea would seem logical, but these cities were either made up of many different sexual orientations or many different religious affiliations. They both claimed acceptance and love, but were always the most troublesome cities throughout Quadra. Simon suddenly had no urge to travel there, regardless of which type of "love" town New Orleans had become.

The iced tea had once again urged Simon to the restroom. When he returned, the instructor asked him to slow down with the tea or they'd never finish his briefing this afternoon.

"The more I drink the tea, the more I like it."

"The SE is the only quadrant capable of growing sugar. You've never tasted it before in this form and the sensation can be quite addictive. There's sugar in your tea and that probably makes it appealing to you," the instructor explained.

Simon remembered the history that tied sugar to obesity and could now understand the urge to overdo.

That afternoon, Simon learned about the co-posts he'd be working with at the museum and was instructed further on the P.O.L.'s expectations. He'd travel to the museum tomorrow and attempt to find a way of infiltrating the suspected resistance group, without arousing suspicion.

Simon tended to be smug and over-confident, but he had no idea how much he was about to learn.

Chapter 3

The passenger van jostled around terribly because no road work had been done anywhere in Quadra for decades. It wasn't necessary now that hardly anyone owned transportation other than bicycles. Simon sat in the second row of the passenger van. He hated anything to do with being cooped up in a vehicle.

"So, how did you get this job as a driver?" Simon asked, trying to pass the time.

"My dad was a truck driver in '32. I was only two at the time, but got to go for driver's training when I was thirteen."

"Do you know why everyone stopped driving? There used to be so many cars on the road," Simon asked.

The driver stopped the van. "I really have to pee. It's almost a half hour to the museum, you better pee, too. C'mon, let's go together. Then we can get back on the road quicker."

Simon thought it odd that the driver would stop so abruptly and insist they go to the bathroom at the same time. But, he looked the driver over and decided he didn't present a physical threat. Another bad habit of Simon's- sizing people up…deciding whether or not he could take them.

Simon also didn't understand customs or traditions in the SE and figured men using the restroom together may be something the instructor missed in the briefing yesterday. He got out of the car slowly, making sure the driver walked ahead of him. About twenty feet from the car, the driver stopped.

"We have about five minutes before a hover gets here. My van has audio and video recording devices and once we lose contact for more than a minute, a hover will be sent," the driver explained, speaking much quicker now. "If they gave you anything, you can guarantee you're being recorded, too."

"During the staged pandemic of 2032, many people lost their jobs. The government told consumers if they were leasing a car or making payments that they could turn it in without any penalty and purchase a car after the quarantine came to an end. You know, like they were trying to be helpful."

Simon began to ask the driver a question, but the driver raised his hand to silence him. Quadra had not educated Simon about their transition to power and the disparities of history and current life fascinated him.

"It seemed all good and well except after the quarantine, there were no cars available to sell and almost all gas stations were destroyed, unless they were Quadra-run." The driver pointed to his vehicle. "That is the only kind of vehicle that's being built, maintained or driven on any road. The Ford Transit. That's it. It carries small amounts of cargo and they also make passenger models. Quadra manufactures one vehicle and only needs to repair one kind of vehicle. That's smart. It cuts down on repair shops, parts needed, etc."

"People's cars began to break down over the years and they eventually ran out of gas. Quadra wouldn't share their resources. Not much you can do then. You're stuck."

"What about Alaska? They had oil and gas," Simon asked.

"People were still talking about that place when I was young, but Alaska and Haway were cut out of Quadra," the driver said. "The government said they could live without them northern lights and pineapples, whatever that means. Quadra's fuel comes from the SW quadrant now."

"Hawaii. You pronounce it *huh-why-ee,*" Simon said.

The driver started at Simon in disbelief. "Doesn't much matter how I say it. As far as we're concerned, it doesn't exist."

Simon looked around. "What is this hover thing you're talking about?"

"You wouldn't see them in bigger cities because everything is easily recorded there. Any time you're in a more rural area, they are sent to monitor your movements and conversations. You can't miss…"

And just like that, Simon heard what sounded like a swarm of bees. The buzzing noise stopped once the hover located itself in a place to observe…about fifteen feet overhead.

"Ya, you'll see a ton of wildflowers in the fall, too," the driver improvised, looking over the field of flowers before him. "I reckon you just missed the azaleas in the spring. They're beautiful…"

The driver could have been imprisoned for the conversation they just had and Simon saw him fidget, becoming uneasy. Simon gained respect for the man in an instant, recognizing his bravery and that he trusted a stranger with this story. Simon nodded his head up and down, playing along.

"Thankfully, there aren't a lot of vehicles on the road, which keeps the flowers healthy," Simon mentioned. "We're lucky Quadra is looking out for us!"

The driver lowered his head and smirked, admiring the way Simon expertly covered over their conversation once the hover arrived. The driver started back to the van, but Simon took a piss and hoped that Bree would see the footage. He looked up toward the hover and winked.

Once they were moving toward Baton Rouge again,

Simon took the disk out of his bag that supposedly carried the picture of his daughter. He placed it on the floor of the van, guiding it under the front seat with his foot. It was the only object they had given him, but he'd leave it behind in hopes he might have unrecorded moments.

He'd never forget her face. Simon briefly entertained the thought of being a father and how that would feel, but pushed the emotions downward, knowing that picture was likely manufactured, only used for manipulation purposes.

When they pulled up to the museum, Simon couldn't believe his eyes. The building sat on a small bluff, overlooking the Mississippi River and resembled a castle, like he'd seen in history books. The museum stood taller than the other buildings in the area and Simon wondered if it was breaking the Quadra law of four stories. Buildings were not allowed to be taller than that…for safety reasons and so Quadra could better control the population.

He had seen pictures in his history books of skyscrapers, but that was no longer a reality or even a word used in the Quadra language. Just more information that Simon knew, but others would describe as fictional tales.

He got out of the van, thanking the driver and immediately felt the heat beat down on him. A bird berated him with a call when he started walking around the circular path. The grounds boasted deep green hues, trees of varying species and a perfect lawn. A breeze lifted the greenery smells up to Simon's senses.

He walked up a few steps, stopping on the landing to look back at the river because it was so different than the Willamette River he knew in Portland. He heard of a Columbia River north of where he lived, but had never traveled there. The river he looked upon now, took its time, earning his respect by the mere enormity.

Simon turned to open the heavy, glass and wood doors so he could enter the museum. The huge cast-iron spiral staircase and the pillars in the lobby were like nothing Simon had ever seen in person, but reminded him of grand stairways in foreign castles. The architecture took his breath away.

To his left, he heard a throat clear. A large, wooden desk made Farrow look much smaller. Simon had studied the dossiers of his co-posts at the museum and it surprised him that only four people were needed to run such a large place. Farrow was the manager of the museum, scheduling tours, overseeing the other two posts and handling special events.

From all accounts, no one had anything nice to say about him except that he took great pride in his post and devoted his life to the museum. He was six feet tall, just a few inches shorter than Simon. Simon pretended not to know who he was speaking to, but recognized Farrow from his pictures.

"Hi, I'm Simon. I'm here to train for the post that's opening. Can you direct me to the manager?"

Farrow came around the desk with his glasses perched in a way where he could look over them in disdain, which is exactly what he did.

"I'm Farrow, young man. We've been expecting a new post. Nice to meet you, Mr. Handler." Farrow extended his hand.

Simon learned in his briefing yesterday that this was called a handshake. The SE was the only quadrant that still used the archaic greeting, as it had been identified as a germ-spread. Simon grabbed Farrow's hand, gripping it, while moving it slowly up and down. He decided the SE was like a different country, not just a different quadrant.

"The facility opens in an hour, so let's get you set up in

your room. Follow me."

As Simon passed by the stairway, he looked up, spying a small portion of a colorful, glass ceiling. He couldn't fathom why a person would make a roof out of glass, but strived to see every last drop…until he bumped into Farrow.

"You're going to have to be more alert if you plan on working here, young man."

Farrow's dossier recorded his age as forty-five, which wouldn't seem to give him license to keep calling Simon, or anyone else, "young." In the south, being older earned a person respect, which would take Simon time to get used to. Youth was king in the NW and, at thirty-two, Simon commonly had the adjective "old" attached to his description.

A velvet rope separated the main foyer with a hallway to the right of the entrance. Farrow unlinked a side to escort Simon through.

"Museum guests are not allowed to be in this hallway. As you can see," Farrow pointed, "there are cameras set up around the museum. This hallway is where the posts live and it includes a gym and kitchen. Each room is outfitted with a private full bath. If you wish to have a private guest, they are allowed, but I will need to be made aware of any incoming guests twenty-four hours in advance."

"So, when I call the escort hub?"

"No problem. Just record the name of the visitor and give the proper notice. You understand the responsibilities and expectations of this post?"

"Yes, I'll perform guided tours and cook because the woman who does that now will be getting married soon."

"Cook?" Farrow said, amused. It was the first smile Simon had seen cross Farrow's lips. "We're lucky if she can make a sandwich. Ordering pre-made meals has kept us alive for the last couple of years. Had we depended on her for sustenance, I dare say, we'd be skeletal."

Farrow shook his head, still tickled by Simon's comment, as he unlocked the second room on the left. He handed a set of keys to Simon. "Welcome home. I'll allow you to get settled. We'll meet at the desk promptly at 10:30 for a quick meeting before the museum opens."

Chapter 4

Simon left his room to attend the meeting a little early, wanting to check out the glass ceiling. He stood by the staircase and controlled the urge to climb up the stairs so he could see the parts of the ceiling that were obstructed from his view. He was sure that Farrow wouldn't approve of him flitting around the museum, without first getting a proper introduction to the place.

The building had a slight musty smell, but Simon breathed in the scents of wood, metal and history. The air conditioner couldn't keep up with the expanse of the building and the temperature hovered close to eighty degrees, but it was an improvement to the higher temperatures and humidity that loomed outside.

"It still takes my breath away," a female voice sounded behind him.

Startled, Simon turned quickly, accidentally knocking the woman to the ground. She landed on her butt and broke part of her fall with her hands behind her. She whimpered in pain and was able to get up with Simon's help. Simon recognized her as April, from her pictures.

"I apologize," Simon said.

"Well, I don't think that's going to be good enough. You're going to have to walk me to the clinic after our shift. I think it's broken."

Simon couldn't believe a small fall had broken a bone, but when April uncovered her tiny, injured wrist, it had already started to swell and discolor. Just as she had come out of nowhere, so did a punch that landed square on Simon's jaw. He fell to the stairs and sprung up, ready to defend himself.

"Stop it, Cass!" April took a step between the two men. "It was an accident. I should have made my presence known. I startled 'im, that's all."

Farrow had arrived at the desk. April pulled her sleeve over the swollen wrist and made her way toward the meeting place. Cass looked at Simon like he would be content to finish him right there and then bury him out back. They slowly congregated around the welcome desk.

"So, I'm glad you've all met our newest addition. You can all get acquainted later," Farrow suggested.

Simon could feel a little trickle of blood run down his chin and he reached up to find it coming from a swollen lip. April held her wrist gingerly while Cass stared at Simon. Simon stood there, realizing he hadn't kicked off this assignment very well, but he never claimed to be the king of first impressions.

"We have only one tour scheduled when we open and another one at 3pm," Farrow announced. "April, you show Simon, here, the ropes. Because it's quiet today, most of his training can be completed. And Cass, you keep working on setting up the house chamber for the Farewell Ceremony next week because it won't be long before we'll need it for April's wedding."

Cass shook his head up and down. He was a huge, hot-headed, country boy and had a temper that could rival Simon's. His dossier didn't have much in it because he was a new post to the museum. The last maintenance man had aged out a couple of weeks ago. Simon decided that if sports were still around, Cass would have played football.

Farrow blinked and widened his large brown eyes, wondering why no one had moved. He then shooed everyone away. Cass sneered at Simon before he went up the stairs to begin his chores.

"Let's get an ice pack on that wrist before the first tour comes in," Simon suggested to April. "Do you know where we can find one?"

"There's a first aid kit in the kitchen. We should get one for your lip, too."

"Don't worry about me, I'm fine."

"I've known Cass long enough to know he can throw a mean punch. Are you sure you don't want something for your lip?"

Simon shrugged even though the side of his face, where Cass landed the punch, throbbed in pain. They walked to the kitchen, which was across the hall from their rooms.

"I'll be fine," Simon reassured her. He found her concern to be sweetly genuine.

April was able to fit an ice pack under her sleeve so Simon wrapped an elastic bandage around it to keep it in place. She wouldn't be able to get anything for the pain until she went to the clinic.

The first tour had arrived and was out in the foyer when they returned.

"Good morning, ladies and gentlemen," April started. "This is the beautiful Baton Rouge museum. My name is April and I'm so glad you decided to join us here today. If you need to use a restroom during the tour, there is one to the right of the entrance, as you came in. It's the only one available for public use."

Simon side-stepped his way into the back of the group to take the tour himself, deciding the experience would be a good way to learn the ins and outs. It didn't take him long to realize that all museums must use the same script and exhibits. Quadra had made sure of it. The tour mostly consisted of P.O.L. propaganda, so questions were rarely asked because the law of the land dare not be challenged.

The tour bored Simon, but the building dripped of grandeur and he could envision southern dignitaries from the past having conversations in the hall or conducting business in the rooms they visited. He also noticed April's smile and how it lit up her entire face. His eyes ran across her figure until Simon remembered he should call the escort service as soon as possible. Wandering eyes were a sure sign he needed an appointment.

"And this is the year that Quadra decided that everyone would have only one or two-syllable names and no longer have a middle name. It cut down on time and money. Quadra is always thinking of ways to improve our lives," April said, as she went along the timeline in the downstairs room.

"What did names sound like when there were more syllables?"

A boy of no more thirteen asked the question. His parent's eyes opened wide with embarrassment. Simon admired the child's curiosity and peered at April, waiting for an answer. She fumbled, not sure what to say. Beads of sweat formed on her forehead, likely from the pain in her arm. Questions were not encouraged during tours and contemplating, wondering and free-thinking anywhere in Quadra was forbidden- especially out in public. The others looked upon the parents with deep disapproval.

"It was quite common for people to have more than two syllable names," Simon spoke up in an attempt to alleviate the tension and rescue April from her awkward state of paralysis. He only knew names with historical significance.

"Benjamin, Elizabeth, Jonathan, Cleopatra, Alexander, Christopher, Abraham…" Simon listed.

The boy smiled as Simon spoke the names. Simon watched the others in the group and made two of them out to be potential snitches. Others seemed dangerously intrigued by the additional information.

"OK, well," April interrupted. "Let's go to the majestic stairway out in the foyer and up to the second floor. Don't forget to look up and view the breath-taking stained-glass ceiling, but hold tight onto the railing."

Everyone followed April's instructions. Simon went on the stairs after April and shamelessly stared at her backside until he caught Cass's death-stare over the second-floor railing. Simon averted his eyes to the ceiling, pretending not to have noticed Cass's glare or April's behind.

The only part of the tour that contained uniqueness was the small part about the city where the museum was located. That information also needed to be approved my Quadra.

"This building is different from most museums as it used to be called the 'Old Capitol' and hadn't been a museum for long, before Quadra came into being," April shared. "Baton Rouge was an important city."

"What made it important?" The curiosity of the young teenager would not be quenched. "And do you know why it's named Baton Rouge? That's a weird name."

April smiled. "A lot of important men came to this building to work and serve the public, just like Quadra representatives work for us now."

"What's the name mean?" He persisted.

"Baton Rouge means 'red stick' in French," Simon said. "When French settlers arrived in this area, they saw long sticks placed in the ground with red on the tips. That's how many of the Indian tribes would mark their territory. These sticks could have been either boundary lines or designated hunting grounds."

"What's French?"

"It's another language spoken in a country besides this one. Kids your age used to learn different languages when schools were still around. We only speak English now that Quadra replaced America, but there are hundreds of other languages in the world."

"America?"

"Oh, I'm sorry. That's what this country used to be called," Simon explained. "The United States of America. You'd think it would have been called Columbus- because in 1492 he sailed the ocean blue and all that. He's credited with discovering these lands, which is odd because there were already people here." Simon rattled on while the boy looked on in amazement.

"But, no. It was named after Amerigo Vespucci, who drew a lot of the maps of the new world and once he started putting his name on the maps, the name just stuck. America used to be made up of fifty states and Baton Rouge was the capitol of a state called Louisiana. And if this is called the old capitol building…"

A very loud "ahem" sounded behind Simon, making him jump and ending the chat with the boy. Simon hadn't realized that a crowd had formed around them. Simon turned to find Farrow with raised eyebrows and anger in his eyes.

Farrow quickly regained his composure and apologized to the group for Simon's behavior. "I have all your names on a list and you're welcome to come back for a free tour. I don't think we need to punish this man. It's his first day and he obviously doesn't know what he's doing. Perhaps he's stricken by the heat."

The guests mumbled things like "fairy tales, myths, ridiculous, insane," as they left. But the young boy couldn't stop smiling. He looked back at Simon as he descended the stairs and waved goodbye. Simon put himself in danger talking about unapproved historical facts, but he also knew he sparked a young man's imagination. He decided sharing his love for history was worth the risk.

Farrow's expression hardened once the last of the guests left. He pushed his glasses all the way up the bridge of his nose with a single index finger, staring into Simon's eyes.

"Please take April to the clinic now, between tours. And if you ever babble on like that again, you will be reported to the P.O.L.," Farrow said, barely moving his lips.

Cass found the scolding entertaining and returned to his chores. April took Simon by his arm and led him down the stairs.

Little did Farrow know, the P.O.L. had sent him here.

Chapter 5

When April and Simon exited the back door of the museum, the humidity made Simon sweat after only a few steps. The sidewalks were not well maintained as they had large cracks and weeds growing through the cement. He noticed that buildings had been demolished to a height of four stories, but mostly stood in disrepair.

They arrived at the clinic in five minutes because it was located only two blocks away. They didn't pass or see one person on the way and he wasn't surprised, given the sun beating down on them.

They were relieved that no patients waited for treatment in the clinic when they entered.

"Hi Jen," April said to the receptionist.

"Hi April, the scanner at the door said your blood pressure is high, what's going on?"

"I hurt my arm and I think the pain is likely elevating my pressure," April answered.

"Who is this handsome young man you're running around with? Does your future husband know about this?"

"Jen, this is Simon. Simon, this is Jen. Jen has been posted here with Dr. Michon for a very long time and she knows everyone and everything for miles."

Jen got up from her chair and shook Simon's hand. He decided he'd never get used to the odd physicality of the handshake.

"Nice to meet you, Simon," Jen said. "Let me get you situated in exam room 3." Simon started to take a seat in the waiting area. "You too, Simon. I don't know how long you'll have to wait for April and she can always kick you out if the doctor needs to discuss anything of a personal nature."

Simon heeded the suggestion, following them to the exam room. "Take this for the pain, you poor thing." Jen handed April a small pill that quickly dissolved in April's mouth and relieved the pain almost instantaneously.

"Better already, thank you," April said and smiled.

Jen left the room as Simon studied April's smile, recognizing its honesty. He looked away when April caught him staring.

"So, tell me something about yourself," April said. "I mean other than the things I already know, like your hobbies of throwing women to the ground and spouting nonsense in museums."

Simon smiled, finding himself amused by her banter. "I'm a history buff," he admitted. "Much of my spouting is true."

Simon had grown used to people not believing even the smallest bits of truth. He imagined April would be no different.

"You sound just like my grandfather." She rolled her eyes. "I love him, but he's a leftover and sometimes wants life to go back to the way it used to be, instead of accepting life as it is now."

Simon found this conversation might be a good way to help identify if April was involved in a museum underground ring. "And what do you think? How does Quadra measure up to the ways of the past?"

April shrugged. "I don't really know anything about the past. Besides, don't turn this on me. I asked you to tell me something about yourself. Why did you decide to go the way of the escort hub vs. marriage?"

Simon found the question quite personal and couldn't remember anyone asking him that before.

"Twenty-five years is a long time to be married to

someone and we only have two choices. Either get married to a woman the computer matches you up to for at least twenty-five years or retain escort privileges for 15 years," Simon said.

April looked at Simon with her eyebrows raised. "Yes, I know how our system works and thank you for so astutely avoiding the question yet again. How 'bout you try to manage an answer."

The door cracked open and the doctor joined the two of them in the exam room. Simon felt a sigh of relief. He wasn't used to thinking very deeply about choices he's made or being peppered with questions. No relational requirements or tedious conversation could be the very reason he opted for the escort hub.

"How is our famous resident doing today?" The doctor asked. He spoke slowly and had a heavy accent.

"My wing is injured, Dr. Michon, will I live?"

The doctor lifted her wrist and examined the discoloration. He poked and prodded the area, until April winced.

"It's a sprain, but you should begin healing quickly. I'm going to give you a brace that I want you to wear for the next two weeks before the wedding." He stared at April, waiting for her to acknowledge his instructions. She reluctantly nodded. It came as no surprise to Simon that April was a stubborn patient. "The pain medicine that Jen gave you should last a week. You won't need any more after that."

"Hello, I'm Dr. Michon," he said to Simon, extending his hand for the ritual touching.

"My name is Simon, I'll soon be an official post at the museum."

"Well, take care of this lucky woman because she is getting ready to marry an extremely powerful man!"

"I know. Cass punched me earlier. He's powerful, indeed!"

April and Dr. Michon exchanged a glance, smiled at each other and tried not to laugh. Dr. Michon said he needed to go get a brace and he'd be right back. Once the door shut behind him, his laughter could not be contained.

"What's so funny?"

"Cass is my brother."

Simon blushed a bit, not remembering the last time his cheeks tingled from embarrassment. The doctor returned in short order and fitted a piece of small, clear, plastic tubing over April's wrist. He rubbed the tubing with a damp cloth and it shrunk to fit, holding her wrist in place.

"Try not to get it wet again for two weeks, so your wrist can properly heal. I'll take it off right before the wedding. And thanks again for the invitation. It will be the event of a lifetime." Dr. Michon exited the room.

"Well, we should get back for our next tour," April said. When she hopped off the exam table, she wobbled, falling into Simon's chest. She righted herself. "I'm sorry, Simon, the pain medicine can make you feel a little drunk at first. It'll get better."

Simon became worried for April's safety. He imagined her stumbling throughout the museum, especially worried about the stairs. Simon was not acquainted with feeling much concern for other people, but this foreign feeling became a priority.

"I'm going to call a transit to take us back to the museum," Simon decided.

"No, you're not. We're not wasting our miles on such foolishness! I may need to lean on you a little when we walk back. Surely, you will allow me this small favor since you're responsible for my predicament."

Simon nodded, noticing how she slurred her admonition.

After struggling to make it one block, April demanded to rest on a grassy slope. Simon could see the museum within reach, but sat down beside her. She leaned all her body weight on Simon and momentarily fell asleep.

Simon sat in silent discomfort and at a loss as to what his next move should be. He could easily carry her the one block. Something needed to be done soon because a group would be at the museum for the next tour. He peered down and his chin touched the top of her head, the dark brown hair tickling his nose.

"Put her in here," a voice came from behind them, making Simon jump.

Simon could only turn slightly, afraid to send April rolling down the side of the bluff. He struggled to hold onto her and twist around. A man stood by a wheelbarrow and Simon recognized him as the groundskeeper on post at the museum. Simon held onto April as he slowly raised her to a standing position.

Earl had a blanket in the wheelbarrow to protect the passenger from the dirt and grime. April stirred and Simon explained the plan, but she didn't want to get in the wheelbarrow, so Simon lifted her up and placed her in it anyway.

"Would you have just given her to anyone walking by?" Earl asked.

"I figured you were Earl, the groundskeeper at the museum. April was talking about you earlier."

"No I wasn't," April protested.

Simon patted the top of her head and told April the pain medicine had made her forget. Earl hoisted up the wheelbarrow and traveled carefully down the road. The dossier listed his age as fifty-four, but he seemed much younger. Earl stopped the wheelbarrow on the side entrance of where the rooms were located. He made like he planned to pick April up.

"Oh, no. Let me do that," Simon said. "Could you hold the door open for me?"

Earl used a key to open the side door while Simon lifted April out of the wheelbarrow and she yelled "whee" like a child. Her room was unlocked and Simon finessed the door open while still holding her.

"Impressive work, Simon," April said between bouts of unconsciousness. "My room is right there!"

Simon got April to her bed and laid her down. The temps were high, so Simon decided to leave her uncovered. He took her shoes off so they wouldn't get the bedding dirty. The small carafe on the bedside table was empty, so he went to the kitchen and filled it with water, grabbing a glass before returning to her room.

He poured some water in the glass. "Sit up, April, and take a little sip of water. I'll handle the next tour and begin dinner after that. You rest."

April followed his instructions and discovered she was parched. She drank a good portion of the water and offered some to Simon. Simon noticed that she watched him drink and as soon as the glass dropped from his lips, she leaned in and kissed him.

The kiss was so gentle that Simon scarcely understood what was happening. When their lips parted, they both looked at each other. April stroked Simon's cheek and touched his lips with hers once more. He wrapped an arm around her, caressing her back. When she let the slightest moan escape her body, Simon pulled her closer and kissed her like he had never kissed anyone. Without warning, in the middle of the kiss, April flopped back onto the bed, turning away from Simon.

His head whirled, trying to understand the situation. He had no clue what to do next, so he slowly got up and went to his room. The scheduled tour would be at the front desk in minutes and Simon needed to change his shirt. The walk back from the doctor's office had left him a sweaty mess.

Simon walked into the foyer of the museum, where Farrow had come out of the front office in anticipation of the group's arrival. He needed to make sure they all had the proper paperwork for entry.

"I'd like to give you notice that I'm ordering an escort tomorrow night, so there will be a visitor."

"I will note that in my log. Where's April?" Farrow asked.

"She's doped up on some medicine the nurse gave her for her wrist. She wasn't able to walk back, so she's in her room resting."

"I'll need to supervise your performance this afternoon. There better be none of that tomfoolery from the previous tour."

Chapter 6

The tour went off without a hitch, which meant Simon was terribly bored and, Farrow, on the other hand, had renewed confidence that Simon would fit in perfectly at his new post.

After the guests were thanked for coming and on their merry way, Simon told Farrow that he would start preparing dinner after a quick shower. He decided not to wake April even though she was supposed to be training him. The events of the day confused Simon and Farrow said she couldn't cook- so why bother. He didn't want to make a wrong move with April…so his plan was to not make any moves. He was thirty-two and far too old to now begin what he perceived as the arduous task of understanding women.

Simon threw both shirts into the hamper. The scent of April hung on the one shirt and wisps of her invaded his senses. He brought the shirt up to his nose and decided April's parents must have chosen her name because she smelled like spring…a new beginning. He quickly threw the shirts in the hamper after his musing and chalked his delirium up to the heat.

In the kitchen, Simon rummaged through the refrigerator and cupboards. He didn't know what the SE had to offer in the way of ingredients, but, to his surprise, the museum was well-stocked. Some of the foods were going bad from lack of use and he threw those out.

He took the fresh chicken out of the refrigerator. He found olive oil, which made him happy, as he wasn't sure olives grew in this quadrant. A small bag of pine nuts spurred his creativity and Simon went out onto the grounds where he had spotted a small herb garden. He leaned down to smell the basil he sought and plucked quite a bit of it off the small bushes.

"Whatcha doin'?" Earl asked.

"I'm gathering ingredients for dinner."

"Well, I'll be. You cook, do you? Come around over here."

Earl guided Simon past the large landscaping shed to a quaint garden that shone in the sunlight. "I was jus' getting' ready to water it, but hep' yaself."

Simon gathered a couple tomatoes and couldn't believe they were already mature, being so early in the summer months. He bent down, unearthing some garlic. He wouldn't have time to dry it out, but it would be great for flavoring.

"Hey, that elephant garlic is a natural pesticide. I plant it to keep the bugs away. You can't eat garlic!"

"What? That's not true. It's delicious *and* good for you. Where I come from, people eat it for health benefits."

Earl furrowed his bushy eyebrows and shook his head at the notion, while he put a wet cloth on the back of his neck. His skin was tanned and rough-looking from years out in the sun. Simon thanked Earl for his produce, telling him to come to dinner at six and then he retreated back to the kitchen with his bounty.

Simon immediately got to work, butchering the chicken and getting it in the oven to bake. He placed the pine nuts, basil and olive oil in a blender to start the pesto sauce. They must not have parmesan cheese in the SE, Simon thought, but there was a firm cheese in the fridge that would suffice. He added some to the pesto, along with garlic, salt and pepper. Ideally, the garlic would be dried, but he would leave most of the head out to dry for the next few days.

He cut a fresh, round loaf of bread in half, rubbing the garlic all over it before applying butter. The tomatoes were sliced and plated. Simon looked for something specific to dress the tomatoes with, but couldn't find it. He blended a bit of garlic, olive oil and salt for a light dressing.

Half way through its baking time, Simon added the pesto sauce to the chicken. He retrieved dishes and utensils to set the lone, long table in the vast room. The whole kitchen was against a wall, to the right of the entrance. A large countertop was a few feet off the kitchen area. After that, the room was filled with a large table and floor-to-ceiling windows with a view of the grounds.

Simon put the bread in another oven to brown the top and prepared to gather the other posts, but the aroma from the kitchen made them trickle in shortly before serving time. Earl arrived very punctually at 6 pm. April offered to help. When Simon looked at her, he held back laughter at all the lines that were deeply creasing her face from her nap. He thought, with relief, that she probably wouldn't remember the events from earlier.

"I do need to know where the trivets are," Simon asked April.

She squinted a little. "What's a trivet?"

"You know those things you put under hot dishes or pans so it doesn't burn the table."

"We use metal or tile for tabletops so they can withstand heat. We do have things called potholders to move hot dishes. Do you know what those are?" She looked at him with a bit of disbelief.

"Yes, thanks. I don't need any."

Simon decided that making tables in heat-proof materials was a brilliant idea and wondered why the NW didn't do that. Slightly embarrassed, he started taking the food to the table. He had put the chicken on a large white platter so the green of the pesto would be pronounced. The sliced bread lay in a bowl and the tomato salad was also on a platter.

Farrow's eyes grew wide with interest and questioned about the green sauce. "We don't get much spinach around here. Is that what's in the green sauce?"

"No, sir. That's basil."

Cass had already started to load his plate up with food.

"Just tell me what all has the pesticide in 'em, I can always make a sammich," Earl asked.

"You put pesticide in the food?!" April shrieked.

"No, no. Earl uses it as a natural way to keep the bugs at bay in the garden, but garlic is a great flavor enhancer and it's really good for you."

Earl tilted his head downward, raising a furry eyebrow in Simon's direction, still waiting for an answer to his question.

"The bread, Earl…I rubbed some on the bread."

Everyone began to dine on the meal. Simon received rave reviews and even Cass seemed pleased with his dinner.

Cass started talking with his mouth full. "This is really good. You mixed up ingredients. We usually just eat ingredients." He smiled, revealing pesto bits in his teeth, but somehow continued to shovel in more chicken. "Can you make other stuff taste good?"

"I think so."

Cass nodded his head up and down. Earl ate everything offered to him, except the bread. Farrow ate his meal like a gentleman and looked on in horror at Cass's table manners.

"You know, I'd say you should teach April how to cook, but I imagine she'll have servant posts to help her around the house," Farrow said. "Once she's married to the chancellor's son…"

Simon almost spit out his food upon hearing Farrow's

statement. Ever since the country was divided into four parts, a monarchy has ruled in each quadrant, alongside Quadra. They were chosen from the richest families before the government took over. The chancellors were allowed to maintain their wealth in turn for pledging their allegiance and money to helping rule their quadrant. Simon now understood everyone's excitement about her pending nuptials.

"What do you know about the monarchy in the SE? Are they good people?" Simon asked April.

She shrugged. "I'm not sure because I haven't met any of them. I went in for an interview and answered a bunch of questions. A messenger showed up a week later and let me know I had been selected. So, now I'm to be married. Do you know anything about your monarchy?"

"Only that there were three or four families in the running, but since the other men became wealthy from computer-related things, and computers would no longer exist, they chose someone named Knight and that family has ruled ever since."

"What's your favorite kind of fish?" Cass asked, apparently bored with the conversation in progress.

"Salmon…without a doubt!"

Everyone at the table looked around at each other, having never heard of such a fish.

"Please tell me you have salmon here," Simon said. "It's a fish with an orange or pinkish flesh."

"Never heard of it," Cass replied, tomato juice dribbling down the corner of his mouth. "How about catfish?"

"Yes, we have those where I come from…Do you have trout?"

Everyone shook their head up and down.

"What does the monarchy do in your quadrant?" April

asked.

Simon shrugged. “They mostly attend functions or court trials. They get invited to weddings and town ceremonies, but their visits with people during the search months were vital to keeping everyone calm. People look up to them for no other reason than their titles.”

“Interesting,” Farrow said.

“So, I was looking for mustard to make a dressing for the tomatoes, have you ever heard of that condiment? It’s mostly mustard seeds and vinegar. It’s delicious.”

“What a funny word, mustard,” April mused. “It doesn’t sound very appetizing. What did you put in the dressing? It’s quite yummy.”

“Olive oil, salt and pepper…a little garlic.” Earl stopped wiping his mouth with his napkin and glared at Simon from across the table. Simon smiled and kept Earl’s gaze. “Actually garlic is in the pesto sauce, too. It’s in everything I made tonight.”

Earl stood, making Simon flinch a little. He threw his napkin on the table. “Much obliged for supper. Everything was tasty.” Earl looked down at the bowl that held the garlic bread then looked back up at Simon. He snatched a piece of bread out of the bowl and left for the grounds.

“You best not play with Earl. He’s a good man, but not one I’d toy with,” Farrow advised.

“You keep cooking like this and we’ll get along just fine,” Cass said, finally with an empty mouth. Once Cass cleared the doorway to the kitchen, his belch echoed in the hallway.

Farrow started grabbing plates and serving dishes, but April insisted she would take care of it. Farrow informed her that he’d be in his office, attending to museum business if he was needed.

"After this is all taken care of, would you join me outside?" April asked Simon. "You can see your first SE sunset."

Chapter 7

April and Simon went out on the grounds to a little bench that had a great view of the river. Between the excitement from earlier today and the prospect of a sunset, Simon became nervous. Beads of sweat formed on his forehead.

"Are you OK?" April asked.

"The night is coming and it's still so hot out! Does it get cooler when the sun goes down?"

"Not really. I mean, sometimes, but the humidity keeps the temperatures high."

"We have humidity in Portland, but not in the summer months." They sat for a time and Simon asked, "Are you excited for the wedding?"

April looked out over the river and then back at Simon.

"You ask too many questions and don't answer near enough. I get that you may be curious and new to the area, but how 'bout we do this. I'll answer any question you ask after you answer just one of mine."

Simon believed he'd easily control conversations while in the SE and keep himself comfortably out of focus. Simon was often wrong.

"OK, go ahead and ask me anything," he surrendered.

"Question number one: Why did you go the way of the escort hub instead of marriage? And I'm not asking this because I'm nosy; this is obviously something that's been on my mind. Everyone around here is thrilled that I'll be marrying the chancellor's son. Everyone, except me."

Simon sighed. He couldn't give too much away about where he was and what he was going through at eighteen, but he wanted to be honest, if possible.

"I registered when I was in Portland, but didn't put too much effort in the process. It's not that I believe marriage can't work, but I knew the history…why this choice even existed. In the age of Quadra, divorce is still an option for people, but only after a 25 year commitment. A long time ago, people could get divorced after being married only a week!"

"My grandpa talked to me about that once. Can you believe people getting divorced after only a week, a month, a year? Crazy! He said people were allowed to choose their own partners, too. They didn't use the algorithm to pair up. Also something about on-line dating and catfishing...it sounded wild."

"It's true. Divorce cost the country loads of money, split up families and clogged the court system. Quadra thought this was yet another way to better society for our own good."

"You don't think so?"

Simon took a break from the conversation, sitting back on the bench. He knew if April was an operative, this conversation would send him away for treason. He looked at her, scanning her face for any deception. Her expression ached of need…the need to understand her own path and Simon decided she was just a young girl, trying to find her way.

"Her name was Haven," Simon started, "the girl I fell in love with...or, at least, I think that's what it was. We kind of grew up together. She helped her mom in a kitchen and even though I would be exhausted at the end of the day, I'd help her cook, clean…whatever. She was beautiful and a year older than me."

"When Haven registered her information and went in for the physical, she got selected for marriage immediately because she was fertile. I never told her how I felt and she moved away to a different quadrant to be married. We're taught not to acknowledge 'feelings,' but I had them for her and haven't felt that way since."

Simon lost himself in his words, embarrassed when he realized he shouldn't have shared quite so much…shouldn't have confessed emotions like he did.

April mused, "When you're in love it can't be hidden and where no love exists, it cannot be pretended. My Grandma told me that. Do you still think of her…Haven?"

Simon didn't want to admit that he did and as the conversation became too personal, he quickly changed the subject. "Where are all these birds that I hear?"

"Those are frogs, bird-voiced tree frogs, to be exact. They're just getting started- nocturnal little beasts that live mostly in the trees." The off-the-wall question wouldn't deter April. "So, do you believe that love is still a real entity, even though it's so discouraged?"

"I believe I answered my one question and, if I heard you correctly, you must now answer all the questions I pose."

Simon smiled, as though he won a major coup, and April sighed in defeat. "I suppose that is what I said."

"If you had a choice in the matter, would you choose the escort hubs over marriage?" Simon asked.

"That's the ironic part. If I wasn't fertile, I'd likely be posted *in* an escort hub. I'd be sent off to school to learn the art of pleasing a man and that would be my life for 10 years. I could get married afterward, but would anyone want me?"

"You're quite beautiful and men are simple creatures. Someone would want you."

"Maybe. But, that's why I kissed you earlier. I'm twenty-two and my life has been on hold for years! I just wanted to do something that was my choice...be a bit rebellious. I shouldn't have put you in that position, I'm sorry. I can't blame everything on the pain meds, but they did encourage me to act on the impulse."

"No need to apologize."

Simon became uncomfortable, as his mind flashed to the kiss. Guilt rose in him, thinking of how he wanted to kiss her again…to kiss her all over. That escort couldn't come soon enough. He needed to take the edge off.

"I'm going to my grandpa's in a couple days, when the museum is closed. Would you like to meet him? We'd stay overnight."

"You just said your grandpa told you about on-line dating, but all that was before Quadra. He must be over 70. Shouldn't he have aged out already?"

April moved closer to Simon and covered his mouth with her hand. She whispered in his ear that her grandpa was born in 2009 and pleaded for him not to tell anyone. Simon nodded and wondered what was with these SE people and their touching habits. Her closeness made Simon long for her that much more and it annoyed him.

Simon removed her hand from his mouth. "Are you kidding?" He said quietly. "I would love to meet your grandpa and learn more about the Quadra turnover."

April hoped he would want to spend time with her, but understood his curiosity. They were face to face as the sunset became dusk and the cliché was too much for Simon. He looked out at the river and mentioned how a sunset used to symbolize romance. April sat back, returning to her spot on the bench.

"Well, we better get inside before the mosquitos come out and eat us alive," April said.

"It's OK; we have mosquitos where I come from. I'd like to sit for a while longer."

This surprised April. She had heard of people that didn't get bit a lot, but the way Simon was sweating, she figured the mosquitos would surely maul him. She went inside, looking out the huge kitchen windows. The outer museum lights shone just enough to watch Simon on the bench.

At first, she saw the shadowy figure swat at himself a couple of times, but it didn't take long for him to flail about. In no time at all, he ran for the museum side entrance. April remembered that she had locked it- not to prove a point; it was merely force of habit.

The door had a square of glass up high and, as April made her way to the door, she saw Simon's eyes, wide, as he loudly banged on the wood portion of the door. She lowered her head, hiding her smile. She started a conversation with him through the door instead of opening it right away.

"Don't you have your keys?"

"No," Simon yelped. "They're in my room. Please open the door!"

April let Simon in as he continued to jump about, trying to rid any trace of the biting insects. He lifted his t-shirt over his head and threw the blood-dotted clothing outside. April saw the tell-tale bumps rising on his skin and continued to tamp down the laughter.

"I think they bit me through my clothes! Can they bite me through my clothes!?"

April couldn't hold it in anymore and bust out laughing. "I told you that we should come in. You assured me you had experience with mosquitos."

Simon pointed outside and started ranting about how these were completely different than the ones he knew and that they were greater in number than he'd ever seen. He started itching his chest. April put her hand on his to stop

Simon from scratching.

"Don't do that. You'll scar."

She grabbed his hand and walked him into the kitchen. She asked him to cut a garlic clove because it was hard to do that with her bum wrist. She then motioned for Simon to turn around and dabbed the garlic on the bites.

"Garlic is not the best remedy for the bites. Aloe is the best, but after that trick you played on Earl, I'm not sure he'll give you any of his."

"Well, I can't smell like garlic. I have an escort appointment tomorrow."

April finished coating the bites on his back. She handed the garlic to Simon and said, "You should be able to get the rest yourself. Goodnight."

Simon finished applying the garlic and headed for his room. He knocked on April's door, after realizing he hadn't thanked her for helping him. April was getting ready to jump in the shower and her blouse was unbuttoned. Simon averted his eyes after the door opened.

"What?!"

"I just wanted to thank you for getting my back." Simon fidgeted, uncomfortable by the thought of possibly upsetting her. "Have I done something wrong?"

"No, I'm sorry. I guess I'm a little jealous that you can phone up an escort and I can't."

"Why?" Simon said and returned his gaze to April's face. He couldn't believe her statement. "It's a Quadra right to have escort privileges."

"Maybe it's different here, but when I received my fertility results after registration, they said I would have to wait for a few influential men to age up, so *they* could choose. I suppose either I'll be marrying a younger man or one that wanted to experience escorts before marriage. There are rumors that the chancellor's family lives by a different set of rules than the ones they demand from everyone else. Either way, I've wanted to order an escort. Friends have even tried to order one for me."

"That's smart, why didn't that work?"

"When the escort arrived he told me he couldn't service me. There's some sort of pictorial training at the hub containing 'protected' men and women…not to be touched. He recognized me. The punishment was so severe for the escort that I never tried to trick the hub again. I couldn't ruin a man's life, trying to fulfill a selfish need."

"It's a need, nonetheless. I've been having a difficult time these last few weeks! I can't imagine a couple years."

"I hope my future husband understands that when I rip his clothes off his body, it's because of my deprivation and not that I'm a crazy person. Above all else, I want to be most compatible while naked. I've heard that the best marriages grow from an inability to keep your hands to yourself." She daydreamed for a second. "Well, now I need to go take a cold shower, just at the thought." April sneered at her musings and shut the door.

Simon had never heard a woman talk of wanting a man like that. Escorts just came and went, performing their duty. He wished someone would long for him, want him in the way April described. He shook away the foolish notion and escaped to his room.

He dreamt of April.

Chapter 8

Simon woke up for his second day in the SE and, upon realizing where he was, stuck a pillow over his face and screamed. He decided he'd get a cup of coffee, but remembered there was no coffee…only something called iced tea. A second scream into the pillow soon followed. The highpoint of his day would undoubtedly be the much-needed escort delivery this evening.

He walked across the hall into the kitchen to find everyone at the table, but Cass.

Earl stared at Simon. "You got a little sompin' on your face, buddy." Earl said, while gesturing all over his own face.

The whole room bust out in laughter. They were laughing long before Earl's joke because Farrow wiped tears from his eyes. Simon shot April a look- the only one who knew about the murderous bugs from last night.

"Have a sweet potato beignet," April said as she slid a plate in Simon's direction. "They are delicious with some mayhaw jelly."

"There are some boudin patties in the oven and a soufflé keeping warm," Farrow chimed in.

"You must've really made an impression on Jen. She's the one that brought all this over," Earl mentioned, as he waved his arm over all the food. "Very disappointed when we told her you weren't up yet."

"You've been good for us, Simon," Farrow said. "We've never eaten better and I can't remember when I've laughed so hard."

"I've known you for over twenty years and I never heard you laugh like that," Earl said.

"Speaking of good things, friend, happy birthday to you," Farrow raised his glass and drank. Everyone followed suit. After the age of eighteen, birthday celebrations were illegal, but Farrow wanted to make a point of recognizing Earl's special day.

A few minutes passed before Farrow rose from the table and checked his pocket watch. He let everyone know the first tour was scheduled for 9am sharp.

Farrow and Earl left the room at the same time. They were bantering with each other. One said "we have skeeters where I'm from" and the other "where are all the birds?" They laughed and split off in different directions once out in the hall.

Simon looked at April. "I did well as the entertainment for this morning?"

"You saw for yourself. You were a hit!"

She rose from her chair, shoving a beignet into Simon's mouth. He enjoyed every morsel. As a matter of fact, for not knowing what most of the breakfast consisted of, he liked everything he tried.

"What's a mayhaw?" Simon asked.

"It's not that similar to anything else. It looks like a small crab apple and grows in marshy land. They're very tart which is why a lot of people make them into jelly."

April and Simon were standing around the large countertop when Cass came in and plopped down a small alligator. Bits of swamp water flung outward and landed on everyone present. A knife was still lodged in the beasts head. Cass realized he forgot to remove it and pulled it out. The sound alone almost made Simon ill.

"What the hell is this?!" Simon asked.

"It's a gator, dumbass. Make it taste good like you did with that chicken. You know, use ingredients and such. I gotta go shower the swamp off'a me or Farrow will be displeased." Cass wiped the knife off on his pants and left as quickly as he had come.

"I've never seen anything like this before!"

"They're very common here in the swamp lands. This is a small one, but they can grow up to twelve, sometimes thirteen feet."

"How am I supposed to cook this monster?"

"Just lop off the tail and deep fry the tail meat. That's the easiest and it will make Cass happy...maybe make a fancy sauce to dip it in. Lots of folk eat gator ribs, too, but that's more work."

Simon nodded. "I can do that. Kinda like rocky mountain oysters?"

"What are those?"

"Oh, never mind, you don't want to know. I guess all the quadrants have their strange foods. What's this going to taste like?"

"Kinda like a cross between a chicken and fish. It's got a little more chew or stretch than chicken. You'll see. All in all, not bad and it's a readily available food source."

"What do I do with the rest of this, once I use the tail?"

"Give it to Earl so he can bury it in the garden for fertilizer."

***

The rest of the day flew by. Cass and everyone else were pleased with the supper of alligator, paired with an aioli dip flavored with dill and garlic. Earl provided a basketful of fresh vegetables early in the day to accompany the meal and in the basket sat a couple heads of garlic. It was Earl's way of communicating he no longer had objections to the tasty bulb being used in meals.

After dinner, Simon hoped everyone would go to their rooms or disperse after eating, but Jen had supplied so many breakfast treats, that they sat around, eating those for dessert. This unnerved Simon because the escort would be showing up soon. When the escorts came to his apartment in Portland, no one paid much attention. He didn't want anyone to see her, to know what would be happening that evening.

"Earl, did you bury the gator yet?" Simon asked.

"Nope. Gotta soon 'cause the flies are becoming in'trested."

"I'll help you. C'mon," Simon offered, in hopes of breaking up the party and scattering everyone.

Once the alligator burial had been completed, they both returned to the museum to take showers. When they entered the hallway, laughter rang out from the kitchen. Both the men ventured down the hallway, curiously poking their heads in the kitchen to investigate. A young woman sat with Farrow, April and Cass- a full plate of food and tall glass of iced tea in front of her.

"This is Cara, she's your escort for tonight," April said. "We were just telling her about your run-in with the mosquitos last night. Didn't want her to think you had an ailment because you're covered in little red bumps."

They all laughed again at Simon's expense. Simon didn't know what to do. Normally, the escort would just wait in his apartment if he needed to shower or hadn't finished dinner. These people had invited her for a meal and were enjoying conversation. The confusion paralyzed him for a second.

Farrow piped up, "Simon, go get yourself cleaned up and we'll keep your lady-friend company."

Simon took the quickest shower of his life and returned. Cara was still eating, so he joined them at the table. Earl had retired, but the rest of the posts were still there.

"Well, we have to get going," Farrow said, eyeballing Cass and April to rise from their chairs.

Farrow walked over and kissed Cara's hand, bidding her good luck this evening. Simon admired how he dripped of class and manners. Cass, before exiting, leered at Simon.

Farrow put his hand on Simon's shoulder, leaned down and whispered in his ear, "This is her first assignment. Be good to her." Farrow patted Simon's shoulder.

Simon hired escorts because it helped him remain distant. He didn't care to know fun facts or information about the escorts. Not getting personal was part of the appeal. Never had he shared a meal with an escort or worried about being good to them. And now he felt like he had a lot to live up to since the rest of the museum posts had been so kind to her.

"So, this is your first assignment, huh?" Simon asked.

Cara nodded, grinning nervously.

"Where were you trained?"

"Sir?"

"You know, when you learned how to be with a man," Simon uncomfortably asked.

Cara blushed and looked downward. "I've been shown pictures and movies, but I have yet to lay with a man, sir."

"And yet they send you out on assignment with no experience?"

"Yes, sir, they said they hadn't received a delivery request in so long that you'd probably be a good first for me…not very nice or obliging. They say it's better that the first time isn't so good. No expectations built up of being pleased and all. I've even heard of some male escorts focusing on the women's needs and not coming to climax, but that's much rarer."

Simon sat flabbergasted by her explanation. He never thought once about making sure to please an escort or even asked if she would like that.

"So you talk about your clients with each other?"

"Well, yes, we are allowed to talk about our clients among other escorts, but no one else. It's our career, after all."

"And why did they assume I wouldn't be very nice because I asked for delivery? Where I'm from, delivery is the only option."

"Don't know where you're from, but here, our escort hubs are centrally located in larger cities. The clients go there because it puts the escorts more at ease to be in their own surroundings and we are able to keep a constant level of cleanliness. The escorts are then rotated within a 500-mile radius to other cities to ensure variety."

"That's quite a good plan," Simon decided. "How old are you?"

"Eighteen, sir."

"Listen, if you're done with your meal, you can go on your way. I won't be having you tonight."

Simon could tell by her expression that she felt a bit rejected, but he decided not to be her first. The night would have gone much differently had he not been aware of her inexperience or had shared so much conversation. A pressure rested on him, knowing he'd be her first- an escort was supposed to relieve his stress, not add to it. He mused if he was anyone else's first over the years and if the escorts had spoken of him after their visits.

He saw Cara to the door and retired to his room.

Chapter 9

In the middle of the night, Simon awakened to a rustling sound, which he thought was coming from below his floor. The noise was not constant, but an intermittent and inconsistent sound that left him straining to hear for the next one. He got out of bed to look out his window, thinking that perhaps an animal might be up to mischief outside. After seeing a gator for the first time, he wondered what other beasts called the SE home.

He grabbed the flashlight and shone it outside only to be blinded by the reflection of light off the window. A muffled sound rose up from the floor behind him. He left his room, to see if he could find the source of the disturbance. Suddenly a sliver of light shone across the floor tiles, near the staircase, but disappeared just as quickly.

Simon clicked off his flashlight and now gripped it like a weapon. He moved silently down the hallway and right before he got to the corner, April rounded it quickly, running into him and dropping a bag. Before she could scream, he covered her mouth with one hand and wrapped his hand with the flashlight behind her back. She pushed him away with her good arm.

"What are you doing sneaking around the museum at night?" Simon asked in a whisper.

April picked up the bag and insisted she wasn't sneaking around.

"What's in the bag?"

"A personal item. None of your business!" She hissed.

Simon believed that he had caught an agent for the underground on just the second day. He gave April a steely gaze, nodded his head and walked past her to find the source of the light, in hopes of exposing whatever secret April was trying to hide.

She grabbed his arm as he passed. "Where do you think you're going?"

"If you're not going to be straight with me, I'll have a look around on my own."

Simon walked out into the foyer and concentrated on the three doors to the right. He opened the first, using the pull-string to the light above and discovered it to be a closet filled with extra ropes and poles for exhibits. Behind the second door, after turning on that light, he saw a small storage space that held supplies and cleaning solutions for the museum. He turned on the third closet light to find a rolling toolbox and miscellaneous items on shelves above.

"You're going to wake Farrow up and we're all going to be in trouble."

Simon took a couple steps away from all the closets and stared at all three, but he knew exactly which closet April had retrieved her personal item. This was merely a test…to see how well she did under pressure.

"It's the third door I opened. You definitely retrieved whatever's in that bag from the closet closest to the window."

Simon appreciated her calm demeanor, but noticed she became increasingly anxious when he turned off the lights and closed the doors to the first and second closets.

He started inspecting the closet with the toolbox.

"If I show you what's in the bag, will you give up this ridiculous quest?"

Simon knew this offer meant he was getting warmer, so he shook his head no, continuing the search. He moved the toolbox lengthwise in the closet and off to the right, giving him more room to explore. He tapped the floor with his foot, shining the flashlight around, hoping he could find something abnormal about the space.

A door opened down the hall. Simon motioned for April and he pulled her in the closet, turned the light off and tried his best to silently shut the door down. She put the bag on top of the toolbox.

"Hello?" Cass's voice rang out.

If they got caught in a closet together, there would be no calming Cass down and Simon would have to fight him in earnest. Cass didn't stay long and they soon heard him rifling around in the kitchen for a snack.

"How long will he be in the kitchen?" Simon whispered.

"Just long enough to fill up a plate. He'll take it back to his room- listen for his door shutting."

They both had their eyes open, but could see nothing in the darkness. The compact area had them smashed up against each other and Simon became intoxicated by April's scent. It made him regret sending the escort away.

After a couple minutes, they heard the door shut down the hall and they both reached up for the pull string to the light. They squinted when it finally came on.

"I figured you'd be sound asleep after the escort visit."

"You're a smart one, but I sent her away. I couldn't be her first."

"That was nice of you." April softened for a moment, then quickly scolded. "Do you have any idea what Cass would have done to you if he found us in here?!"

"It's so nice you care." Simon touched her sides, not realizing she was ticklish.

She pushed him backward with her good hand, as a reflex to his touch. When he bounced off the back wall of the closet, a click sounded and April closed her eyes in anguish.

Simon turned around to find a portion of the back of the closet protruding towards him. He grabbed each side of the panel and moved it to the right- the only way it would go. Behind the opening was a stairway leading down into the darkness.

His expression was a victorious one. But when he turned to look at April, she had started crying. Generally, tears didn't faze him, but he felt a compulsion to wrap his arms around her and try to soothe and understand the pain.

"Fine," she said, quickly releasing herself from his embrace. "I really screwed this up, so let's get this over with."

April took Simon's flashlight, turned it on, led him through the opening and closed the panel behind them. At the bottom of the stairs, she flipped a lever that turned on rows of lights, illuminating the contents of the basement. The amount of items in the belly of the building overwhelmed Simon, making it hard for him to focus on anything other than the vast quantities of "stuff."

There were rows of display cases, furniture and larger pieces that were approachable by small, cleared aisles. If the sight wasn't the most amazing thing he'd seen, he would have thought it more reminiscent of a condition he learned about at Quadra- hoarding.

Slowly, as his senses returned, he ran his hand over some beads lying on a glass cabinet and picked up another item.

"Do you know what this is?" Simon asked.

April shook her head.

"It's a clay pot made by the native people of this land," he said. "These beads, baskets, moccasins, arrow heads..." He was going down a row of items. "Look at this headdress! It's the most beautiful thing I've ever seen."

"Shh. We have to go now!"

"You can't show me something like this and tell me we need to go."

She started crying again and begged, "Please! I'll explain when we get upstairs."

Simon and April went back up the stairs, righting the panel and toolbox. April grabbed the bag and Simon quietly followed her into her room- the one right behind the closets and first off the museum foyer. Her quiet crying turned to sobs. The fact that she had been caught red-handed must be weighing on her. Simon touched both her shoulders and tried to get her to look at him, but she continued to hang her head while wiping away her tears.

She pushed his arms away and sat on the corner of her bed. Simon saw her torment and wanted to erase her pain, but could only bring her a tissue in a lame attempt to make everything better. Maybe if *he* told her everything…that he knew she was part of the museum underground and even though he was sent here to investigate- he wouldn't say anything.

"I'm sorry we had to come upstairs so quickly," April said. "Quadra monitors power usage and those lights downstairs use a lot of energy. We only get so many kilowatt hours a week at the museum, but we're lucky because lights can stay on our exhibits during the night. So, when I need to spend time in the basement, I just make sure the exhibit lights are off for a couple nights during the week."

Simon moved toward the bed and sat down beside her, wondering if they monitored his energy usage in Portland.

"I swore to my grandpa that I'd never let anyone know his secret, but I've let him down."

"I won't say a word," Simon said, not knowing if that promise would be kept. "What's all that stuff doing downstairs?"

"Back when Quadra was coming into power, there were rumors that all museum artifacts and exhibits would be destroyed. Quadra wanted a clean slate under their regime…an opportunity to make new history, untethered to the old. A big fire was started, the museums were emptied and history burned for days."

"How did the items in the basement escape the flames?"

"My grandpa belonged to some group. He told me the name of it once, but I forgot. They selected and gathered important things from museums in the area, relocating them here before Quadra arrived. From what grandpa says, the group did this all over the country."

"Wasn't this place a museum back then?"

"Yes, but the placard outside still read 'Old Capitol Building' and it was a newer museum, compared to the rest. The building plans logged with the city were switched with plans that didn't show a basement, making it the perfect place to hide everything. Quadra decided to keep this building because it was so unique and use it for the Quadra history museum. They took everything else out of here that hadn't been hidden in the basement and burned it with the rest."

It seemed as though April and Simon realized simultaneously that she had shared too much information. Simon thought maybe she had loose lips because of her youth or lack of experience with secretive protocol. April felt relief in thinking that she could share her burden, finding a person to trust.

"So, you won't tell anyone?" April asked, looking at Simon in a way that made him uncomfortable. "Don't even say anything to my grandpa."

"OK."

She flew into his arms, hugging him. She kissed him on the cheek before backing away again. Simon moved in for a real kiss, but April had already sprung up from the bed, escorting him to the door.

"I have to get some sleep. It'll be morning soon," April said. "Tomorrow we go to my grandpa's house so you can sleep in for a while, but we should leave around ten, so we'll be there in plenty of time for lunch."

Once Simon lay on his bed, he began assessing the situation, wondering why April would be part of a museum underground organization when she was to be married in two weeks…to a chancellor's son!? Why had she told Simon so much about the hidden basement?

He hoped the trip to see her grandfather would put things into perspective because there were so many unanswered questions.

The most pressing question of all…why couldn't he stop thinking about April?

Chapter 10

Transportation arrived outside the museum at 10am sharp. Simon had been at the roadside waiting, but April came running out of the building five minutes later. They got in the transit.

When April had finally caught her breath, she said, "Sorry, Beau, I didn't mean to hold you up."

"I would have waited a long time for my favorite passenger," Beau responded, winking in the rearview mirror.

April smiled at the flirtation, but Simon was irritated, unappreciative with his tone.

"So, are we going all the way today?" Beau asked.

Simon was about to reach in the front seat and throttle this man, but April answered Beau quickly.

"I'd like to, Beau, but it's not safe. Maybe just at the entrance would be best and then we can walk the rest of the way."

Simon calmed down once he realized "going all the way" meant the distance to April's grandpa's house. He wrestled with the thought that he may be jealous. It was only ever a word to Simon, but now it had silently crept into his existence, becoming a reality. He wondered how it could be stopped or reversed.

"Who's this guy?" Beau asked April.

"My name's Murphy. Nice to meet you," Simon lied.

The driver just grunted, obviously not keen on talking to anyone but April…or, at least, that's the impression Simon got.

April and Beau chatted the entire time until they reached their destination. It couldn't have been more than 10-15 miles outside of Baton Rouge, but it might as well have been out in the middle of nowhere. The driver told April that he would only charge her for the miles of one passenger. If anyone asked, he'd say she had a really heavy bag in the other seat. She giggled and thanked the smitten driver. Simon stood duly impressed by how April not only knew the affect she had on men, but how she expertly wielded the advantage.

The transit driver removed April's two small bags out of the trunk, barely acknowledging Simon or his bag other than to navigate around them both. He told April he'd be back tomorrow at 9am to pick her up. When he looked like he was going to hug April, Simon stepped between them, shaking Beau's hand and thanking him for the ride. The driver departed, waving out the open window.

"He's a little infatuated, don't you think?"

"Beau is harmless. He's my brother's friend and we've known each other since we were kids."

Simon couldn't decide if April was a beautiful mastermind or a naïve beauty.

"Welcome to Shenadoah," April said, as she put her long hair up in a bun. "We've got about a three-mile walk in. Do you have room in your bag for this?"

April held up the bag that she had carried last night. Simon still didn't know what it held, but hoped to find out and agreed to carry it. Neither of them had much to carry as they only planned for a 24-hour stay. April removed something from her bag and held it out to Simon.

"This is peppermint oil," April said. "It helps repel bugs. You should put some on your legs." Simon didn't take it right away. "Remember the mosquitos? There are things out here on this trail that won't be very forgiving…spiders, red velvet ants, chiggers, boil beetles…you name it."

They both applied the oil.

After walking a mile down the road, beyond the first couple of bends, they came to a solid, wooden gate about seven feet tall and eight feet wide- the same width of the road. There was no fencing around the property and people could go around the gate, even though each side of the gate had thick vegetation. The "No Trespassing" sign seemed unnecessary and Simon couldn't imagine anyone wandering on this land uninvited. April opened the gate with the passcode.

"My grandpa will get notification that we'll be there soon."

Directly past the gate, on the right side of the road, stood a large safe. April entered a combination and withdrew a gun belt that she asked Simon to help fasten around her waist. She then took a gun off a shelf, and placed it in her belt. Lastly, she grabbed a type of long spear that was folded, but when she snapped it into place, the spear stood taller than Simon.

"Are you sure we're going to your grandpa's or to war?"

"Just precautionary. I've been coming here for years and never needed to fire the gun, but this spear has seen a use or two on every trip. Not sure I'll be able to use it well with a bum wrist, but I'm going to try."

Just by having that gun in her possession, April could be punished. Guns were expressly outlawed in 2040 by Quadra…unless you were Quadra. Simon wanted to protect her.

"Why don't you let me carry the gun?" Simon suggested.

"Have you ever shot a gun?"

"No."

"Do you even know how to load a gun or what kind of

gun this is?" April removed the gun from its holster and showed it to Simon.

"No."

April squinted and gave him a side-glance, as they walked. "Then why would you think it's better that you hold the gun? You city boys make no sense."

"Why do you need a gun?"

"There's wild boar in these parts. They mostly want nothing to do with us, but if they're startled or ornery, they can be aggressive."

"And the spear?"

"That's to shoo snakes or kill 'em if they won't move. They like to sunbathe on the path. We have a lot of poisonous species here, but if you do get bit, grandpa has plenty of remedies."

Simon wasn't the kind to spook easily, but even the sounds of the birds rustling in the brush made him jump on more than one occasion. The first snake they encountered seemed put out that he needed to move, but slowly gave the intruders a path. There were two more before they made it to the house and one of them didn't go quietly. April expertly got the spear under the snake and launched it quite a distance away.

They came to another gate that was short and the same height as all the fencing that surrounded the entire homestead. The sign on the fence read: Benton Oasis and that's exactly what it looked like…a little slice of paradise in an otherwise vermin-littered area. The cleared area had to be a couple acres large and was circular. There were offshoots that connected to the main area which included a small garden and a barn.

A fire pit was the focal point of the oasis and there were old, overseas, shipping containers that formed a decoration like the sun's rays away from the fire. Simon recognized them because so many people in Portland had repurposed them into homes. He counted five and they were all painted in blue or green color tones that reminded Simon of different bodies of water.

"C'mon," April said to Simon, as she opened the gate and ventured forward, "just don't stand there." April shouted into the air, "It's us, grandpa! Hello?!"

A tall, thin man emerged from around one of the containers. He had on overalls and looked the very picture of a man that belonged in this setting. He raised an arm up high.

"Buttercup!"

April ran to her grandfather and they hugged. Simon stood back, moved by the sight of their reunion. As Simon slowly approached, April started the introduction.

"Grandpa, this is Simon, Simon this is grandpa."

"The name is Clifford. I don't think you have much need to call me grandpa," Clifford said, extending his hand for a traditional shake. He sniffed the air and turned toward April. "You must like this one, he smells like peppermint."

"Sir?" Simon questioned.

"She brought another post out here and never offered 'im the oil. Poor bastard had chiggers ravaging his ball sack." Clifford laughed, slapping his knee and Simon found that his thick accent and twisted sense of humor immediately put him at ease.

April showed Simon to his container which was outfitted as a guest room and, by the looks of things, where April stayed when she visited. It was located in the back of the property and slightly to the left- with the number 5 painted on its exterior. A small path led to the outhouse which stood behind the container area. The ground and pathways were decorated with the most beautiful landscaping. The plants and flowers were dotted around the property, giving the outdoor space a cozy feeling.

Clifford came to ask if Simon would like a tour of the property and they all walked past the smoldering fire pit, heading toward the barn. A small patch of yellow flowers caught Simon's attention and he walked toward the outer fence. He recognized these flowers for some reason, but never saw them in Portland, so they must be from his lessons at Quadra.

April got ready to shout at Simon, but Clifford touched her arm and put his finger over his lips to keep her silent. He and April went and stood by Simon as he looked over the patch of flowers.

"This flower…these plants," Simon started to remember; "they're illegal because people were allergic. These are peanuts, aren't they?"

"Well, I'll be. Yes they are. Should be ready to harvest in a month." Clifford looked over the field. "Got some peanut butter in the cupboard if you'd like to try some later. I guarantee you've never had anything like it. It's delicious!"

"But, if I'm allergic, won't I die?"

"Maybe," Clifford said. "Tell you what, I'll give you a small taste so you'll only die a little."

Chapter 11

Clifford showed Simon his property, obviously proud of the homestead. Apart from the containers, there were a few outbuildings and attached acreage on all sides.

Technically, all land belonged to the government, but Quadra wasn't big enough to police all areas…not yet. Once the tour of the property concluded, they all ended up by the fire pit.

"Why do you have a fire going on such a hot day?" Simon asked.

"I had a hankerin' for some pig and since we were havin' company, I trapped a wild boar a couple days ago and it's in the ground, by the fire pit…cookin'. Been there since yesterday. It'll be ready for supper around 1."

He swore Clifford said "we." And no sooner did the thought cross his mind, that a woman rounded a container with more firewood in her arms. Clifford introduced the woman as Rosa. It made sense now- all the touches around Benton Oasis, the flowers, the stone paths…decorations. Clifford didn't seem that concerned with such fanciful things.

Obviously surprised, Simon told her it was nice to meet her. She placed the wood on the fire.

"April, here, doesn't know what to make of Rosa," Clifford shared. "I can understand, she's not her grandma." Clifford put his arm around Rosa's shoulders. "But Rosa is sixty and much too old for me." He then slapped her on the butt and the two of them laughed.

Rosa smiled and joked, "I'm fixin' to leave him soon anyway."

April smiled, but was visibly uncomfortable. Rosa left

as quickly as she had come, respectful of April's feelings- not wanting to come between her man and his family. Clifford suggested they all get out of the afternoon sun for a bit of iced tea.

"April, why don't you go get the museum piece you brought and meet us in number 3?"

A wash of cooler air felt heavenly to Simon when Clifford opened the door to container three. It was set up like a large living room, complete with seating areas and book shelves. The large windows all around gave a good view of the grounds. Simon expected life out here, in the middle of nowhere, to be less civilized, but this container reminded him of his apartment in Portland.

April came in with the bag, handing it to Clifford. He smiled, immediately taking an item out of the bag which was wrapped in a burlap material. He carefully unrolled the item and revealed the contents. Clifford's smile disappeared and Simon lowered his head, knowing full well what purpose the item once served.

"What's the matter?" April asked. "This is from the museum's basement. It's rusty, but it looked really old, as far as the design of it."

"No, honey. You did well. I'll catalog this with all the other items you've brought me. Let me get your return item."

Clifford grabbed a small picture album off one of his shelves.

"May I?" Simon asked.

Clifford was surprised that Simon took an interest and handed him the album. Simon riffled through the album of twenty or so pictures, studying the contents before handing the album to April. She folded it in the burlap material and put the album in the bag. Clifford had watched Simon intently.

"So, wha'cha think, ole boy?" Clifford asked Simon.

"The Great Depression was a difficult time for the whole country," Simon answered.

Clifford's mouth went slack with surprise. "What do you know about that?"

"I don't mind saying that prohibition didn't help the problem and may have even caused it. The country's budget was practically funded by the alcohol taxes and so many jobs were lost in distilling, bottle-making, label-printing and saloons."

"You're right. Did you know that before Quadra outlawed alcohol, it was considered an essential business during the first quarantine?" Clifford asked.

Simon couldn't believe it at first. But then again, any government decision made to benefit itself seemed plausible.

Clifford took out a bottle and three glasses. Alcohol was banned under Quadra law almost 50 years ago. Most people didn't know much about the stuff, but Clifford was raised by a family with moonshine in their blood. He poured a small amount into each glass and held his up- April and Simon followed suit. They all drank up in one large gulp.

"And this, Simon," Clifford said, putting his hand on the item April had delivered. "Tell me what you know about this...without mentioning painful particulars, 'cause my grandbaby doesn't need to hear about such atrocities."

Clifford had thrown down a gauntlet...some sort of test. Simon wondered to what end, but he was always up for a game.

"Being as cryptic and vague as I can, it was a tool used to transport valuable cargo long distances. It is a very shameful part of our history but, our country is forever indebted to the hard work and suffering..." Simon's voice trailed off, not wanting to divulge too much.

The straight piece of iron had been flattened out on one end and had a loop on the other. Both of these ends were meant to keep the two u-shaped pieces of iron, in the middle of the bar, from slipping off. They were ankle shackles…shackles that were used to transport Africans to the new world.

Simon could see the picture in his head of the men and women laid out in the cargo bays of the boat. Laid in such a way that ensured more "cargo" could be shipped. The illustrations of whips, auctions, civil rights, the KKK and inhumane treatment flooded his memory. The idea that a person could be property was beyond his comprehension. But, he was also aware that he now sat in a part of the country that used to think just that…and with a person that knew racism and had heard of the country of Africa.

He saw Clifford smile and couldn't understand the motivation behind it…did he agree with slavery? But now Clifford knew his thoughts and Simon felt a little exposed and wondered if he should keep his mouth shut for the rest of the visit.

They spent the afternoon dining on an amazing meal and continued to drink as the sun set behind the fields. No bugs bothered them as they sat by the fire. The combination of the smoke and the plants (mint and garlic) dotting the area did much to keep the bugs at bay.

April talked about her upcoming wedding, with all the excitement of a convicted inmate, waiting to be sentenced. Clifford continued to quiz Simon on his historical knowledge, but Simon decided the time was right to ask some questions of his own.

"So, why did you leave Cape Canaveral? Wouldn't it be better to live out your days there than live here illegally and in fear of being caught?" Simon asked Clifford.

"Why, are you going to turn me in, Mr. P.O.L. agent?"

April and Rosa froze. Even though Simon was shocked by the response, he wouldn't insult Clifford's intelligence by trying to deny the accusation. He studied Clifford's face before answering, staring into his eyes. Regardless of his age, Clifford's eyes still burned with life and vigor…still sought the truth and housed the passions of a man half his age. Simon found him compelling as he wasn't altogether sure his own eyes were that full of life.

"I asked first," Simon joked. "You answer my question and then we can talk about yours."

The silence was replaced with hearty laughter and Clifford poured everyone another round of drinks. He raised his glass and toasted "to the truth."

"Just for the record, I did go to Cape Canaveral. I attended a going away ceremony when I aged out in the very museum you're posted at." Clifford got up and poked at the wood in the fire, staring at the flames.

"When we arrived there, it looked like the beaches went on forever. There was a fancy welcome dinner, but I couldn't eat. I'd tied one on the night before, knowing alcohol wouldn't be available there. I gave my meal to the guy next to me. Everyone was hungrier than a tick on a teddy bear because no one had eaten since our farewell ceremony."

April interrupted his thought. "I'll never understand why you'd come back. All your meals provided for you, the beaches, friends…"

Clifford smirked. "I suppose you wouldn't, without the full story. The food and drink at that welcome meal contained powerful time-release drugs in the food and drink. After a couple of hours, everyone was retiring for the evening. They could barely keep their eyes open. Since no one stayed up, I went to my room, too, to get settled in."

"It wasn't long before the gas started seeping in my room through the vent…I recognized the smell. I tried to leave the room, but the door was locked from the outside and the window had been screwed shut. Not that the window would have been much of an escape route- I was almost twenty floors up. I guess Quadra only allows their building to be taller than four stories. Anyway, I was getting woozy from the gas and needed fresh air."

April gasped.

"I took my belt off and whipped my buckle at the window until it broke…just in time. I stuck my head out the window, gasping for fresh air."

It wasn't long before Clifford heard rattling at his door, leaving him to assume some kind of alarm had given him away.

Chapter 12

Before the door could be opened, Clifford slid beside the armoire that stood a couple of feet from the window so he was out of sight, not visible from the doorway.

Clifford thinks the person who entered his room said "hello" out loud, but the sound of his beating heart muffled the words. When the person walked by, to inspect the broken window, he grabbed an arm, shoving it up their back and leaned the person out the window. He glanced back at the door which had closed automatically.

"What's with the gas? Is it to put us to sleep? Knock us out for some purpose? You better start talking," Clifford sneered, leaning the worker further out the window.

"I just work here," the voice answered. It was a woman's voice, which surprised Clifford and even made him instinctually loosen his grip. He spun her around.

"You have minutes to tell me what you know about this place or I'll throw you out this window."

"This is the E.S.!"

"What does that stand for?"

"The Euthanasia Sector."

The realization of what that meant startled Clifford. People being sent here to die, reminiscent of the holocaust. He had no words, but shook her and told her to explain this place as though he was getting trained to be posted here.

She explained that people over the age of 70 were no longer adding value to society. They had out-lived their usefulness and would merely put a drain on the economy. The E.S. was formed to help right some of the wrongs that humanity had inflicted on the planet.

After the gassing was complete, which was intended to

kill the seniors, a roller would come to retrieve the bodies. The corpses were categorized as seafood or fertilizer. This is why the "aged" brought their medical records so they could be properly classified.

The young girl pointed out the window to the half-mile pier, jutting out from the base of the building. She explained it was actually a long conveyor belt and went a half mile off shore to dump the bodies into the ocean, past a drop-off.

"We've so badly damaged the oceans that this is a great way to give back. If the sea life doesn't eat all the remains, the bodies rest on the bottom and the bones are developing into a beautiful reef."

Those that were not in the best health or on too many medications, got sent to the fertilizer station, where they were bled to make bone meal fertilizer- their bodies cremated afterward.

"Their blood will help grow beautiful flowers and plants to help feed Quadra and make it beautiful!"

After hearing the explanations, Clifford couldn't fathom the insanity of such a place. "This should be called the Twilight Zone, not the E.S.," Clifford told her. She was too young to understand the reference.

He let her stand upright, but blocked the pathway to the door.

"Do you know what I was classified as?"

"Yes. You are on the seafood floor. Congratulations! You're a charitable contributor to the sea!" It was said with such excitement that Clifford knew it would be lost on her if he tried to explain the atrocity of the E.S.

She told Clifford how the bodies were retrieved from the rooms by posts known as rollers and explained the whole process. Clifford asked her if she could keep him a secret and not let anyone know he was still alive. She hesitated too long, so Clifford ripped up a t-shirt he had brought and fashioned it into strips of cloth to tie her up.

He gagged her and placed her in the bathroom, but checked on her frequently. They would find her when the clean-up crew came in, after the bodies were removed. They needed to prepare for the next batch of aged this evening. The killing must go on.

Sleep was out of the question. He closed the curtains to hide the broken window, ran over his plan of escape in his head and decided if this was his last day on Earth- he should go out fighting. Clifford couldn't remember when time had passed so slowly. Although, the hot Sunday mornings when he was a kid, waiting for church to end, came darn close. He counted the minutes before he could strip off his "Sunday best" and jump in the river.

He lay in his bed at Cape Canaveral, waiting to assume a corpse's identity, deciding to act a little stiff as though rigor mortis had set in. After paying all his taxes, abiding mostly by the laws, and being a good man, this is how he's rewarded- with a death sentence.

A beep broke the silence and Clifford recognized the sound of the door unlocking and opening. The sun had barely started rising. He lay still. Through his eyelids, he could tell that an overhead light switched on. The bed was bumped and the roller, as they were called, had arrived.

The unknown equation tied up in the bathroom started making noises, mumbling loudly and banging her leg against the bathtub. Clifford had asked her to keep quiet and felt betrayed after he had let her live. A swish of cloth brushed by him and Clifford knew the person coming to pick him up was going to check on the noises in the bathroom.

He opened his eyes and saw a man passing by the foot of the bed. A gurney blocked his way to the left, so Clifford jumped out of bed on the side closest to the window. He moved quickly, knowing the next few minutes were vital to his escape.

Clifford took him by the collar, stripping the roller out of his lab coat which dropped to the floor. He lunged to take hold of the roller's T-shirt. The man in his grasp stood slightly taller and was quite young, but the adrenaline running through Clifford made it easy to wrestle the man to the window and lean him over the opening.

Clifford's eye caught the sight of the huge conveyor belt, disguised as a pier and watched as the naked, dead bodies that dotted the belt, slowly moved toward the sea. The man beneath him struggled, but Clifford held him down more forcibly as he stared in horror at the belt.

A gurgling sound floated up and there was blood gushing down from the window. Clifford turned the man toward him, seeing that he stood clutching his throat- his eyes wide and fearful. A shard of glass still lodged in the window had cut his neck, leaving a fatal wound.

Clifford laid him on the bed, recognizing that he was barely a man at all. Wanting to end his suffering, he placed a pillow over the dying's boy's face.

Clifford knew what he had to do and rolled the lifeless body on the gurney meant for him. The body landed on its stomach which was preferred, as the blood would absorb in the small mattress below. His plan quickly changed and he would now need to pretend he worked for the E.S. and haul the body to the pier.

He'd only been here less than 24 hours, but it wasn't lost on him how young all the posts were. He grabbed the lab coat off the floor and buttoned the top button. After ripping up more of the T-shirts he had packed, he fashioned a bandana-type face mask and a head-covering to conceal the grey hair and his age.

Clifford covered the body with a bed sheet and moved the hospital bed toward the door, pressing the button to automatically open it. Some intermittent noise could be heard from the bathroom, but the traitor's mumbles fell on deaf ears. She was to blame for the death of the boy now being rolled away.

Everyone on this floor had been classified as seafood, so he followed the other gurney's headed to the elevator. Luckily, no one spoke or maintained eye contact. Perhaps a shred of shame ran through the posts. Clifford didn't have time to dwell on the possibility of redeeming qualities in the posts because the elevator door opened and he got on, quickly pressing the button labeled "dock" and barring any more passengers by also clicking "private ride."

The elevator stopped on the second floor and the door opened behind him. Clifford watched as the bodies were uncovered and the gurneys clicked into a lift mechanism on the end of the "pier." The beds ascended to a little over six feet, tilted the bodies off at the top, where they fell a couple of feet onto the conveyor belt and returned the empty gurney back to its "roller" to repeat the process. A Ferris wheel of death.

Mercifully, there was a high guard rail around the beginning of the pier and once the bodies were dropped on the belt, they could no longer be seen. This would work in Clifford's favor if he timed it right. He waited until the last roller had entered the elevator and clicked the bed he had brought down into the contraption.

Looking back at the four elevators, he saw one getting dangerously close to the second floor. He started to hide until he spotted a button that would disable them, so he ran to press it and climbed on top of the dead boy on the gurney, with only a sheet to separate them. He willed the lift to move faster, realizing the button he pushed only stopped two of the four elevators. His eyes were fixed on a button as it lit up and just as he heard the ding of the elevator door opening, he was falling onto the belt.

Clifford held onto the white sheet once he landed and quickly covered himself. He mostly did it in case the pier was watched, but realized his luck when the sound of the pier motor was replaced with screaming gulls, looking for an easy meal. They landed on the bodies, pecking at the remains. When he peeked from under the sheet, Clifford was thrilled to see that the gulls would probably camouflage not only his leap from the pier, but even the sheet he used as they circled above in a cloud of white.

***

"So, I jumped off the middle of the pier, swam a safe distance and high-tailed it back to Baton Rouge. And I'll be damned if I've ever been a drain on society! That was eight years ago."

Chapter 13

April walked over to her grandfather, with tears in her eyes and hugged him tightly. Clifford patted her arm as a way to say thank you, but also to discourage a lengthy display of affection.

Rosa wrapped up the remains of the small pig. "I will save this for pozole."

"I love it when you talk dirty to me, Rosa!" Clifford hooted.

Lifting a pack by his chair, he spoke, "Would you ladies mind if Simon and I had an opportunity to chat alone?"

The question made Simon feel nervous for the first time in years. He secretly hoped the request would be denied.

By now, the sun's only light reflected off the moon, making the fire and a small bulb on each container the sole source of illumination. Simon watched as Rosa and April made their way to separate containers. April looked back at the two men before turning a corner; her worried expression concerned Simon.

Clifford dropped the pack in Simon's lap and motioned for him to look inside. The bag held two T-shirts, a pair of shorts and some toiletries. The item that caught Simon's attention was a metallic disk that he removed from the pack. When he clicked it on, a picture of a little girl rose up. It was a different woman pictured, but the same little girl that smiled and played on Simon's disk. The P.O.L. didn't even bother to upload a different image.

Simon smirked and shook his head, not surprised that this proved his initial suspicions of the POL's deception.

"You know the girl in the picture?" Clifford asked, as he sat down.

Simon shook his head no. He put the disk back in the bag and tossed it in the old man's lap. "Who's stuff is this, anyway?"

Clifford pointed to his right and said, "He's down yonder."

"In hiding, like you?"

"No, not exactly. That's where I buried him…down that path a-ways."

As Simon stared in the direction of the path, he heard a gun cock. He only knew the sound because of an old western he watched in his studies, but he found the loud click as eerie now as the first day he heard it.

Simon looked at Clifford and the gun he held. "So, you shoot me? Is that the plan? You should've at least killed me before I ate so much of that delicious boar. What a waste!"

"Have you always been such a smart ass?"

"Yes," Simon answered, coolly.

Clifford squinted, but Simon recognized the look. Good old Clifford was trying to get a read on his guest…size him up and figure out whether or not Simon could be trusted.

"So, convince me why I should let you leave here. You know where I live and that I escaped from the E.S.," Clifford prodded. "By Jove, in the eyes of Quadra, I'm a regular criminal, merely for being alive at this age. I bet the P.O.L. would show their appreciation for anyone who turned in a left-over like me."

"They probably would," Simon agreed.

Clifford sat there waiting for Simon to defend himself, to start sweating or babble, but Simon stared into the fire waiting for a bullet to arrive. He hoped it would be quick and painless. Minutes passed with the gun still aimed in his direction.

"I'm not a patient man, Simon, but I'd like to know my

ammo isn't going to waste and I have good reason to shoot you."

"I hate the P.O.L. Maybe I'll be able to fully explain why that is, but not today. Not even at the risk of a bullet to the head. I'm not sure what you want me to say. The truth is that I'm here at their request." Simon paused. "I don't mean to say here on your property, but in Baton Rouge for the same reason the last post was assigned."

"Something about history leaking out," Simon continued. "I'm a history expert and if anyone could identify historical artifacts or truths, it would be me. Quadra thinks there is some undercover operation in the area. I'm to find the key players and report back to Quadra. Anything to forward the cause." Simon raised his hand, flipping the bird. "Hail, Quadra."

Clifford smiled. There was a salute for hailing Quadra, but that definitely wasn't it. He sat back, marinating on the info.

"So, how do you feel about your assignment? Do you hate history enough to try and stop them?" Clifford asked.

Simon looked at him in disbelief. "I love history. The powers-that-be have managed to dig up, burn, tear down or destroy any ties to the past. The same past that would help us to understand how we've gotten to this point in our world and how far we have yet to go."

Simon raised his voice to almost a yell as he fought the urge to become overly emotional and continued, "Why did Quadra have to get rid of every statue, monument or historical marker? If you don't like something or agree with it, spit on it when you walk by- but, never forget why it stands!"

Simon couldn't remember the last time he had spoken so passionately. It flushed his cheeks with embarrassment.

Clifford lowered the gun, holding the hammer back and engaging the trigger on the revolver to bring it back to a safe position.

"Well, look at that, you're one of us," Clifford said, surprised by Simon's convictions. "I should've known you'd be different when I heard your name."

"What do you mean?"

"Well, no one uses names from the Bible anymore because it's been deemed offensive. Used to be, you couldn't throw a stick without hitting a John, David or Matthew."

Simon asked, into the air, "When did it become that a differing opinion meant anarchy?"

Simon asked the question rhetorically, but Clifford responded. "It happened over time as self-proclaimed, open-minded people thought their ideas rose above that of others and should be made the law of the land." Clifford raised the gun he held. "Owning a gun shouldn't equate to being a criminal. A lot of country folk used guns to hunt and feed their families. City folk didn't care nothin' about that because they had the government providin' meals at soup kitchens or food pantries. A well-aimed bullet meant a rural family could eat through a long winter."

"Removing guns seemed like the only good decision that Quadra made..." Simon challenged.

"You're wrong," Clifford interrupted. "Any time a government takes away something from its citizens, but keeps that item for their own purposes- you have to wonder why. They still use computers. Quadra militia is armed with guns…the bodyguards of high-ranking officials have guns. It was a crime the way they unarmed the citizens. I think they called it the 'food for arms' plan, basically starving out gun owners."

"Crime is non-existent now. Don't you think that has

something to do with outlawing guns? I haven't heard of any criminal activity in years," Simon argued.

"And how would you hear of this 'criminal activity,' dumbass, now that internet and television haven't existed since 2036? Who's going to say a bad word about Quadra when they tape so many conversations? Why, it's illegal to distribute any news publication that isn't Quadra-approved! No one saw that coming down the pike. Used to be everybody had an opinion about somethin'. I've lived in this world longer than most and I guarantee criminal activity of some sort still runs rampant. If nothing else, the government is taking away our rights. Can't get more criminal than that!"

"What does 'down the pike' mean?"

"Sorry, I still use a lot of old terms. A pike was a long highway where you should be able to see things comin' from out a-ways."

Simon grinned, enjoying the explanation, trying to picture different vehicles traveling on the roadways while Clifford remembered cars and trucks rushing past- the sound of the speeding vehicles as they passed. Vroom…vroom. Dust kicked up behind the tires, while random pieces of garbage lifted up into the air. The men sat quietly within their own imaginations.

"Well," Clifford broke the silence, "I can't very well shoot you now that we've had our chat. It's obvious you're not a puppet."

Simon understood the puppet reference. Quadra had been trying to outlaw the use of the word, but resistance organizations had kept it alive. The visual of having Quadra's agenda up your ass, controlling your every move was too accurate to let go. Neither of the men understood that brainless existence.

"Follow me," Clifford said, springing out of his chair

like a man half his age.

Simon did what he was asked, trailing after Clifford to the barn. Clifford started a small generator before turning on the lights. He looked back at Simon and smiled before reaching the wall of tools which had been meticulously outlined on a peg board. Shadowing tools was an old system, but it still worked. The camouflaged door to the secret back room was impossible to spot, but Clifford opened the door and the two men entered.

A small, shed-sized room no more than 20 by 10 feet housed book shelves all around. A small table sat in the middle of the room with only one chair. Clifford took a seat while he watched Simon circle around the room. Simon discovered the pages of the tomes were filled with pictures of museum artifacts, diary entries, historically relevant newspaper clippings, encyclopedia pictures of statues and historical landmarks. There were notations inserted to describe or explain pictures.

Simon held up one of the entries. "This is about Brigham Young and how the Mormons settled in Utah." He slowly looked around the room, one hand still elevating the entry, while the other pointed to the bookshelves. "You're getting this history from all over Quadra. The P.O.L. is right to be worried about you guys! I'm impressed with the organization. Are there libraries like this all over Quadra?"

Clifford nodded while Simon waited for more information about the Museum Underground that never came.

"How many people in town help you with this? There's no way you can have all these entries sent to one address without raising suspicion. And your home isn't even a legal mailing address."

"I'm not giving away all my secrets just yet, but there's

a loyal group of people that support the cause."

A smile slowly crossed Simon's lips.

"Why do you look so proud of yourself?" Clifford asked.

"One of those people is Earl," Simon surmised. "He's probably the most experienced groundskeeper and gardener I've met and yet he doesn't use the one ingredient that helps everything grow- the fertilizer. He knows what it contains. You must have told him. I helped him bury an alligator in the garden the other day for fertilizer and didn't see one bag of Quadra fertilizer anywhere."

Clifford got up out of the chair. "It's about time I hit the hay." He turned off the light and motioned for Simon to follow him out. On the way back to the containers, right before they parted ways, Clifford said, "Be careful, boy, don't get too big for your britches…I just might shoot you yet."

When Simon approached container number 5, the door was slightly open and he could hear what sounded like muffled sobbing. He slowly made his way to the other side of the container to find the source of the sounds and spied April with her face in a pillow.

He touched her shoulder and she quickly flipped around to face him. A look of disbelief shone through her eyes and, then, pure joy. Simon may have been terrible with social cues, but this was unmistakable. She sprang from the bed and put her hands on Simon's shoulders, ensuring this wasn't some sort of cruel trick of her imagination.

"You thought I was dead…" Simon whispered.

April let her arms drop to her sides and lowered her head, nodding, while another whimper escaped. Simon didn't overthink, size her up or question motives. He simply cupped her cheeks in his hands and lifted her lips to his. He knew as soon as their mouths touched that this is what he had been missing all his life- true desire and longing.

Simon found that as he tried to be gentle with April and respect her inexperience, she invited every opportunity, making him feel more like a man than ever before. The natural order of things overwhelmed him. She wanted Simon just as much as he wanted her.

And she got what she wanted- again and again, until sleep overtook them.

Chapter 14

April woke up enveloped in Simon's arms and nuzzled her face into his chest. She moved up to his neck, kissing him awake. Whatever her plans may have been for the morning, a loud knock on the container brought them to an end.

"Hey, Simon, up and out in fifteen. We need to talk about what happens now," Clifford barked.

Simon wasted no time, springing from the bed and jumping in the shower. When he got out to dress, April had already left. For the slightest moment he thought the night could have been a dream, but the smell of her lingered.

Breakfast was laid out by the fire pit. Eggs, bacon and fresh-baked biscuits quickly re-fueled Simon's drained energy. He couldn't remember a time when he had a fresher or better tasting meal. He washed it down with some iced tea. The drink was growing on him and he found that he liked the beverage better without the sugar.

"A P.O.L. agent will come through the museum soon, disguised as a visitor or a delivery person," Clifford said. "They think they're fooling everyone, but you'll know within a couple of minutes exactly who they are. Just act normal. You were right- Earl is my inside guy and he's smart as a whip. April helps out, but she has no idea of the full scope of our operations because she won't be of much use once she's married."

That last sentence made Simon choke on the bit of food in his mouth. April couldn't go through with the wedding after last night, could she?

Clifford interrupted Simon's thinking. "Cass is about as useful as a mirror to a blind man. He still thinks I'm living the high life in the E.S. and would only mess things up if he got involved. You keep to your post for now and I'll see you next week, after the wedding."

April joined the men at the fire pit, with her backpack. She explained they had to get going if they were to meet their transit. "I'm going to go get the gun and stick," she told Simon. "Can you throw things in your pack so we can go?" April grabbed a biscuit and walked toward the gate.

"You know Beau would wait for you until winter, if you asked him to," Clifford yelled after her. He smacked Simon on the knee. "That one has been in love with her for years. I imagine he may just weep at her wedding."

"Be right there," Simon shouted after April. He stood up and shook Clifford's hand.

Clifford held onto Simon's hand. "You're one of us, now, you hear? You don't get to come through here unscathed and not join the underground. During the wedding, right before the 'I do's,' are exchanged, go to Earl's shed so you can be introduced to the others."

Simon nodded, went to retrieve his belongings and started down the trail with April.

Beau hadn't arrived to pick them up yet, but Simon and April got to the road much earlier than expected, given they didn't talk at all and it was too early for the snakes to be sunbathing.

"I'd like to say I'm sorry about last night, but I'm not," Simon broke the silence.

"I'm not either. I had a wonderful time." April smiled at Simon.

Beau drove up before any other conversation could be had.

The ride back to Baton Rouge was quiet. Beau tried, but

failed to have a conversation with April. He only managed to get an answer about her wrist brace. April simply said her wrist didn't hurt anymore and continued to stare out the window.

Simon wanted to reach over to hold her hand, but he knew it would look suspicious to Beau if he witnessed that.

They arrived at the museum where April quickly retired to her room. It wasn't even noon yet, but Simon decided he could use a nap after the long night and big breakfast. He was exhausted and he hoped to later have a serious conversation with April. A clear head would require some rest.

Simon got a couple of hours sleep and woke to Cass hovering over his bed, jarring the mattress with his knee.

"You need to make dinner tonight," Cass demanded. "We ordered out last night and it wasn't too good. Get up."

"I have the day off, Cass," Simon said, almost whining.

"Nope, technically, you had one day off, so you're back on the clock. Now, get up and make us dinner."

Cass lacked self-awareness, but may have recognized how rude he sounded, adding a weak "please" as he exited the room.

Simon splashed his face with a little cold water and went to the kitchen. He cooked in peace for an hour, but just as he got dinner in the oven, Cass came into the kitchen for a chat.

"Smells good already. So, where did you go yesterday?" Cass asked, with eyebrows inquisitively raised. "Were you spendin' time with Jen from Dr. Michon's office? I bet she's quite the welcome wagon!"

Simon shook his head and chuckled, knowing Cass would want to kill him if he responded honestly. Simon excused himself under the guise that he needed more ingredients from the garden. He felt the need to connect with Earl and let him know that he met with Clifford's approval and might be joining the underground group.

"Hi Earl," Simon waved, as he rounded the shed. "Can I help myself to a couple of things for tonight's salad?"

Earl gave a quick nod and went back to hoeing a line of soil for a new row of seeds. Simon picked a couple of tomatoes, a bell pepper and some greens before he blocked Earl's path. Earl stopped his chore, put his elbow on the top of the hoe, waiting for Simon to move or explain his actions. Simon did neither.

In a whisper, Simon said, "I just want you to know that I met Clifford and I'm in."

Earl stood there with his elbow still perched on the hoe, waiting for Simon to get out of his way. Simon waited for a response, but Earl only pointed impatiently to the path in front of him. Simon stepped out of Earl's way and then started back toward the museum. He didn't get two steps in before his legs were swept out from under him, sending the salad fixings flying in every direction.

Simon quickly rolled over and kicked his leg against the weapon of attack. The hoe rose in the air, but Earl held on tightly. As Simon kept trying to get up, Earl would use a different technique to trip him up. Simon waited for the next rush of the hoe and grabbed it, pulling Earl down on the ground.

He thought if they were both on the ground it would give him an advantage, but it did no such thing. Earl proved a skilled opponent.

"I'm on your side, Earl!" Simon yelled, as they exchanged blows.

"Anyone on my side keeps their mouth shut," Earl said calmly, his eyes squinting with disapproval. Earl rolled over

Simon and got him in a chokehold. Simon struggled, making the situation worse, until everything went dark.

When he came to, Simon found himself in the middle of the garden with his head in April's lap. Simon initially thought his hearing had been lost because of the quiet, until everyone sighed in relief. Even Earl, covered in dirt, pretended to give a damn.

"Welcome back," April smiled.

"Thanks," Simon squeaked, his voice temporarily affected by being choked. "I thought I heard you yell and rushed out here to find Earl with his hands around your neck."

"Like I said…thought he was a thief," Earl explained as he collected the salad ingredients on the ground. April glared in his direction.

"I'll go get a cool washcloth for his forehead," Farrow offered.

"No, no, I'll be fine," Simon said, slowly rising from the ground. He was covered in just as much grime as his adversary. "I'm going to go shower before I get dinner out of the oven."

Earl handed Simon a bag of the vegetables he had collected before the scuffle.

"Thank you, Earl. Dinner's at 6 p.m., like before," Simon reminded.

"I'll be there." Earl answered.

While Simon showered, he played back the scene in the garden. He knew Earl wouldn't have stopped choking him if April didn't come out. He rubbed his neck and recognized this as the second day in a row he survived the threat of death.

After all the posts had gathered in the kitchen for dinner, Simon put a platter and bowl on the table.

Cass looked at the platter filled with the dark brown contents, unsure of the meal to be served and asked, "What's that? It smells mighty fine, but can't say it looks too appetizin'." He scrunched up his nose a bit and waited for an answer.

"It's a favorite of mine. It's called French onion soup stuffed chicken. I thought you might like to try it.

Cass continued to look at the platter, unconvinced. April took a piece as did everyone but Cass. They passed around the salad bowl and started eating. Slowly, Cass came around and managed to finish two pieces of chicken and his salad before anyone finished the first piece.

"So, Beau tells me you were running around with some guy named Murphy yesterday and today. What's that about, Sis?" Cass interrogated. "Does your fiancé know about this boyfriend of yours?"

April just shook her head as Earl glanced in Simon's direction.

"Now, that's enough, Cass," Farrow said. "I'm sure April has more important things to do than respond to your foolishness. She has a wedding to prepare for next weekend."

"Everything will be delivered here and set up," April corrected. "I only need to get ready and show up. That reminds me, Simon. You're invited!"

"But, you only get twenty five guests. I don't need to come."

"You'll be guest number nineteen. I didn't reach Quadra's cut-off of twenty five," April said. "Besides, because I'm marrying into the chancellor's family, they can have as many guests on their list as they want."

"Oh, April, you are a lucky young woman," Farrow remarked. "A marriage to a chancellor's son will bring you so much happiness."

Everyone looked at April's expression, which conveyed a lot of things- happiness wasn't one of them.

Cass piped up, "This stuffed soup chicken was delicious, Simon. I apologize for doubtin' yuh."

"Lemme guess, this dinner includes garlic somehow." Earl pondered.

"No Earl," Simon shook his head and smiled ever so slightly, "only in the main dish and the salad."

Earl grinned, let out a huff and excused himself from the table. Simon watched him leave, not knowing what to make of his interactions with the groundskeeper today. Earl choked him out an hour before they shared a civilized dinner and did so with a fascinating consistency in demeanor. Simon found that oddly impressive.

Simon and April cleaned up the kitchen alone. He was oddly at ease in her presence.

"I'm going to return the item to the basement tonight," April whispered. "If you'd like to go, too, meet me in my room at midnight. I'll leave the door unlocked."

She put down her drying towel and left the kitchen.

Simon mulled over the last few days before retiring to his room: Guns, a crazy old man, alligators, death grips, passionate sex, betraying the POL, and secret museum artifacts. It was all good and well, but he appreciated one thing above the rest- he was no longer bored.

Chapter 15

He opened his door at 11:45pm, hoping to get in a quick conversation with April before they returned the photo album to the basement. But when he snuck out of his room, he saw April exiting her room at the same time.

He whispered, once he got close to her, "You said midnight."

"I didn't think you'd come," April lied. She put her finger over her lips to shush him.

They quietly slinked down the hall and made it down to the basement without issue. April took the photo album out of the burlap bag and put it away in a nearby dresser. She handed the bag to Simon.

"I think my grandpa will expect you to bring the new artifacts after I'm married."

"You're still getting married?"

"Yep," April answered easily. She shifted the conversation. "So, tell me all about the artifact we left at Benton Oasis."

Simon looked surprised at how effortlessly April moved past the question about her marriage. He decided to focus on her second question. "Your grandpa didn't want me saying too much about that. It's ugly history."

"Please," April asked.

Simon had heard the word please before, but never like this. He thought she could have asked him anything and he'd be powerless to deny her. Realizing he had been staring at April, Simon abruptly broke eye contact.

"They were shackles."

"For prisoners?"

"No…for slaves. People who were owned by other

people. Bought and sold, used as sexual objects, whipped, beaten, degraded, divided from family, worked to the bone, having no rights and barely regarded as human…they were property."

April shook her head in disbelief. Slowly, the thought of such atrocities sunk in and made her eyes well up with tears. Simon was affected by the tears just as much as the "please." He went to hold her, but she stopped him.

"That couldn't have happened here, not in my town," April decided.

"Where we stand right now is an area that could be considered one of the worst anywhere in all four quadrants. I remember being shown a picture of a man from Baton Rouge with his back covered in scars from being whipped. And down in New Orleans is where many slave women were prostituted or sold for concubine use. It wasn't unusual for a twelve or thirteen year old girl to be up for sale. But, in fairness, the mistreatment happened everywhere. Mostly the slaves were used on plantations to farm cotton, tobacco or other crops."

"How did they decide who would be slaves?!"

"Men sailed to Africa, stealing the native men and women from their shores before transporting them to this country. The shackles we brought to your grandfather are an example of what the slave-runners used to keep order. The slaves were laid in the hull of the boats under horrible conditions. Many lost their lives during the trip or became very ill."

"Well, why didn't they just join society?! Refuse to be slaves? I don't believe any of this! You and your wild, fantastical stories!"

At that moment, a noise broke the brief silence, startling them both. Simon grabbed April and stood in front of her in an attempt to keep her safe. On the other side of the basement, a form revealed itself, stepping out into the light. Slowly, Farrow emerged, his face lined with tears.

"It's all true," Farrow cried out.

April nervously looked upward, straining to hear if Earl or Cass were roused out of their sleep, but only an eerie silence followed Farrow's proclamation.

"As a boy, I used to sit on my grandmother's lap and listen to tales similar to these. She told me of the struggles suffered to get equal rights. She spoke of hangings, whips and second-class treatment. It's true." Farrow waved his arms around. "All of it."

"Farrow," April whispered, "of all people, you cannot lose your good sense and start listening to all this nonsense."

"You asked why the slaves couldn't join society? Just refuse to be servants?" Farrow repeated, as he moved closer to April and Simon. "It was the color of their skin. The color of my skin. I'm black, African-American…colored…a Negro. Those were the words they used to call us, before we were merely citizens. That is how they differed."

"You're Farrow!" April raised her voice.

She ascended the stairs. Between her upcoming nuptials to a proponent of Quadra and the personal discomfort at the thought of slavery being a reality, she left.

"Thank you for believing me," Simon told Farrow.

"If it was just you, I'm not sure I would, but what I just heard lines up with my grandmother's tales and this journal." Farrow raised an old, tattered book. "I'd be a fool to deny the truth."

"What's in the journal?"

"A long time ago a woman from this area named Sarah Morgan wrote a number of journals about life in Baton Rouge, during something called the Civil War. I've been making my way through them over the past few months. Very interesting."

Simon nodded.

"So people used to be treated differently, based solely on the color of their skin?" Farrow asked, feeling heartbroken.

"Unfortunately, yes. But, don't worry, Farrow, my thinking that you can be an ass sometimes has nothing to do with the color of your skin." Simon attempted to lighten the mood.

"I appreciate that," Farrow said, smirking.

Farrow patted Simon on the back and they both made their way up the stairs, righting the tool box and the secret door in the back of the closet. Farrow entered the basement a different way, but he planned to keep that to himself for now.

"How long have you known about the basement?" Simon wondered.

"For more than a year. After the discovery, I fully intended to report it to Quadra. But, after stumbling across the journals, there was not one word…one page that my eyes could miss."

As Farrow and Simon walked down the hall, they saw that Earl sat in the kitchen, snacking on leftover chicken.

"C'mon in here, you two," Earl said.

Through the kitchen windows, they witnessed a storm inching toward them, as it traveled across the river. The trees whipped around outside. Earl had only turned on the light over the stove, but the room intermittently illuminated with lightning.

Earl motioned for them to take a seat. Farrow did so without hesitation, but events from earlier in the day made Simon think better of it. He dragged a chair away from the table and sat at what he considered to be a safer distance.

"That journal in your hand, Farrow, it gives you some knowledge and understanding that not everyone possesses," Earl pointed out. "I need to know how you feel about that." He wiped his mouth with a napkin, eyeing Farrow.

"In the end, I believe it makes me angry, as though I'm being denied the truth," Farrow answered.

"Understandable," Earl nodded. "What if I told you the lies don't stop there? Would you want to know more or do you prefer to be a Quadra puppet?"

"You've known me for a long time, Earl. It takes some time with decisions and I have a family to consider."

"Well," Earl said, getting up from the table and taking his plate to the sink, "you have a week to decide. Let me know before April's wedding. You can go with us the day of the wedding or…" Earl trailed off, never expressing more options.

A lightning blast lit up the whole room and the thunder clap followed. It served as the missing punctuation mark to Earl's sentence. There was only one option available. The men dispersed into their rooms. Farrow only went home on his days off, when the museum closed for two days.

Simon lay on his bed, disappointed by April. First, that she still planned to marry and, second, that she dismissed Simon's wisdom. A light knock on his door stirred him from his thoughts. April entered the room and locked the door behind her. She joined Simon, sitting on the edge of the bed.

"I need to start locking my door," Simon mentioned, not knowing what else to say.

They sat in silence for a while, listening to the droplets of water beat against the window.

"I should go," April said.

She moved to leave, but Simon put his hand on her leg.

"Why are you still getting married? You don't love him. It's irresponsible."

"If we want to talk about irresponsible, I believe you're the very definition of that word. You slept with a woman who will marry into a chancellor's family, you tried to get me involved in a history conversation with Farrow and you and Earl were rolling around in the garden this afternoon!"

"You don't love him."

"True, but I don't love you either."

That comment stung.

She continued. "We had an amazing night and I don't regret a thing. Being able to make a choice all my own felt exhilarating…you felt exhilarating. But, at the end of the day, I've made a promise to marry. The idea of marriage is comforting to me and how lucky am I that a powerful family wishes to welcome me? Marriage isn't for you, like you've explained, so you don't understand."

Looking at her, Simon almost broke down, wanting to take back all his negative remarks about marriage and propose they run away together. But, he refrained. He'd never given her a reason to believe he was worthy of such an opportunity.

"Simon, you need to understand something about this area when it comes to loyalty," she warned. "There are only two sides to things: Quadra or Resistance. There is no in-between. You would be wise to remember that. After I'm married, my allegiance will be to Quadra. I'd never give away my grandfather, but I can't support his cause anymore."

Simon appreciated April's wisdom. Where he came from, Quadra was the only game in town. The very idea of being part of a resistance pleased him. He fell back on the bed and let out a sigh, knowing she was right. They looked at each other for a time while he ran his hand through her hair.

"I'm not sure which bewitches me the most," Simon shared, still slowly combing her hair with his fingers, "your beauty or your mind."

April leaned down by Simon's ear and moved his hand that had been in her hair to her chest. She whispered, "I think if you're up for it, you should be irresponsible one more time."

The storm outside became barely noticeable.

Chapter 16

Simon went through the motions leading up to the wedding. He gave most of the museum tours and cooked all the meals to keep busy, averting his eyes to the constant wedding preparations surrounding him.

He had a new buddy in Farrow, who respected Simon's knowledge. They started going for walks after dinner so their conversations wouldn't be overheard. Farrow dispelled his straight-laced reputation with Simon as he asked probing and highly illegal questions. Simon answered every last one.

Earl stalked around the property, uneasy with the bustling activity. He often squinted at Simon, looking for another opportunity to pounce. Simon knew his cooking saved him from harm…both where Earl and Cass were concerned, but garlic jokes had stopped, now that Simon had a healthy dose of fear when it came to Earl.

The night before the wedding, many of the guests were staying in tented quarters that had been erected up and down the street behind the museum. The chancellor went all out on his son's wedding and fashioned the tents with beautiful furnishings, food baskets and, most importantly, air conditioners.

A power shut-down in Baton Rouge for five hours the day before the wedding made up for the power usage of the guest tents and the wedding itself. The needs of an entire town were nothing in comparison to the chancellor's son getting married.

Simon didn't have to make dinner on the eve of April's wedding. The chancellor's family brought in their chef and cooking team which distributed meals to everyone throughout the grounds around 8pm. He internally scoffed at the dinner hour, thinking it was too late, so he ate a sandwich around 6pm in protest. The chancellor's guests and families ate dinner upstairs in the museum. But, because April could not see the groom before her wedding day, she stayed in her room.

Knowing only a door stood between him and April made Simon antsy. He escaped outside to the bench that faced the river. He remembered their first real conversation and how it felt to share thoughts and feelings…tell her about parts of his life.

It wasn't long before a man joined him on the bench. "This seems a good place to be alone with your thoughts," said the stranger.

"It's as good a place as any. I'll leave you to it," Simon said, getting up to leave, not looking at the man.

"No, please stay. I need someone to talk to and a stranger is a better option at the moment," the man said.

"So, you're in town for the wedding?" Simon asked, not caring one way or the other.

The man started laughing, "My name's Marshall, Marshall Walton."

"Well, we can't very well talk as strangers if you go and introduce yourself, Marshall. It doesn't work that way," Simon joked, still focusing his attention on the river.

"I'm the groom," Marshall said. "Didn't you recognize the name?"

Simon played along. "I thought you might be a family member…not the actual groom."

Marshall nodded his head in understanding. Simon would have liked to be anywhere else. He sat uncomfortably next to Marshall for a couple more minutes. Out of curiosity, Simon was compelled to take a closer look over at the man...the man he assumed was a spoiled, undeserving, ass of a human being. Instead, a good-looking, young, well-dressed man sat at the other end of the bench.

"Are you married?" Marshall asked.

Simon shook his head no.

"I'm so excited and nervous, all at the same time. I've only seen her when she came for the interview, but she was beautiful!" Marshall looked over the river, remembering April.

"I'm sure you've had your fair share of women," Simon assumed. "A handsome man like yourself."

Marshall looked over, surprised by Simon's statement. "No, that's what worries me…that I won't know what to do."

Fearing that Marshall may ask Simon for advice on how to please April, Simon mumbled something about good luck tomorrow and left, barely making his way up the property and getting around the garden shed before throwing up. It was proof, that in the short time he'd known April, she had penetrated his marrow.

Bent over, with his palms still on his knees, Simon felt unable to move until a hand on his shoulder startled him upward. Earl handed him a handkerchief. Simon blew his nose and then used a corner of the cloth to wipe around his mouth. Earl took a shovel, covering up the vomit with dirt.

"You wanna leave here tonight instead of waiting until the wedding?" Earl asked.

Simon searched Earl's face, looking for any sign that Earl understood why Simon had thrown up. Earl was impossible to read, but Simon answered, "More than anything."

"Go pack a bag, clean up, and meet me out here in fifteen minutes," Earl instructed.

"What about Farrow? He won't want to miss the

wedding."

"Farrow needs another couple o' days to make a decision and Imma give it to him. Go on, now. Fifteen minutes." Earl shooed Simon away from the shed.

After splashing his face off and stuffing some clothing into a bag, Simon closed his door and checked that it was locked. He paused in the hallway because he heard April crying. He closed his eyes, putting his forehead on his door. Out loud, he whispered, "I love you. Have an amazing life."

***

Simon estimated they had been on the road for an hour. The sun set to his left, so he surmised they were traveling north. The small roadway, engulfed with foliage, was barely visible which prompted anxiety in Simon, knowing he could never mimic the route on his own.

Suddenly, the view became otherworldly, as a low-lying fog traveled off the river to the left. Simon could see a small brick building ahead, but beyond that, the world could have dropped away for all he knew.

"Welcome to the resistance within the weeds," Earl announced, raising his voice.

Strange that those would be the first words spoken on the entire drive, especially given they picked up another passenger right outside of Baton Rouge. In fairness, the vehicle groaned and complained so loudly, it hardly encouraged conversation.

The whole valley-like area basked in the light pink twilight as they approached and the sun fell lower. Whatever lay past the entrance, started becoming illuminated with small lights and fires. Earl honked his horn a couple hundred yards from the entrance, announcing their arrival. Birds squawked and took flight, startled by the sound.

Two men exited the small brick building with weapons

drawn. One of them was the biggest man Simon had ever seen. Not only was he tall, but his clothes could barely contain the muscle mass.

"Listen to me," Earl demanded, looking over at Simon. "You're here as my guest. Don't call me by name or use your name. Don't speak at all if you can help it. If you don't draw unwanted attention to yourself, we have a good chance of leaving here alive."

Earl stopped the car in front of the gate with the motor running. He got out, approaching the guards while speaking to them, but Simon couldn't make out what Earl was saying due to the vehicle noise. Then, the passenger in the back got out and nodded to the guards as he passed into the compound.

A weathered sign stood to the right of the little guard shack, still trying to get its point across after years of neglect. It held Simon's attention, as he eyed the remaining letters: A-G-L-A. He scrambled miscellaneous letters around in his head, until he arrived at the only possibility that made sense.

Given how long they traveled from Baton Rouge and the fact that they headed north, he had no doubt the sign once read "Angola." It was the most infamous prison in America at one time, housing incredibly dangerous criminals. Simon closed his eyes and saw the numbers. Ninety-five percent of all prisoners that went to Angola would die there. 18,000 acres were home to the prison, a town for Angola employees and acres of land for crops or animals.

A tap on the car brought Simon's attention back. The immense guard had approached without making enough sound to alert him.

"Get out," the gruff voice demanded.

Simon did as instructed, while the guard backed up in the direction of the shack, lifting his gun to take aim. The other guard ran over to give Simon a rigorous pat down and inspect the bag he had packed back at the museum. The guard found nothing incriminating and seemed disappointed.

"He's good, Banner," said the smaller guard. Looking at Simon, he said, "Nice to meet you. I'm Logan. Good luck this weekend."

Logan reached across the passenger seat and retrieved the car keys. Banner lowered his gun and motioned with his head that Simon follow him into the complex. Their destination was close to the entrance and one flight of stairs up. Simon became uneasy after realizing his accommodations for the evening consisted of an old, operational cell. The bars clanged shut and Banner's smirk gave away his lack of compassion.

To be fair, the cell had all the comforts of home, including a platter of cheese and crackers. He'd missed dinner and found his stomach had settled enough to introduce food again. While he ate, he looked past the bars of the cell and across a walkway. Out a window, he could see that fog covered everything, leaving him to wonder what daylight might reveal as only small breaks of orange light from fire pierced the low-lying murk.

It seemed an early bedtime, but given the fresh air and full belly, Simon couldn't keep his eyes open. The excitement he felt for what tomorrow might bring reminded him of the children in stories Dr. Shane would read to him about something called Christmas.

He hoped April was excited for her tomorrow.

Chapter 17

The clang of the cell, as it opened, roused Simon from slumber. It was early and looking out the window revealed little more than the night before. Earl appeared at the open cell and invited Simon to breakfast before his tour got started. Conversation and laughter of all types could be heard rising from below.

As they walked down the hall, eventually descending the stairs, the noise level increased and the various aromas in the air made Simon's stomach groan. Upon entering the cafeteria, two lines immediately formed to the right or the left of a huge buffet line that ran down the middle of the room. The kitchen was abuzz at the far end of the buffet, busily supplying more food for the lines of hungry patrons.

At first, Simon thought this was similar to the eatery where he used to work, but he watched as men and women pointed to what they wanted and, in some cases, the amount they wanted. The servers filled the plates as instructed.

Not being comfortable with this new freedom, Simon asked for some scrambled eggs and toast which was his standard breakfast fare. He passed by mounds of breakfast meats, fruits, pancakes and muffins. At the end of the buffet sat a supply of cups for the drink stations that were located on the outskirts of the room.

The men and women in the cafeteria wore Quadra clothes, but they had been altered. Many of the men had long hair which was illegal. Their eyes seemed bright and alert which was nothing like back home where a sullenness hung in the air. People were lively, smiling and energetic.

Simon followed Earl to an adjoining room where they both set their trays down and grabbed their cups. When

Simon approached the machine and saw that one of the spigots on the beverage cabinet was marked "coffee," he almost stuck his head under it. The brown liquid came steaming out and he leaned in to inhale the smell. No matter what happened next, this was already a good day.

The cafeteria filled to near capacity, holding a couple hundred people. There were rooms off the main dining hall and no way for Simon to estimate a true head count. While they ate, people came by to greet "Rock" (Earl), intrigued by his guest, but Simon was never introduced. Simon wondered if this was Earl's nickname or last name, but he thought it better not to ask, remembering the instructions to keep his mouth shut.

"Today, you're going to get a tour and be evaluated," Earl told Simon. He raised his hand and waved someone over. "This is Parker and he's going to give you the grand tour today." Earl looked at Parker. "You don't need to know the pledge's name, Parker- call him X for the day." Earl looked down at Simon's plate that held only crumbs. "Go on and start the tour, there's a lot of ground to cover."

Before Simon got up, he downed the rest of the coffee. He had hoped to have one…or even five more cups. He rose from his seat and followed Parker out of the dining hall. Parker stood a couple inches shorter than Simon with a similar sandy-brown hair color. His slight build still boasted strength. Parker unplugged a small vehicle that had no windows or doors, but a ragged canopy overhead. He called it a cart, instructing Simon to get in.

They didn't go far, arriving at a tower where Parker leaped out and waved at Simon to do the same. After using a stairway, the two men came out at the top. The guard posted there was unconcerned with their presence.

"You can see the grounds up here better and I want you

to get a feel for the place," Parker said. "You can't really see the Mississippi river between the pesky fog and all the overgrowth, but it winds around and covers the area on almost three sides." Parker pointed to the southwest and ran his finger around to a northern position. "Over there to the East are the Tunica Hills. This area is protected on nearly every side."

"Do people live here or just come here when they can?" Simon asked.

"Most of us two-dayers stay in the barracks or old cells on our days off. There are loads of people who have relocated here, but they have to do it smart," Parker answered. Parker walked around the tower platform and pointed to the east. "You can see the neighborhood there. The farming and animal fields are between here and the river," Parker said as he pointed to his left.

The fog dissipated quickly as the sun and temperature rose. They first toured the eastern side of the acreage where the neighborhood was located. There was a run-down hospital being renovated into mostly living quarters, but a small portion would be used for injuries or illness. Parker explained that they hadn't found any doctors yet, but had plenty of nurses, which were just as good.

Moving north, Parker drove by a large cemetery nestled against the woods. Huge trees swayed at the entrance, looking as though they were warning people to keep out. Turning west, they passed a sign that read: Prison View Golf Course. Pictures of former presidents flashed in his mind playing the sport and Simon remembered where he had seen this cart they were riding in…transportation for golfers.

Soon they arrived at Lake Killarney where Simon would experience his first test.

"Follow me," Parker said, cheerily, parking the cart

near a solid, 2-story, cement wall.

The building was unremarkable other than its immensity and that the windows were located very high up. When they walked around to the front, a huge door opening revealed a gym and training area. The men and women didn't pay much attention to the visitors as they made their way to the back of the field house to a huge climbing wall.

"This is your first challenge, X," Parker said, pointing upward. "No safety ropes or anything. You need to scale this wall, grab that flag and come back down with the flag as fast as you can. I'll be timing you."

"How high is that?"

"At its highest point, about thirty feet, give or take."

Simon felt a little uneasy about the task, never having enjoyed heights, but he wasn't going to screw up the first challenge. He made his way up the wall quickly, put the flag in his mouth for the descent and carefully retraced his steps back to terra firma. Parker clicked the timer, obviously unimpressed by the effort.

Simon underwent weight-lifting tests, flexibility exercises and speed drills. He managed to complete everything asked of him, but didn't think he'd be able to move in the morning. When taking a break at the water cooler, Parker realized he still had the flag from the rock wall.

"Can you hold this for me?" Parker asked. It was a small bag with a notepad and timer.

Simon nodded, taking the bag. He hoped there'd be an opportunity to see what Parker had scribbled about him on the notepad, but Parker climbed up and down the wall in seconds. Simon choked on the water he drank, while he watched Parker practically perform a cartwheel against the wall and do a backflip to safely land on the ground.

"What the hell was that?!" Simon asked.

Parker shrugged as they left the field house. "It's my thing. Everyone here has a talent or ability that makes them valuable to our community. I can climb better than anyone. That's how I got my name. Climbing is obviously not your thing…or weights…or speed."

"I get your point!" Simon barked, embarrassed by the judgment. As they motored on along the lake, Simon asked, "What did you mean back there when you said climbing is how you got your name?"

"In the neighborhood we visited earlier, someone found a huge stash of something called comic books. They're filled with people who have special talents. That's where we all got our names."

"Why don't you use your real names?"

"Because if we're on a mission and get caught, we don't know anyone's real identities. It's safer this way."

Simon agreed it was a good philosophy and began to think he should start taking this organization more seriously, wondering exactly what Parker meant when he used the word "mission."

They arrived at a pier where two small houses sat on the shoreline. Parker got out and knocked on one of the doors. Out came a shirtless man in shorts with very long hair and a beard, both of which defied Quadra law. He held a pair of swimming trunks in his hand and tossed them to Simon.

"Hi Curry," Parker greeted. "This is X and he's here for a tour and evaluation."

"Aye," Curry responded, with a strange accent. "I don't care who ya be. Put on the shorts and swim to that buoy." Curry pointed to a white buoy in the middle of the lake.

Simon began to take off his pants and both Curry and Parker whirled around in order to avoid any unwanted sights.

"Do I swim back, too?" Simon asked.

Curry turned around, squinting. "Well, I dunno, unless you'd like to stay out there for the remainder o' ya life, I suggest you might wanna swim back." Curry looked at Parker. "See what I told ya? Stupid questions do exist."

For whatever reason, Curry's tone and attitude enraged Simon and he ran toward Curry, tackling him to the ground. Simon sprung up and maintained an old martial art stance from his youth, like it was second nature.

Parker swiftly jumped between the two men, spreading his arms out wide to separate the man standing and the one still on the ground. "I suggest you take that swim now, X."

As Curry rose to his feet, with the first smile Simon had seen from him, Simon got in the water and walked out as far as he could before starting to swim. Both men on shore watched him struggle to stay afloat. The inability to swim had become common in the age of Quadra, but Simon must have had some experience…enough to get him out to the buoy. He clung to the floating marker, trying to catch his breath and gain the confidence to swim back to shore.

"Well, you don't have to worry about him taking your place as the strongest swimmer," Parker said, chuckling at Simon's attempt to return. "You're going to suggest his initiation exercise tonight, aren't you?"

"Yep," answered Curry.

"He may not live through it," Parker mentioned.

Curry shrugged his shoulders. "After the shit he just pulled…I hope not."

Chapter 18

Simon swam closer to the shore where he could touch the bottom and walk the rest of the way. He jumped when something brushed by his leg. He got to the shore quickly, remembering the beast Cass had brought him to cook, wondering if they were in these waters.

"Are gators in this lake?" Simon asked.

"No," Parker shook his head. "This lake is filled with sacalait. If we find gators in here, we relocate 'em if they go willingly. We swim in here. This is where you'll learn to swim if you join the cause." Parker tossed Simon a towel.

"Didn't you see me get to the buoy and back?" Simon asked as he dried himself off.

"Um, ya, but that wasn't swimmin'," Parker joked. "Don't be offended, but Curry could have made it across the whole lake and back by the time you got out and back from the buoy. I'm beginnin' to wonder what it is you're good at, X!"

The men went into the second house and Simon realized that it wasn't dedicated to one person or a family, but open to anyone passing through or wanting to stop and fish. Parker took out some fresh fish from the cooler and cooked it up on the stove for their lunch. He got a tomato/cucumber salad out of the fridge and they feasted.

"This is delicious. What kind of fish is in the lake again?" Simon asked.

"It's called sacalait…it's a white croppie. Supposedly, this lake has always had the best sacalait, even before Quadra."

Simon nodded and continued eating the tasty fish. It came close, but salmon still reigned as his favorite. He'd allow this to occupy second place. They cleaned up the dishes, leaving the house exactly as when they had arrived, minus some food. All the activity of the day had increased their appetite.

When they got into the cart to continue on, Parker looked at Simon with a serious expression. "Listen, if you ever get tired in the water, when you're swimming, the trick is to float on your back and rest." Parker gave Simon a little punch on his arm.

"Why'd you do that?" Simon asked.

"I heard that if you punch someone after an important statement, they're more likely to remember it."

Simon smiled. And that's when Simon thought that maybe his historical knowledge was the special talent he'd contribute here. Clifford and Earl knew each other and maybe they talked about his background coming in handy, although Simon couldn't understand how.

The next stop was a large swamp, teeming with alligators. Parker explained these animals were farmed for meat. The area was fenced in and Simon gasped when he saw a man walking inside the caged area.

"Don't worry, that's Tarzan and the gators think he's their leader. As long as he keeps them fed, he has nothing to worry about."

Simon watched Tarzan as he gracefully moved among the beasts, keenly aware of his location and the reptile's individual temperaments. Tarzan shot an arm up and waved at the two visitors, smiling to expose perfectly straight, white teeth. His wavy, jet black hair that pulled back into a braid and perfect tan caused Simon to stare.

"I hate him, too," Parker laughed, waving back at Tarzan. "He's perfect. Strong, handsome and not just the animals, but every woman who's ever met him becomes smitten. We all hope he falls in love, so some of us have a shot." Parker tapped Simon on the leg. "C'mon, let's check out the gators."

Parker and Simon exited the cart, walking closer to the fencing and saw one of the large, male gators, known as a bull, enjoying the afternoon sun.

"That's Ernesto. He's the other ladies' man around here…successfully breeds every year. Older than you are."

Simon didn't appreciate the comment in regard to his age, but realized Parker was probably ten years younger and didn't know any better. People in the SE viewed age differently.

The alligator opened his mouth wide, shocking Simon by the number of teeth and sheer immensity of his mouth. After a couple of minutes, Ernesto snapped his mouth shut, hissing at the intruders.

"Don't worry," Parker said, "Ernesto is all talk."

The fence between Ernesto and Simon brought little comfort and he walked back to the cart, Parker closely following. Tarzan once again waved at the two men as they left. This time Simon returned the wave as well.

"There's gotta be something wrong with him," Simon hoped.

"Nope," Parker responded, "nicest guy you'll ever meet."

The rest of the tour consisted of acres of farmland and livestock pens. Simon saw many familiar animals, but he asked Parker about one in particular he had never seen before.

"That's a horse. They're used for transportation more than anything. It's not an animal we eat or see much of anymore. They're almost extinct. We're trying to breed them, releasing a couple into the nearby forests every year.

It's been a successful program so far. We hope they'll breed in the wild."

The men stopped at the stables where Simon rode a horse for the first time. A beautiful, chestnut-colored horse named Sissy. Simon was overcome by how expressive her eyes were. He learned the general commands and navigated the pasture, while Sissy graciously tolerated his company.

When they returned to the cart, Parker steered toward the Mississippi River and they went to a place called Angola Landing. There were a few dilapidated homes that were being swallowed up by the weeds and overgrowth, but a small maintained path led to a pier that extended a short distance out above the water. They walked toward the pier, Parker picking up a long stick. Simon realized why when he saw the alligator at the end of the pier.

The animal, not wanting anything to do with the human visitors, abandoned his spot with a slow dive into the water. Both men looked up and down the mighty river, a slight breeze rustling the brush along the banks.

"The Mississippi has always meant a great deal to the people of this area. It's still used for travel and a rich food source to this day. Can you imagine the adventures people had on this water?" Parker mused as they watched the water travel past. "I can't support all that Quadra is doing, but at least the river is clean again. Do you know my grandma told me that parts of this river were called the 'chemical corridor' and 'cancer alley?' The pollution made the water smell bad. Now, look at how it's recovered." Parker lifted his arms.

"I imagine there are more wild miles than before, too," Simon added.

"What's that mean?" Parker asked.

"When people used to travel down the Mississippi, on the water, there are parts of it that looked untouched by humans. They used to be called wild miles. If I remember right, there were about 500 miles of them in this lower part of the river."

Parker became astonished. "Five hundred miles?! Just how long do you think this river is, X?"

"It's over 2,300 miles."

Parker found the number hard to believe, but also recognized a confidence in the answer. He threw the stick in the water, patting Simon on the shoulder. "Maybe that's what you're good for…random facts and information."

Simon smiled. "Maybe."

"We should head back to get cleaned up for the dinner. We need to be at the rally tonight. If I remember correctly, you're the only pledge this weekend. So special…" Parker laughed, amusing himself. Both men donned sweat-soaked clothing, dirty from the day. A shower sounded like a welcome endeavor.

As they drove through the main grounds, Simon noticed that the amount of people in the complex had grown in numbers. People chatted with one another or made their way to other areas. The smells from the cafeteria once again permeated the air. Parker stopped the cart outside the cafeteria and plugged it in. He told Simon he'd come pick him up for dinner from his room a little before 6pm.

If he didn't reek of sweat and animals, Simon would have suggested they eat now to calm the rumblings of his stomach. Simon went to his room, grabbing a change of clothes before meandering down the hall in search of a shower. Most of the cells that were empty this morning were now occupied or had belongings strewn about.

Simon reached a deserted shower area and felt relief that he was the only one there as it was a wide-open space with showerheads protruding from opposing walls. He showered quickly, returned to his room and waited rather impatiently for Parker. He didn't know what about this place riled him up or why he tackled Curry earlier, but he felt more alive than usual…in touch with his senses.

He wished that April could have toured Angola with him today…or, better yet, could join him for the shower.

Parker arrived and they rushed to the cafeteria. Simon asked the servers for exactly what he wanted, no longer concerned about portions. He poured himself coffee. Not that drinking it late was a good idea- he didn't care. It was coffee.

No sooner had he and Parker sat down, they were joined by a woman that sat directly across from Simon. Parker greeted her as Quinn, but Simon never forgot a face. It was Jen from the clinic back in Baton Rouge. She had helped April with her wrist and sent along a nice breakfast to welcome Simon to the area.

"You look good today, Quinn," Parker commented.

Jen stared at Simon when talking to Parker. "I had a fancy occasion to attend earlier today. It required my best Quadra clothes." This reminded Simon that April was now a married woman and he fought the urge to cry. He decided being in touch with his senses also had a down side.

Parker noticed Simon and Jen staring at each other. "Quinn, this is X, he's a possible newbie. He's the only one up this weekend for the rally."

She looked at Parker. "You don't say? If he passes rally, who do you think will call it?"

"Definitely Curry," Parker answered.

"How do you think…," Quinn couldn't finish the question because she saw that Parker immediately shook his head.

"Well, that's too bad, X," Quinn said. "I'd rather hoped

to get to know you better." She lowered her voice. "It's faster and safer in the middle. If you don't remember anything else, remember that."

Before Simon could ask about the cryptic message, Quinn got up and left the table as quickly as she had arrived. Parker's eyes followed her out of the room, exposing some private longings.

When the meal concluded, Parker led Simon to a stadium. People slowly filed in until no space remained. There were greetings and discussions all around. Many of the herd sat on metal benches, but others remained standing. Simon suddenly became nervous by what tonight may bring.

The festivities started with a man climbing the stairs to an elevated platform. When people saw him raise his hand, a hush came over the crowd.

"I pledge…," the man shouted.

Voices in the stadium rose up in unison after the prompt. "I pledge to resist the…," everyone made a hand signal. "I honor this…," another hand signal, "and I'll die for my…," the last hand signal was made to complete the statement.

"Before we start the rally, we must determine a pledge's value and dispatch him for initiation," the man said. He walked down from the platform as Earl (Rock) made his way up. They shook hands as they passed.

Parker nudged Simon, pointing toward Earl. "You need to go up there."

Chapter 19

Earl began to describe the pledge as Simon made his way up onto the platform. "This specimen is fit and easily able to gain strength with continued training, but I vouch for him because he has a special talent that could further the cause." Earl looked at Simon. "Have you ever been here before, X?"

"No."

Simon looked out over the crowds of people and immediately noticed the diversity. He saw that the ratio for men to women was about 4 to 1. Simon stopped scanning the crowd when Earl spoke to him again.

"Has anyone ever told you about this place?"

"No, but I've read about it."

A few chuckles ran through those in attendance. They knew books had been destroyed well before Simon's birth.

"Tell us what you know about the land you saw today from your books," Earl encouraged. He backed up, so Simon could speak to the crowd.

"This place used to be called Angola, after a country in Africa where many of the men and women that came to this area were from." Simon paused briefly, wondering if that information would suffice for an answer, but continued after receiving no guidance. "This area was originally called the Angola Plantation, mostly acres of cotton fields. It became a prison in the early 1900's and had a reputation for housing extremely dangerous criminals. If a man was sent to Angola, he would likely die here."

Earl stepped forward. "And the cart that transported you around today?"

"It's a golf cart. North of the eastern neighborhood, it

looks like a golf course used to be there," Simon answered. The crowd looked quizzically at Simon. "Golf was a sport played a long time ago. A small ball was hit with a metal club and the goal was to get the ball into cups all over the course."

The crowd laughed loudly at such a foolish notion, but Earl raised his hand and immediately silenced them.

"And what of the field with the white stones in the ground?" Earl asked.

"That's something called a cemetery. Long ago, when people would die, the custom was to bury them in a grave and mark the spot with their name. Quadra probably never repurposed that land because it's so remote."

This elicited a collective gasp. All bodies were immediately cremated for cleanliness under Quadra law. The thought of bodies in the ground made the group uncomfortable.

A hand rose in the middle of the crowd.

Earl pointed at the raised hand in the middle of the crowd. "It's not yet time for questions, but I'll allow yours, Clark."

Simon noticed that Earl had a special level of respect for Clark, making Simon wonder if Clark held a position of power here.

"More a statement than a question," Clark yelled, so the crowd could hear. "Even if what this pledge says is true, I'm confused as to how this would be an asset to our cause."

Earl smiled. "Let me show you."

Even Simon stood curious to find out what Earl would present to the crowd.

"It's been almost three weeks that this man has been off drug-laced Quadra foods, making his mind clearer and sharpening emotional responses. We learned through our channels that he has a photographic memory."

Simon knew he could remember things well, but decided long ago that it was a gift of his youth which he only possessed for a time. He tried to communicate with Earl to stop the presentation, but Earl persisted. He placed Simon in the middle of the platform, instructing him to close his eyes until told otherwise.

Many of the people Simon had met or been around during that day came up on the platform, with large pieces of paper folded in their hands. Parker handed Earl a couple when he passed by. Simon heard the rustling, but fought the urge to open his eyes.

"X, when we arrived at the complex, I honked my horn. What is the next sound you heard?"

"A bird cawed near the river," Simon answered.

Earl unfolded one of the papers he held, moving it from one side of the stadium to the other, trying to make it visible to as many attendees as possible. It read: "bird."

"What letters were missing on the sign outside of the complex?"

"N and O." Earl held up the paper with the matching answer.

"You passed a man bench-pressing in the gym on your way to the back wall. How much weight was on the barbell?"

"210 pounds," Simon answered, surprised that he remembered, but easily pulling up the scene from memory. An unknown man raised the paper that read 210 and left the platform.

"On the rock wall you climbed, what color were most of the climbing holds?"

"Gray." A sign again matched the answer.

The name of the fifth server on the breakfast buffet line.

How many teeth in Ernesto's mouth. What fish could be found in Killarney Lake. The brand name of the cart. Names of all the people you met today, in order. The color of the dot on the white buoy. The number painted on the tower door. How many cells were located in his hallway. The color of the shower gel.

He answered them all correctly. Simon didn't know he could recall so much, but hadn't been put in a position to do so since Dr. Shane. Earl told him he could open his eyes. When his eyes adjusted to the scene before him, he witnessed a more convinced people, murmuring to each other.

The same hand raised in the crowd. Earl pointed to it and nodded with permission.

"When I first came to this place," Clark started, "it was fall. I had traveled down the Mississippi river from outside Natchez and walked around these deserted grounds for a couple o' days. No one left." Clark spoke slowly…deliberately.

"I picked out a house I liked in the neighborhood and set out to gather firewood to combat the chill in the air. A lot of wooden signs dotted this property, so I started taking my axe to 'em…using 'em for kindling. They were dry and saved me the energy of cutting down the trees. Worked real well."

Clark nodded, remembering the early days. "For some reason, I could never get the name of that stone garden out of my head…I think you called it a cemetery."

Clark made his way up on the platform, taking a piece of used paper out of Earl's hands, asking him for a marker. Earl snapped his fingers at Parker on the ground level, who quickly produced a marker. Clark wrote on the paper, folding it in half when he had finished. He gave the marker back to Earl.

"So, X, if you know so much about this place, what was the name on that piece of wood that I burned in my hearth? Cause no one but me could know." Clark added.

Simon breathed deep, as the documentary he had seen about Angola played in his mind. He became nervous that the name didn't pop up in his head immediately.

"The prisoners that didn't have family take them home for burial were laid to rest in a cemetery on prison grounds," Simon said to himself, although many around him could hear his words. "The prison was not only self-sufficient in life, but also in death and the prisoners were guaranteed a spot at point lookout if they had no other options available." Simon smiled, raised his voice and shouted, "Point Lookout."

Clark opened the paper and it read: Point Lookout. He threw the piece of paper in the air, taking his hands open in front of him and pulling them toward his chest, while closing his fingers to his thumb…sign language for "accept." The crowd followed suit with the hand gesture, chanting "pledge." Clark enthusiastically shook Simon's hand and welcomed him.

"O.K., pledge," Earl said in Simon's ear as the crowd continued to chant. "You've passed this part of the entry process. Follow me."

Earl walked back toward the cafeteria, where he and Simon got into the cart. Curry and Tarzan drove up in another cart and they all started driving south in silence. The sun had just started to drop and the colors in the sky were beautiful. Simon felt quite smug by the outcome of the rally, but had so many unanswered questions for Earl when they went back to the museum. Simon hadn't forgotten the instructions to keep his mouth shut while in the complex.

The main entrance could be seen about a mile to their

left as they continued to head south. It took ten minutes to arrive at their destination. They all got out of the carts and walked out on the beach. The river splashed at an angle onto the sand.

"Seriously?!" Curry complained. "Rowe's Bayou…could you get him any closer?"

"Shut up, Curry," Earl calmly demanded. "He still has around 65 miles and you know this is overkill because he wounded your pride. I'm not even sure you could do this."

Curry, obviously insulted, went back to sulk in the carts.

"Alright, X, in ya go," Earl said.

Simon looked at the water and back at the two men. "What do you mean? In there?" Simon asked as he pointed into the river.

"Yep. You need to make it down to Baton Rouge by morning. The river runs about 5 mph now that the local dam was removed. It's about a 12-14 hour trip, but I suggest you swim a little 'cause you can't be in the water more than twelve hours or hypothermia could set in." Earl explained. "Lucky it's summer."

Usually confident, Simon seemed horrified at the notion. He looked at the river again. "I'll walk."

Tarzan shook his head. "No, amigo, it would not be a good idea. Poisonous snakes, alligators and you'd never be able to sustain that speed on land."

"But aren't there alligators in the water?"

"Yes," Tarzan answered, with a quick nod. "Many."

"They probably sleep at night, though," Simon said, hopeful for confirmation.

Tarzan had a quizzical look on his face. "No, they are most active at night." Tarzan could see that his comment didn't please Simon. "They can also hold their breath for 30-

45 minutes."

"Stop helping," Earl said, patting Tarzan on the shoulder.

"I'm not doing it!" Simon said, flustered. "Take me to the person in charge of this place…someone who can make a decision. This is like murdering me- I'm a terrible swimmer!" Simon yelled in Earl's face. "I mean it. Take me to the person in charge. Maybe he'll listen to sense."

Earl didn't move and ignored Simon's demands. "You're losing daylight. You better get going."

"This is crazy," Simon reiterated. "Just let me talk to your leader."

A flash in Earl's eyes gave away that patience had left him. He tilted his head and slowly asked, "What can I do for you?"

"No, I want to…," Simon froze, becoming keenly aware in that moment that it was Earl who ran this complex.

Curry had stormed back down on the beach, charging at Simon. "Just get in the water, you pussy," he insisted.

Before a word escaped anyone's mouth, Curry grabbed one of Simon's arms and twisted it behind his back, leading him into the water. When they were deep enough and the current strong, Curry shoved Simon into the river.

The men nervously watched the surface of the water until, not far from where he went under, Simon's head broke the surface, gasping for air. He now had no other option, but to travel with the current.

When Curry joined the men back on the beach, they busted up laughing.

"Now that we've seen how amazing his memory is, I hope he makes it, but he swims like a rock," Curry said.

"We had Parker and Quinn give him hints on how to accomplish it, so maybe that will help," Earl added.

“Did he really tackle you?” Tarzan asked Curry.

“He did. When he got back on his feet, I recognized a martial arts stance. So, Quadra probably did train him, like we presumed. He could be a huge asset.”

“Martial arts are a plus, but he still has to learn that we don’t use our strengths against each other. Teaching a man his age about respect is not an easy thing,” Earl said, looking down the river, no longer able to see any trace of Simon. “Well, let’s get back to the rally. Maybe we can catch the end.”

Curry and Earl walked toward the carts.

Tarzan paused at the edge of the river before leaving. He quickly made a sign of the cross and whispered out loud, “Vaya con dios, amigo.”

Chapter 20

Simon gasped as he wrestled with the water to stay afloat. Not long after he had been rudely introduced to the Mississippi, he started aiming for shore, but envisioned the inhabitants of Tarzan's alligator pen waiting for him.

Jen's cryptic words now made sense: "It's faster and safer in the middle." Even Parker had words of wisdom: "The trick is to float on your back and rest." They were trying to help. Simon's momentary thankfulness evaporated with the knowledge that they must have known he'd be in this predicament.

The intermittent starlight was a poor substitute for the setting sun at the start of the watery journey. There were clouds that eerily swept across the skies, momentarily allowing stars to shine against the water. With every bend or change in the river's course, Simon hoped to see the lights of Baton Rouge as a symbol that the hellish experience would soon come to an end. He longed to be dry and safe.

Floating on his back wasn't easy, but he fought to keep his feet in front of him. He'd momentarily give in to the exhaustion and let his body fall beneath the surface of the river. Everything went silent and he'd initially be at peace with the thought of dying, but soon pushed his head up for air.

His feet hit something hard and the object grazed his side as it turned into him. He hoped an alligator had come to put him out of his misery but instead, he grabbed onto a large log. It was an immense help keeping him afloat even though it had lost some buoyancy from taking on water.

All track of time was gone and he figured he must be about halfway to his destination when a small light shone in the distance. Simon became overjoyed, letting go of the log by accident. He immediately went under, taking in a combination of air and water while desperately grasping for the log. At one point he had the log with both hands, but foolishly moved it slightly to one side, allowing the current to whip him around.

When he stabilized the log and his trajectory, he concentrated on the light. The light was not in a fixed position, but moved around. When within about 50 feet of the light, he could make out a person waving their arms. His ears strained to hear the words being yelled, but couldn't make them out until about twenty feet away.

"Grab the rope!"

A rope was soon visible a foot above the water, tied between two protrusions exiting the water. When the time was right, Simon pushed against the log with one hand and reached up with the other, grabbing ahold of the rope. As the log drifted away, he gripped the rope with his other hand, too. He lifted himself up as much as possible because the water slammed against his neck and traveled around his head. There was a small boat of some sort twenty feet to his right, also attached to the rope.

"Can you get to me?" The person on the boat called.

Simon didn't answer, but quickly sidled along the rope to the boat. He looked up, blinded by the light.

"Listen carefully. Hold onto the rope and let your legs go slack with the current. It's going to seem counter-intuitive, but you need to trust me. I'm risking my ass doing this for you."

Simon followed the directions and his legs were grabbed and lifted into the boat. He heard a grunt as the boat moved closer to him, being pulled against the current. Soon Simon had his butt on the boat.

"This needs to be fast. Grab my hands and I'll pull you in. Don't help too much or try to lurch into the vessel or we both get tossed in the water. Stay low. On your knees. Do not stand up. Smooth transition, Simon…smooth. Are you ready?"

"Yes," he groaned.

"Now!"

The movement was quick and Simon hesitated slightly when removing the second hand off the rope until he thought his body weight would be supported. He fell to the right side of his rescuer who was tossed back by the effort. The boat rose on one side, but quickly righted itself.

Now that Simon's head was above the light source, he could see that Jen was his hero. She wasted no time in turning off the light on her chest, cutting the line that attached the boat to the rope and grabbing an oar as they began to glide down the Mississippi.

Once Simon could regain his composure, he said, "Thank you, Jen."

She smiled. "You're welcome."

"This is certainly a better way to travel down the river. Where did you get this thing?" Simon asked, patting the boat.

"It's an old, inflatable drift boat that's been around forever. It's seen better days, though. I'm not sure I can put another patch on it. Most of the vessels around here are inflatable because it makes it harder for Quadra to find."

Simon began shivering. "How can I be cold? It has to be at least eighty degrees out."

"The water is cooler and drops your body temperature, but you weren't in there for that long- you'll recover quickly."

"Not long?!" Simon said, outraged. "Baton Rouge has

to be around the next bend!"

"That rope was tied between the columns of what used to be the Audubon Bridge," Jen explained, "which is four hours of river travel, give or take, from Angola." She chuckled. "We have about six hours 'til we reach Baton Rouge. The good news is that the boat will be faster than swimming."

Simon watched as Jen masterfully navigated the river. At a point soon after they started, she paddled toward the left side of the river. A large piece of land appeared to cut the waterway in half.

"Is that an island in the middle of the river?" Simon wondered.

"Yes. Technically, this waterway is called the Fancy Pointe Stream. It's just quicker. We come up to another split at Profit Island and bear left again. Let me show you something kinda cool."

Jen turned on the light that hung around her neck and pointed it toward the shore. Several glowing balls moved around. Simon squinted, trying to see their origins.

"Are those lightning bugs? I remember those when…" Simon stopped mid-sentence, not wanting to disclose his time at Quadra in the Northeast.

"Those are the eyes of alligators. They have tapetum lucidum at the back of each eye that reflects light so they can see better in the dark. The farther the eyes are apart, the longer the animal."

"I'm impressed."

With amazing speed Jen smacked the top of the water with the oar, shaking the boat. Simon spanned his arms out, taking hold of anything, fearful to return to the water. She turned off the light, deciding it was better not to see what lurked in the stream or attract attention. The boat eventually traversed through the chute that once again connected them to the Mississippi.

Simon and Jen both seemed exhausted. Luckily, the small boat flowed with the current, not requiring much work.

Simon watched Jen until she noticed him looking at her. "Why did you help me?" Simon asked.

"The way Parker shook his head in the dining hall meant you were a terrible swimmer. Doubtful you'd make it. And you deserve a shot if you can contribute to the resistance."

"After this, I'm not sure I want to join your little club."

Jen's face grew more serious and menacing. "I should throw your ass right back in the river. Don't say things like that or you'll be eliminated and my effort here tonight wasted. You no longer have a choice. You've been there…met Earl- received a tour, for God's sake. You've already joined, make no mistake."

"What is with Earl, anyway? He's kind of an ass!"

Jen ignored Simon's question and asked her own. "What's with you going after Curry like you did?"

"I'm not sure what got into me," Simon responded, wringing his hands.

Jen softened. "It's not what got into you- it's what's getting out of you. You haven't eaten Quadra-provided foods in a while. The food has levels of tranquilizers based on your testing, to keep you calm and subdued."

"Based on my testing?"

"When you went in for feasibility testing to determine potential marriage matches, they ask a bunch of questions…take your blood. You would be shocked at what blood can tell us about a person and those hundreds of questions are aimed at personality traits and behavior patterns." Jen said as she raised her eyebrows.

"Everyone takes those tests before they turn eighteen," Simon said, unconcerned.

"Don't you see? That's the problem," Jen raised her voice. "If I choose the way of the escort hubs, why should I take a test that I don't need? And what are the tests for, exactly? Seems to me they are a means of social engineering- breeding out defiance or used for other unsavory schemes. They're playing God!"

Simon almost made fun of Jen for being so dramatic until he remembered Dr. Shane coming to him right before he turned eighteen…not long after he had taken the feasibility test. That's why he risked his life to transport Simon. He quite possibly saved his life because Quadra spared no threats earlier in their reign.

"That's where we find resistance candidates…people who have been deemed "unfit" for marriage. Most of the time it's because they are individualists or prone to free thinking. Quadra wants none of that. I tried to pull your test, but I couldn't find anything."

They traveled a long distance in silence until finally, after rounding a large bend, the lights of Baton Rouge could be seen farther up ahead. They weren't like the photos Simon had seen in his studies of New York or Chicago, but he was grateful all the same. He smiled wide with relief.

"You're quite handsome, Simon," Jen complimented. "Maybe now that April is married, we can see each other from time to time."

Hearing April's name stopped his heartbeat for a second. After gaining his composure, he weakly nodded in response and before he was able to speak the boat lifted up momentarily. Jen grabbed the oar, paddling swiftly toward shore.

"What's the matter?" Simon asked.

“We must have floated over a piece of the old bridge. It ripped a hole in the boat. Help me paddle toward shore.”

Simon quickly stuck his arm in the water and rowed on one side of the sinking vessel. The thought of being cast into in the water again renewed his strength. All the furious work from both parties removed them from the strongest current, but the boat would be under soon.

“You choose,” Jen said to Simon, their eyes locked with intensity. “We go through the mouth of the Monte Sano Bayou and walk the five miles or we stay in the river.”

“Bayou,” Simon answered, as the boat continued to take on water.

Jen grabbed his hand and they fell into the water. What was left of the boat floated down river. Jen held onto Simon and pulled him to the surface.

She impatiently instructed him on how to float. “You have to arch your back! When we get in position, kick your feet and leave your arm out to help you float.”

She locked arms with him on one side, soon floating on her back. The unfortunate-looking backstroke got them to shore.

Chapter 21

Hitting landfall coincided with the darkness slowly disappearing, making for an uneventful walk to the museum.

Jen waved goodbye to Simon as she headed up the street. It wasn't long before Simon ran up beside Jen.

"Can I catch a shower at your place?" Simon asked. "I think I lost my keys in the river and I can't get in the museum or my room. Showing up like this would be suspicious."

"Sure," Jen agreed. "I have a couple hours before I have to be at work, but I'm taking a shower first."

Work, Simon mused. How he spent the last twenty four hours made work seem a bit mundane. Jen grabbed a hidden key and climbed the outdoor stairs to her apartment. She lived above the medical clinic which was expected. Most posts were within a half mile of their workplace.

What Simon didn't expect was a studio apartment with a shower in the corner, encased in glass. When he turned around to talk to Jen about formulating a game pan, she walked past him completely nude.

"Take your clothes off, Simon. We only have access to so much water and I can't have Quadra nailing me because of water usage. I'll get in first and then you have to shower immediately after. Three minutes for each of us."

He took his wet, smelly clothes off as he fixated on Jen in the shower, wondering if he never noticed her beauty because of April. Jen jumped out, allowing Simon his turn. She smirked seeing that Simon enjoyed the view. Men were so simple.

Jen applied lotion, which was merely for Simon's entertainment and further suffering. He gaped at her from the shower until she got dressed. Jen had laid out men's Quadra clothing for Simon to wear. Quadra's dress code was the same for everyone and only consisted of four differing outfits for public wear.

"Where did you get these?" Simon asked.

"From a friend. They should be your size. You can't wear what you came home in. And I'll need that towel back, too."

Simon smiled as Jen walked toward him, wrapping her arms around his waist. She maintained eye contact and a slight grin. She undid the towel from the back, where it was twisted over and purposely pressed into Simon, while running her hands over his bare backside as she retrieved the towel. He went in for a kiss, but Jen moved away.

"You better get dressed. They'll be looking for you at the museum."

Simon arrived at the museum relieved that no trace of a wedding remained. Before his first tour, he had enough time to hoover down some breakfast and make a glass of tea, wishing it was his beloved coffee instead. Farrow replaced Simon's lost keys, but not without complaining about the length of time he'd had them before misplacing them. Their conversation tapered off when Earl sauntered into the kitchen, followed closely by Cass.

"Did a little fishing this weekend," Earl told Cass. "There's some sacalait in the fridge. Threw a big one back yesterday!"

Simon's face flushed red with anger, certain that the "big one" referred to him.

Earl poured a glass of tea and the two of them left, talking of hunting and fishing escapades. Simon expected Earl to congratulate him for surviving the initiation or reward him with a look of surprise, but Earl gave him no such satisfaction.

On the first tour of the day, Simon identified a man in the crowd just like Clifford warned him about. It made sense that a Quadra agent would arrive in Baton Rouge around the time of a special event, where strangers would be less conspicuous. The agent would expect a progress report or information to bring back to his superiors.

At the end of the tour, the Quadra agent asked to speak with Simon outside. Simon followed him to the bench.

"Denton sent me," the agent said, once they had been seated. "Tell me what you have."

Simon compiled quite a bit of information over the last month, but he decided that nothing of accuracy would be relayed to Denton. Only one person Simon had met didn't have a tie to either Quadra or the resistance, so he thought it best to lead with that, possibly throwing them off.

"Cass is a potential problem, but I need more time. He's edgy and prone to violence. Also, I've seen a boat crossing the river at night sometimes," Simon lied. "Everyone is leery of outsiders in this town so it's been difficult to garner trust."

Without saying a word, the agent got up and walked away. Simon sat on the bench, waiting for him to return. After ten minutes, Simon went looking for the agent in the museum and on the grounds. He found Earl, tending to the garden.

"What'd you tell him?" Earl asked.

"I threw him off by mentioning suspicions about Cass and that I'd seen boats crossing the river at night," Simon answered.

Simon flinched when Earl bolted by him. Simon followed Earl toward the museum until Earl noticed a car speed away, heading south. It was too late. They had taken Cass.

Earl turned around and put a finger in Simon's face. "If anything happens to that kid, I'll kill you." He smacked into Simon's shoulder when he passed. "Be out here after dinner. We need to discuss some things."

Simon watched the car until it could no longer be seen. A pang of guilt came over him as he'd never meant to heap trouble on Cass. April would be sorely disappointed with him if any harm came to her brother because of his idiocy.

The noise from the next tour group that waited outside the front door of the museum diverted his attention. Farrow would be letting them in soon, so Simon returned to give the remaining tours for the day. His mind wandered amid the boredom, thinking of the many colorful characters in his current life story, but mostly Jen. The bold, naked and gorgeous Jen.

Simon prepared dinner, forgetting to account for April and Cass's absence, so there was plenty of food for the three of them. Farrow mentioned that the POL had borrowed Cass for a 24-hour period. A sigh of relief escaped Simon and Earl. If the POL had documented a "borrow," then Cass wouldn't be harmed, merely questioned.

While they were finishing up with their meal, Farrow said, "I'm joining you, Earl. Whatever you're doing. I've known you for a long time and I trust you."

Earl smiled and nodded his head. Simon wanted to warn Farrow about being thrown in the river or tests he'd have to take, but he kept his mouth shut in front of Earl. After the dishes were cleaned up and the remaining food put away, Earl nodded to Simon to follow him outside.

A small, metal table and two mismatched chairs were set up on the garden side of the shed. Simon didn't think they were there previous to tonight. Earl put a small cloth over the table and set up two cups, inviting Simon to have a seat until he returned. Earl went into the shed for a few minutes when a familiar smell traveled to Simon's nostrils.

Earl joined Simon at the table and poured him a large cup of coffee.

"It's not as good as fresh, but even re-warmed, it's better than tea. I imagine you must be fairly exhausted," Earl said.

It was the first sign that Earl had any sympathetic leanings. He held his glass. Simon wasn't sure what to do, so he mimicked the gesture. Earl tapped Simon's glass with his and drank.

"So, we couldn't find anything out about a Simon Handler until the age of eighteen," Earl said, after returning his coffee to the table. "Can you explain that?"

Simon told Earl almost everything about his life, omitting his dalliances with April and the new-found lust for Jen because they lacked pertinence. Earl listened, nodding in response at times as the sun began to set over the river.

Jen sauntered past the garden. Simon turned to watch her walk to a tree on the museum grounds and did his best not to give away his level of interest. It occurred to Simon that he didn't mention Jen's river rescue. He'd keep that to himself, not wanting to get Jen into trouble.

"I've heard talk of missions and anti-Quadra rhetoric, but what is the end game here?" Simon asked. "What do you hope to achieve?"

"I think freedom comes to mind more than any other cause. The ability to choose things for yourself and live a life more as nature intended. No drugs in your food. No death at 70. Deciding on your own spouse and when it's a good age to marry. Traveling outside the 500 mile rule. Maintaining a post of interest…" Earl trailed off.

"But who says Quadra hasn't chosen a good life for

us?"

"You could be right, but it's my life and I should have the right, within reason, to screw it up without interference." Earl chuckled. Then, becoming more somber, he added, "Or make it beautiful."

"Is your resistance group trying to take down Quadra?" Simon asked.

Earl cocked his head. "Do you know why we threw you in the drink?" Earl asked, ignoring Simon's question.

Simon shrugged, still traumatized by the thought of the water.

"Now that the Quadra drugs have worn off in your system, many of your true reactions are burgeoning to the surface. But you need to learn how to direct these in a beneficial way for you and the resistance," Earl explained. "When you went after Curry that was improperly placed energy. He's not the enemy. When you just said 'your resistance group,' that makes it seem like you're not a part of it and puts distance between us."

The men sat in silence, while Simon realized everything Earl said bore truth.

"You're at a crossroads, Mr. Handler with a unique opportunity to either work for the most powerful organization known- Quadra. Or you can join the resistance. But, when Clifford contacted me about you, he guaranteed that you were a man who desires to make a difference. I'm counting on that."

Earl stood up and cleared the table while Simon looked out toward the river, his eyes darting to catch glimpses of Jen.

"Well, goodnight," Earl said as he passed, making his way toward his room in the museum.

"Do you really think I can make a difference?"

Earl turned around and moved toward Simon, lowering his voice. "If I didn't, I'd never have sent Jen to fish you out of the river."

Chapter 22

The weekends that followed were used for training at Angola. Simon made his decision to back the resistance based on learning about the three main goals of the movement.

1. Whatever the government denies the people (rights or specific advantages), we will attempt to deny the government, while only taking lives when necessary.
2. Learn truth. Share truth.
3. Record history prior to the Quadra government, for future generations.

Simon and Jen traveled to Angola together, using a cover story that they were seeing each other and getting away for the weekends. It didn't take long for the two of them to start a secretive, physical relationship that they'd enjoy every Friday night before reaching their destination.

One such evening, as they were holding each other in the sweaty afterglow, they talked for hours and covered all manner of topics. Simon mentioned how surprised he had been at Earl's level of intelligence, complimenting his leadership abilities.

"I mistakenly thought he was a simple country boy when I first met him. We hear tales up my way and they are an unfair portrayal. Why did Earl never marry?"

"He did marry," Jen informed. "An amazing, beautiful woman that he loved dearly." Jen teared up at the thought of her. Simon became uncomfortable because Jen usually wasn't prone to such emotion.

"What happened?"

"Earl and Ann knew each other since they were children

and decided to marry outside the rules of Quadra," Jen started. "But when Quadra got her test results and saw that she was fertile, they came for her. She'd been married to Earl for five years when she was taken. They didn't recognize the marriage as legal, even though they had a child together."

Jen apologized, as she wiped her flowing tears away.

"That's criminal!" Simon said. "But, Earl makes more sense to me now."

They gathered themselves, starting back toward Angola on a little dirt bike. Every week it was a different form of transport. Many weekends horses were left halfway and they would have to ride a bicycle north to reach the horses.

The noise of the dirt bike made any conversation impossible. Simon had not yet learned to drive this mode of transport, so he held onto Jen's waist as she maneuvered the cracks that dotted the road. By the time they arrived at Angola, Simon's ass was sore.

During their weekend stays, Simon and Jen carried on like they barely knew one another. The training schedules left little time for socializing anyway. Simon's assigned mission was a fuel depot in Beaumont, located almost 200 miles west of Baton Rouge.

Reconnaissance convoys deployed to Beaumont in the past, discovered the area was not as heavily guarded as they expected, only storing the fuel- not mining for it there. Houston, on the other hand, another eighty-five miles west of Beaumont, mined the fuel for every quadrant. Surveillance found that Houston maintained high security and would be impossible to hit. The Quadra border between the SE and SW fell slightly west of Houston, making for an extra line of protection.

The main objective hinged on destroying all the stored

fuel that would soon be distributed. If there was an opportunity to grab some fuel and transport it back, all the better. The fuel storage levels in Beaumont were the highest of the year. The more they could destroy, the harder it would be for Quadra to patrol.

"The key on this one, gentlemen," Clifford instructed, "is that we make it look like an accident. A storm is supposed to hit next weekend and if we can pin this on lightning strikes and go unnoticed, that would be the best outcome possible."

Banner raised his hand, waiting for Maestro (Clifford's Angola name) to acknowledge him.

"Don't we want to leave a calling card or let them know who's responsible?" Banner asked.

Clifford shook his head. "That's a young man's game. There's no room for prideful foolishness. The only thing that would accomplish is to alert Quadra of an enemy presence or possibly heighten their security, leading to more attempted infiltration of our communities. They already know something's amiss- they sent Rogers here." Clifford pointed at Simon.

Simon was named after the comic book character that had America in the title. He knew so much about that timeframe that it seemed the right choice.

"We good, Banner?" Clifford asked.

"Yes sir."

Clifford would head up the tactics portion of the operation, naming Logan as his second in command. The Beaumont crew consisted of Clifford, Banner, Logan, Parker and Simon. Not a large group, but a capable one.

Simon and Parker were the only men needed at a post on Monday morning. The time frame would be tight with the inclusion of so many miles. The men reviewed, studied and practiced their plans the entire weekend. They'd be ready.

Over the course of the months Simon had been visiting Angola, he had increased in strength, exercised his gift and, with the help of Curry, became an impressive swimmer. It would soon be November, but the weather was warm enough to continue swimming.

The men, resigned to the fact they couldn't speak one more word about their mission, went to the dining hall before Sunday night's rally. Simon convinced himself that the food at Angola had helped him bulk up at the gym. Tonight would be no exception because the venison and sweet potato pie may have been the best thing Simon ever ate.

He scanned the room to see if he could find Jen anywhere and decided having her for dessert would be a perfect ending to the day. Even though he had a scheduled return with Earl this Sunday night, he'd see if he could convince her to take him to Baton Rouge.

The crowds formed for the rally and Simon could fully participate now that he'd learned quite a bit of sign language. When the moderator of the rally went up to the podium, he began the pledge. Everyone repeated the beginning in unison and went on to finish the rest of the pledge. "I pledge to resist the," they yelled, signing the word for lies. "I honor this," signing the word army. "And I'll die for my…," they finished, signing "freedom."

The beginning of the rallies, Simon came to learn, consisted of resistance business, but the best part of the rallies were when the announcements were over. The Sundays that showcased music talents were the camp favorites. Because music had been outlawed by Quadra, the resistance took even more pleasure in the musical melodies.

Simon approached Jen, speaking loudly in her ear once

he reached her so she could hear over the music.

"I'd really like to go home with you tonight. Maybe we can make a stop before getting to Baton Rouge?" Simon posed the idea with a wicked grin and glint in his eye. He was sure Jen couldn't reject the offer.

"Sorry," Jen answered. "I have a date tonight after the rally with Tarzan. We usually see each other on Sunday afternoons before the rally, but we were both so busy today."

Without thinking better, Simon grabbed Jen's wrist and led her away from the noise of the rally. She asked him nicely to let go of her wrist after a few yards. When Simon didn't comply, Jen swept his legs out from under him. As Simon twisted to the ground, Jen pulled her wrist to the right, making sure Simon would land on his back.

His mistake was not employing a defensive posture as he fell because Jen pulled her knee up, aiming it directly at Simon's crotch. She rarely missed her targets and this time was no exception. All air left his body as his face turned red with pain. Tears dotted the dirt on each side of his head while Jen went to retrieve some ice from the close-by dining hall. She returned with a small bag, tossing it on his chest with very little compassion.

After a couple minutes, Simon could speak. "Why would you hurt me like this?"

"I asked you nicely to let go of my wrist," she answered flatly. "Do you want help up?"

"Not yet," Simon said, coming to a sitting position on the ground with the ice bag gently positioned. "I still don't understand..."

Jen squatted down, looking directly into Simon's eyes and said, "No man is allowed to touch me unless they are invited to do so. I killed a man once for less and I'll kill you if you ever do something like that again." Jen shrugged.

"That's as plain as I can explain it."

"Can you help me up?"

Jen escorted the limping Simon to a set of stairs that led up to his room where they both took a seat. Simon had been so taken with Jen's sexual talents, that he didn't notice this dangerous side of her.

"So, what, you see me on Friday nights and Tarzan on Sunday? Busy girl."

"And Dr. Michon on Wednesdays," she added, not the least bit ashamed. "That's how all his records are available to us. He's a valuable resource."

Simon wasn't sure if he was jealous of the other men or that Jen got to have sex three times a week. As long as Simon could remember, he was allowed to order from the escort hubs twice a month. Now that the drugs in the food were completely out of his system, his testosterone wanted more.

"But, I can see how three might seem like too many," Jen agreed. Her tone was laced with sarcasm. "Tarzan was my first love, not to mention that he's amazing in the sack and we need Dr. Michon's connection. Looks like I'll have to give up my Friday night lover."

Before Simon could object, a voice interrupted their conversation.

"Ah, amor, shall we go?" Tarzan kissed the top of Jen's hand as he stood in front of her bare-chested.

Simon understood his charm, watching as Tarzan bent over, staring into Jen's eyes. She jumped onto his back for a piggyback ride, leaving Simon to witness their exit.

"I think he owns a shirt, but we're not sure," Parker laughed as he strolled over and sat down. "If you're trying to score with Quinn, it's an impossible task. Tarzan's smooth voice, tanned skin and magical dick are no match for mere mortals, my friend." Parker patted Simon on the back a couple of times.

"No, no," Simon lied. "The hubs are more my pace. No emotional attachments."

"The emotional attachment is what makes it better, though," Parker said. "One time, Quinn and I went on a mission together and were stuck in a cave for almost two days. We've never kissed, but I've been in love with her ever since. She lives life with abandon. It's so attractive."

"What do you mean?"

"She enjoys life and wants more than what Quadra offers us. When we were in the cave, we talked about everything. Her life motto that she stole from her father is: It's not how long you live, but how wide. Isn't that amazing?" Parker looked off in the distance and sighed.

"I've never heard that before," Simon said. "I need some time to mull that over."

Chapter 23

Simon and Earl sat in the back of a transit vehicle, jostling their way toward Baton Rouge. Simon, thankful that his crotch had gone numb with cold, still winced when the vehicle went over a bad bump.

Earl noticed the ice pack and asked, "What happened to you?"

"Hurt myself in training. I'll be good as new in the morning." Simon figured it wasn't a lie because he did receive training on Jen's tolerance levels.

"Why don't you stay at Angola?" Simon asked, changing the subject. "Instead of going back and forth."

"You have to age out or fake a death in order to stay up there," Earl answered. "Dr. Michon has completed a few death certs for us, but we don't want Quadra to get suspicious. Plus, I enjoy my life at the museum and the money I make helps support the cause."

When they pulled up on the street, rear of the museum, they grabbed their bags and exited the transit. Earl walked around the side of the museum, but quickly pushed Simon back behind the building. He signed "be quiet" and "hover." Since Simon had reported the mysterious river crossings at night, hovers had started patrolling the area.

Earl signed for Simon to stay put. He then turned the corner of the building, dropped his bag by the side entrance and headed for the river. Once Earl had almost reached the river, he started making noise so the camera would be targeted on him. A loud noise thundered from above before the hover exploded into pieces.

Earl turned around and smiled toward the museum. Simon started walking toward the bench when Cass flew out the front door with a shotgun in his hand he had just used to take down the hover. He ran to see if there was anything to salvage. Simon decided to go into the museum; he'd pretend he arrived after the excitement.

Once it was decided nothing of value remained on the hover, they threw it in the river and immediately ran toward the museum in case another one was scheduled to arrive. Earl hated littering in the river, but he'd retrieve the hover before his next trip to Angola.

If Quadra caught anyone with a hover, in any condition, it constituted treason. The punishment for treason? Whatever the judges felt reasonable on that day…using any logic he or she wished. All crimes were considered a crime against Quadra; therefore, all crimes were treasonous.

Cass and Earl busted into the kitchen, reliving their story of man vs. hover. Simon came in to the kitchen later and put on a kettle so everyone could have tea while they talked. It took Cass longer to tell the story than the length of time the entire drama unfolded.

Simon watched how Cass and Earl spoke to each other, realizing that Earl cared for Cass, but must not trust him completely to keep the resistance from him. It would be hard for Simon to trust the big meathead, too. Farrow soon joined everyone in the kitchen and the story was retold.

"We don't have any tours scheduled for tomorrow," Farrow announced. "So, Cass, I loaned you out to the old LSU campus. There's some work that needs to be done in the dorms. I guess that's where Quadra will be staying for their search month in November. The three of us," Farrow announced as he pointed at Earl and Simon, "have a project to accomplish here."

"Why can't I help you guys tomorrow?" Cass practically whined.

"Take the experience, meet new people…you know my motto…" Earl said.

Both Farrow and Cass recited Earl's favorite saying, "It's not how long you live, but how wide."

Simon's eyes widened as he leaned over the tea- his mind racing. *Son of a bitch*, Simon thought. The memories all lined up neatly in his head like little soldiers.

On the day Jen sent the fancy breakfast to the museum, it happened to be Earl's birthday and it was Earl that mentioned that Jen seemed impressed with Simon! The breakfast wasn't meant for Simon at all. Earl also gave the order for Jen to fish him out of the river. The two of them are probably the only ones that know about the rescue. Jen cried over Earl's wife being taken away because that was her mother! Simon continued to cuss in his head.

Earl's life motto, the final clue, erased any doubt and led to one conclusion- Jen was Earl's daughter. Simon, dumbstruck by this new information, headed straight for his room. Farrow yelled after him that he wanted everyone up early so they could finish their task. He responded with an indistinct mumble before he shut the door to his room.

Simon paced back and forth in his room, working things through. Did anyone know that Jen and Earl were related? They certainly didn't act like family. Was Simon in danger if he figured it out? Unwelcome flashes of Jen in compromising positions made their way into his head. Then, his mind would imagine Earl letting the alligators rip him apart in the pen, while he and Tarzan had a good laugh about it.

Simon stressed himself out thinking about tomorrow's project and working with Earl. He decided the time spent with both men would be a good time to gather information. He'd play it cool. Be observant.

Slowly, Simon's heart rate returned to a manageable pace. He was able to calm himself down just enough to start nodding off to sleep…the worst night's sleep since he arrived in the SE.

***

Cass was already gone when the men moseyed into the kitchen for their morning cup of caffeine. Earl took out a small device, raising an attached antenna, and began walking all over the room. The lights on the device glowed red near the kitchen island, which led to a closer investigation. Earl grabbed a radio, placing it under the island. The Quadra propaganda poured out of it at a medium volume.

"Let the bastards listen to their own programming, if they want to listen to something," Earl said, before joining the men at the table. "If we speak in regular tones, they won't hear anything."

Farrow showed concern. "Shouldn't we just get rid of it?" he asked.

"No," Earl answered. "They are counting on Cass to perform his duties."

"You mean Cass is working for Quadra?!" Simon said, shocked at the realization.

"Yup. When they borrowed him for questioning, they thought he'd be a perfect candidate. He has a sister married into the counselor's family, plus his test identified him as compliant and in need of affirmation. He's a model candidate," Earl explained. "He will toe the line."

"Doesn't that make you nervous?" Simon asked.

"Psh. No. Cass is a lot of things, but he's not that bright. He already told me about the interview and everything else he should have kept to himself. All the reasons I never trusted him to keep the resistance a secret. He'll be useful…if we use him right." Earl looked at Farrow. "So, what is this project we'll be working on?"

"The basement," Farrow said.

"What basement?" Earl asked.

Simon thought that Earl knew everything there was to know about the museum property.

"The museum has a basement, Earl. There are artifacts down there from old museums before Quadra took over," Farrow explained. "Simon has been bringing Clifford some pieces to catalog and filling in the historical significance, if necessary."

"That old som'a'bitch," Earl said, with a loud pound on the table. He looked at Simon, "So you knew about the basement, too." He smacked Simon, who sat beside him, on the back before clapping his hands together. Earl smiled from ear to ear, likely the most emotive anyone had seen him.

Before Farrow spoke, he shot Simon a look, concerned about Earl's strange reaction. "I've been told Quadra has been using new gadgets during their searches. They have an X-ray wand that can see through floor coverings, walls, furniture…you name it. It only has about a two-foot range, but we must protect the basement's secrecy. Follow me."

Farrow led them to the large stone fireplace at the far end of the museum. He bent slightly to enter the hearth, but stood up after inside. An awful sound rang out that made Simon and Earl bend over to see the metal door scraping the floor. Farrow turned on his flashlight and waved them inside, shutting the door.

"This is where slaves were hidden," Farrow said. He pointed to a ladder with the flashlight and the men started downward. "They would hide down here and a fire would be lit in the hearth to further protect the hiding place. I found an iron grate for the fire place that has metal wheels on it for easier movement. If it happened to be a warm day, where a fire would be out of place, they probably wheeled it in, filled with wood and kindling."

One by one, they reached the bottom. Wherever they had landed, the flashlight was the only source of light. Farrow shone the beam on a small handle directly opposite the ladder. When the door opened, Earl and Simon stayed put, still not able to see. Farrow switched on the lighting that illuminated the basement from end to end.

Instinctively, now that a small bit of light had been cast into the room, Earl and Simon glanced back toward the ladder, practically jumping out of their skin. A skeleton, wearing a tattered outfit was propped up into a sitting position in a corner.

Farrow stuck his head back in the room. "That's Chance," Farrow said. "I found him down here and didn't want to move him. It's his resting place.

"Chance?" Earl asked. "You knew his name?"

"No. I just figured whoever he was, he must have taken a chance to get this far, so that's what I named him. C'mon."

It was now Earl and Simon who shared a glance of concern.

Chapter 24

Farrow showed the men the pile of metals that he had collected over the last few months. He explained that the X-ray machines couldn't scan through the metal, so if they were able to line the basement ceiling with it, they wouldn't be found out.

The men started the chore, but since Earl had never seen all that the basement contained, he found it difficult to stay on task. Farrow told him that he could come down later, but that he needed to focus- no one knew for sure when Quadra would perform their search. Mentioning Quadra re-focused Earl immediately.

Farrow had been collecting different types of metal since he had become aware of the basement. Metals were not something readily available, but he collected all he could find. The men nailed old cooking sheets, farming tools and mostly unidentifiable pieces to the ceiling. Farrow's wife worked at a food factory and supplied him with a couple rolls of aluminum foil, which covered any open spots on the ceiling after the bigger pieces of metal were hung. It took them all day to complete.

When the ladders were put away, the men started looking at the basement treasures. Earl lifted up an artifact. "What's this?" he asked.

"That's a cell phone," Simon told him. "A communication device, but mostly used for other things. People would line up for hours trying to get the latest and greatest."

"I remember those," Earl said. "My momma cried for days when these were shut off and kept checking to see if it started working. I mean this," Earl said, pointing to what the phone was stored in.

"That's a plastic bag," Simon said. "They were outlawed well before the final quarantine. It started with light-weight plastic shopping bags and then all plastic bags. That one in your hand," Simon smiled, "was called a Ziploc."

"Why would you ban those?" Farrow wondered.

"What's shopping?" Earl asked.

The floorboards creaked above them and they heard Cass call out a greeting. He kept repeating "hello" as his footsteps could be heard above.

"Follow my lead on this one," Simon said.

The men went to the stairway at the alternate entrance. Simon switched the lights off and started sliding the panel at the back of the closet. They all knew that the fireplace wasn't an option because of the loud noise the metal door made when it opened.

Simon pushed the toolbox to the left and ushered Earl and Farrow inside. Once he backed into the closet, he shut the panel behind him. He pulled the light cord, not worried about it being visible because it couldn't be dark in the museum yet. Simon edged past the others, closer to the door, and started to whisper a plan to the men.

Their eyes grew wide, when the unexpected sound of the doorknob interrupted all talking. Simon turned around when the door was barely cracked, pushed it open and jumped out of the closet to yell "BOO!"

Cass fell backward, losing all color in his cheeks. Simon had scared him so badly, that Cass had pissed himself. The men pretended not to notice as Cass lowered his shirt over the wet area.

"I'm sorry Cass. I was explaining how I used to play hide and seek with a friend of mine when I was young, trying to show them examples of places we'd hide. When we heard you come in, I thought it would be funny to get in the closet to hide on you," Simon explained. "How did you find us? We were so quiet!"

Simon smiled at Cass, doing a great job at playing it cool. Cass fidgeted, his eyes darting over to the toolbox. All three men realized that Cass didn't "find" them at all. He thought there was no one at the museum and he was trying to secretly get to the toolbox.

"Cass, I'm so sorry this happened," Farrow said. "Can I help you up?"

Cass probably wanted to kill Simon, but because Earl had been in on the shock, he got off the floor and excused himself to shower. Farrow locked the closet with a skeleton key until the toolbox could be checked out.

Farrow led the men to the welcome desk. Before he spoke, Earl checked the area with the device that detected listening bugs, but it remained unlit. He nodded at Farrow, letting him know he could speak.

"Thank you for helping with that project. I'm going home, but I'll be back tomorrow morning to let the first tour in. Here's the skeleton key for the closets," Farrow said and handed it to Simon. "Earl, keep Cass busy with something this evening and let Simon know when it'll be a good time to check out what's in the toolbox."

Farrow heard a honk outside so he left to get his transit.

Earl huffed, shaking his head as he went outside. Simon watched Earl walk to the bench, sit, and let his head collapse into his hands. This seemed an oddly emotive day for Earl so Simon joined him, standing at the end of the bench.

"Are you OK?" Simon asked Earl.

Earl sat upright with tears marking his face. He shook his head, half laughing, like insanity had taken root.

"I'm getting too old for this, Simon…too tired," Earl confessed. "It used to be there wasn't anything I didn't know. I knew who I could trust and why people did the things they did, but now- I'm not sure I can keep things straight- not like you."

Simon didn't expect the compliment.

"Last night, I could see it in your face. You figured out that Jen was my daughter, didn't you?" Earl asked as he looked in Simon's direction.

Simon nodded, not caring to elaborate on the extent of his relationship with Jen, wondering exactly how much Earl knew.

"I figured," Earl sighed. "See, I've known Farrow has been team Quadra since he came here twenty or so years ago. Today only confirmed that conclusion because he never could have known about the x-ray machinery they were using for inspections otherwise." Earl turned on the bench to face Simon and raised his finger. "But, today, he went out of his way to protect something Quadra wants desperately to destroy. It makes no sense to me."

"There are pieces of his history in that basement. Pieces of himself," Simon said.

Earl squinted, waiting for further explanation. Simon took a seat on the bench.

"Farrow didn't know anything about that basement until a few months ago. He found a local woman's journal who wrote during Civil War times. She chronicled the societal make-up of the day, most notable to Farrow- slavery." Simon smiled and added, "He's pieced a lot together in a short time. Look at how he's named Chance and discovered that the room was a hiding spot for escaped slaves. He's a smart man!"

"Why would he want to learn about something so

atrocious?!"

"Because it's the truth and most people have a desire for it, no matter how ugly. What Quadra gives us is bullshit."

Earl looked at Simon with a new-found respect. "How did we get here…so far from the truth?"

Simon shrugged. "People. People picking their truth…or being taught what to think versus how to think. Simpletons deciding their truth is more important, while calling themselves open-minded, but judging with such ferocity and hypocrisy that they prove their claim of acceptance a cheap lie."

"If you can keep people pitted against each other, they can't look past their enemy where the true danger lies," Earl said.

"I like that. That's truth…Quadra was definitely the unforeseen danger."

"You're going to be the next leader of the resistance, Simon," Earl said, before standing. "We need to get you fully trained." Earl looked quickly toward the museum. "Here comes Cass. I'll keep him busy for a few minutes, fishing out the hover from the river. Go check the toolbox."

Cass glared at Simon as he passed him on his way toward Earl. Simon decided it would be funny to whisper "boo." Had it not been for Cass's growl, Simon would've never known that Cass turned to come after him. Cass wasn't able to land his first punch because Simon instinctively used a foot sweep to drop his larger and stronger opponent. Cass rolled down the slope of the grounds toward the bench, but dug his hands in the grass to stop the momentum.

"Cass, I need your help," Earl said.

Cass got up and followed Earl down by the river. Simon thought for sure that the rage he saw in Cass's eyes meant he'd come after Simon relentlessly until exhaustion came over him or injuries made it too difficult to continue. Simon invited the opportunity to fight, hoping it would release bottled-up frustrations.

He watched as the men almost reached the water's edge before he went to check out the toolbox. After unlocking the closet door, he rolled the toolbox to its normal place- in front of the door. When he opened the second shelf down, he found a box of ten listening devices. He quickly removed all the batteries and decided if Cass wanted to play spy, he would be hard-pressed to hear much without a power source.

If Cass did notice the batteries were missing, which seemed unlikely, it wouldn't be an easy thing to explain to Quadra. It'd be best to wait for more batteries than be thought of as careless. Simon stuck the batteries in his pocket, hoping to find a use for them at some point. He went to the kitchen to remove the battery from the listening device Earl had found earlier.

Simon started making some sandwiches for the three of them as Earl and Cass came into the kitchen with the dripping hover. Cass put the machine on the table.

"It's so quiet," Cass said. "If April was here she'd be screeching about taking this off the table." Cass let out a big sigh. "I kinda miss it."

Cass grabbed a sandwich and went to his room, leaving Simon confused by the sudden mood shift from just a half hour ago.

The two men grabbed their sandwiches, deciding to sit on the other end of the table.

"What happened down at the river?" Simon chuckled. "Did you medicate him or something?"

"No, I told him that watching him fight or act up takes a lot out of me."

Simon looked at Earl over the table. "I don't

understand."

"It's complicated. I'm like a father to Cass," Earl explained. "A couple of weeks ago, I told him I have cancer. His dad died of cancer when he and April were very young. My disease wasn't found early enough and the treatment would be lengthy."

Earl paused as the realization of all he explained washed over him. Earl verbalized not only Cass's condition, but his own, when he said, "He's scared and anxious."

Suddenly, so was Simon.

Chapter 25

Farrow let Earl and Simon leave the museum early on Friday. He clocked them out at the end of the day so no suspicions were raised. The Beaumont team hoped to depart from Angola while the sun still shone. They planned to make it to Opelousas, about two hours away, where they had a contact. Traveling through Lafayette would be a mistake, given the high Quadra presence in the city.

They couldn't risk being stopped or questioned by Quadra. Simon and Parker were the only ones with genuine papers and they were not wearing standard Quadra garb.

Earl dropped Simon off at the training room near the field house. There were many training facilities, but this one would be closer to their exit point. Their points of entry and exit had all been carefully planned out. Clifford left nothing to chance when it came to the team's actions.

It was almost five when Parker finally arrived. Simon followed their lead as all the men got suited up in black garb for the first leg of the trip. The river-crossings and road travel could be dangerous.

Banner and Logan carried huge backpacks, while the other men only brought small duffels to the waiting carts. The two drivers took the men to the most northwest spot on the grounds, dropping them off.

The team reached a pole on the river's edge that stood over thirty feet high. It blended in with the other trees and wouldn't seem out of place if viewed from the river or land. Clifford grabbed harnesses and equipment out of an old freezer that had been camouflaged with dirt, instructing everyone to put the harnesses on. Once Banner had his harness on, he rotated a crank attached to the pole. Above the men, a metallic line became visible and moved across the water. A clear, plastic line was attached to it as a guide, keeping the mode of transport virtually invisible when not in use.

"This is called a trolley," Clifford informed Simon, while handing them out. "This goes over the cable and then you put this handle through the bottom. Clip the ring on your harness line through the hole in the bottom of the trolley and let go of the post," Clifford told Simon, pointing to their destination. "There's another zip-line on Shreves Bar that will take us across the rest of the river. I'll go first so you can see how it's done."

Clifford climbed up the metal stakes on the pole like a teenager. He fished under the canopy of leaves and branches that hid the beginning of the line and did exactly what he just explained to Simon. In no time, he was traveling across the water, disappearing into the foliage of Shreves Bar.

"Go on, first timer," Parker said. "It looks fast, but you practically come to a complete stop before your butt hits the ground. Just hold onto the bar on the trolley and try to keep your legs lifted straight out in front of you."

Simon did what he was instructed, finding the ride across the river enjoyable. There were a couple branches that brushed his face on Shreve's Bar, but he kept his legs lifted and landed safely in a huge pile of leaves. Clifford told him to get off quickly, so Simon pulled the handle through the pulley and lifted it off the cable. The cable traveled another fifty feet past the leaves and attached to another post about ten feet off the ground.

Soon after, Parker, Banner and Logan followed. Because of Banner's size, his landing was not as smooth as everyone else's. The weight of the large pack didn't help. Banner hid the first cable. The men quickly went to the western shore of the bar and repeated the ride to get to the other side of the Mississippi.

Simon looked between the last post and across the river as Logan turned the crank to hide the cable.

"It's a one-way trip," Logan said. "When we come back, we use a raft to cross. You'll see, Rogers."

The men collected their zip-line gear and placed it in an old footlocker for safe keeping. A Transit sat under a brush-covered tarp. Quadra may not have been actively patrolling this area, but it was suspected that they had access to satellite surveillance and could spot larger pieces of metal.

Logan and Banner shoved their bags in the back before the others threw theirs in.

"Why are your bags so huge?!" Simon asked. "Nothing on the list took up that much space."

"We got different lists," Logan joked.

The men piled into the car and started down the Mississippi River Trail Road. There were no turns or stops until they arrived at another river. The men covered the car with a tarp and brush. Clifford was the first to strip down to his skivvies, as Simon looked on, confused.

"We swim across this one," Parker said.

"It's safer to keep your drawers on so the fish don't think there's a worm for the taking," Banner added. All the men chuckled.

"Clothes in here," Parker instructed, holding out a plastic bag.

Both Banner and Logan retrieved two large inner tubes from near the tarp and tied a line from them to their waists. They got into the water, while Parker loaded everyone's bags on the tubes. And, just like that, all the men started swimming across. Simon couldn't believe the improvement in his swimming ability from just a couple of months earlier.

They were half-way across when someone started heckling them from the opposite bank.

"Those strokes look like shit! My daughters swim better than you. Let's go, ladies, I don't have all day!"

The taunting sped Banner across, but everyone else continued at their initial pace. Parker retrieved the bag of clothes from one of the inner tubes and distributed them.

"O.K., lads, wet undies in the bag," Parker said.

After all were dressed, they followed the heckler to a waiting transport vehicle. The fit was tight. The man who picked them up couldn't possibly be in regular society. His gray hair was tied back in a pony-tail and his beard ventured in all directions.

"My name is Sherlock," the man said to Simon. "What's your name, newbie?"

"Rogers. Nice to meet you," Simon said.

Logan elbowed Simon, shaking his head. "He's an ass."

Sherlock feigned shock, before a hearty laugh escaped him. "So how did you all enjoy your swim in the Atchafalaya?"

"Same old leg of the trip, Sherlock," Clifford chimed in.

As he drove, Sherlock passed a large bag to Clifford who sat up in the front. The bag was full of sandwiches, cookies and cut-up vegetables. He doled the food out to the men. Everyone was hungry, making quick work of the meal.

Unlike the previous drive, this one contained many turns and twists. Simon felt himself getting queasy. When he couldn't stand it any longer, he asked Sherlock to pull over and promptly threw up beside the car door. He felt miserable and the raucous hooting from the men didn't help.

Another half hour passed before Sherlock exclaimed, "Welcome to Opelousas." Simon lifted his head long enough to see a dilapidated sign with the same greeting. "This is the zydeco and spice capital of the world and used to be home to one of the top ten racetracks in all four quadrants…my home: Evangeline Downs."

There was one road leading to and from Evangeline Downs. When they turned on that road, they met with armed guards about a half-mile in, but the guards immediately recognized the driver and opened the fencing that blocked their path.

Simon couldn't understand how Sherlock hadn't been raided by Quadra because he was so close to Lafayette. He figured there is either hush money being exchanged or Sherlock was able to make this place seem on the up and up, when necessary. Either way, Simon didn't trust the man.

Sherlock slowed down for the safety of the horses that grazed all over the grounds. He pulled up to a hotel which sat just past an old casino, the neon light barely standing to identify the building.

"Someone will check you in at the desk," Sherlock said, as he stopped the car. While the team grabbed their bags, he continued to shout instructions, "Keep to yourself. Don't start any trouble. There are all kinds of people here and everyone needs to mind their business and be peaceable."

Clifford could be heard saying "ya, ya," under his breath. The men got three room keys at the desk. The room assignments were never discussed. Logan and Banner shared a room and Rogers and Parker, while Maestro got his own room.

The men were assigned to the third floor. Clifford explained how the second and third floors were the worst because noise from all sides invaded the rooms. They climbed the stairs and Banner's bag bumped a man descending the stairs. He turned around, cussing at Banner and acting like he wanted to fight- until he fully realized the size of the man holding the bag.

The carpeting was such a wild pattern that Simon was afraid if he looked down for too long, he'd get dizzy and fall. The halls stunk of a combination of body odor and the cleaner that attempted to mask the smell.

A cloud of dust rose into the air after Parker opened up the curtains in the room. No light came in from outside as the sun had long disappeared. Parker coughed and opened the window to air out the musty smell. One lamp in the room worked, but it emitted a buzz.

"You get that bed, since you decided to rain down on it with dust," Simon said, pointing at the bed closest to the window.

Parker and Simon decided to sleep fully clothed. It was a common practice for people who may need to react at a moment's notice. Both men were exhausted, planning to shower in the morning, hoping light would flow into the bathroom. They lay in bed, making idle chit-chat, waiting for sleep to come.

"Have Logan and Banner been friends for long?" Simon asked.

"They're cousins," Parker told Simon. "You won't find two closer friends, but they have completely opposite personalities."

"How so?"

"Banner is a good guy and even though he could easily take a life, he thinks about things. Whereas, Logan...," Parker paused, shaking his head on the pillow and looking upward. "He'd rather kill someone then have a conversation with 'em. That's why they're often together. One, without the other, leaves you kinda lopsided."

"That's weird," Simon said. "When I was coming into Angola for the first time, Logan seemed like the nicer of the two."

"Ha! He's been trying lately, but he is not a nice guy. Believe that."

Chapter 26

A loud thumping on the door roused Simon and Parker.

“Rogers…Parker! C’mon, we have to go.”

This wasn’t the planned way or time to leave so Simon and Parker quickly got up, grabbing their belongings and, after a quick bathroom stop, were on the road in less than five minutes.

Logan drove. Clifford passed out dry bread from the passenger seat, conducting a quick brief.

“A storm has been spotted, coming up from the south. If you look in that direction, you can see the dark sky. We don’t know the window of opportunity, but if we can make our strike during the storm, it bodes well for us. This weather might interfere with the traveling times, so we needed to get on the road immediately.”

Simon’s nerves were on edge, but the hum of the tires on the road lulled other passengers to sleep. Logan pulled over at some point to fill the tank with more gas. A small container of fuel was stored in the back.

“You dumbass!” Logan yelled, waking everyone up. “Look who decided to join us?!”

Everyone looked toward the back to find a petite woman nestled among the bags and supplies. Her beautiful eyes blinked with apology. Banner closed his eyes with disappointment, while Clifford shook his head. Parker smiled, clearly entertained by the circumstances.

“When I told you that you could use my room last night, it was to say goodbye,” Clifford said, facing the front of the car in irritation.

“Della, what are you doing?! I said we’d get you on the way back,” Banner scolded.

"I know, Banner, but after you fell asleep, I heard Clifford and Logan in the next room talking about taking the northern route back to highway 1," Della explained. "That wouldn't take you through Opelousas."

"Is that true?" Banner asked.

Logan and Clifford nodded.

"Get out and wait here," Logan barked. "We'll pick you up on the way back."

Before Logan could lay a hand on her, his feet had left the ground. Banner hoisted him above his head.

"I'm positive you weren't going to touch her," Banner snarled. "Positive!"

Logan was visibly shaken and assured Banner that was not his intention. Banner placed Logan back on the ground before extending his hand to help Della out of the cargo area. A clap of thunder could be heard in the distance as the wind picked up.

"The storm is moving in. We're not leaving her here." Banner said, walking to the door.

"But there's not enough room in the car," Logan complained.

"You can wait here if you want," Banner suggested. "Once we rid ourselves of the explosives, there will be plenty of room. And she will sit on my lap for now."

Logan didn't push any farther, knowing that if he made Banner choose, Della would win every time. That fact enraged him and was exactly why he had convinced Clifford to take the northern route back to Angola.

Once everyone got situated and the doors were closed, the rain started to patter against the car. Within a minute, the rain went from patter to downpour. The wipers couldn't clear the sheets of falling water fast enough and the noise on the roof made it hard to hear people speaking in normal tones.

Banner introduced Parker and Simon to Della. She had met the others. Parker had heard a lot about her and tried to update Simon with the latest news about their relationship.

"So, they've known each other since they were kids," Parker told Simon. "Banner is actually from this area. They tried to figure out how to take the personality test in a way that would match them up perfectly, but it didn't work. Della was assigned to the escort hubs because she's beautiful, but infertile. And Banner was labeled as a great fit for Quadra. He got a death certificate and joined the resistance. Della is supposed to report to the Lafayette hub next week, which is why she's stowed away in the back."

After Parker had finished his background update on Banner and Della, Simon looked over at the pair. Banner did not look happy and started to say something to Parker…or kill him, judging by the glare.

Della put her hand on the side of Banner's face and whispered something in his ear. He smiled, lowering his head and moved her long, brown hair to the side so he could give her neck a quick kiss. Simon wondered how they could possibly be intimate with each other without Banner's immense size harming her.

Simon's thoughts drifted to April and then Jen until the rain began crashing down in waves, interrupting his train of thought.

The weather impeded their progress as they had to stop to move debris off the road or slow down until the road became visible. They arrived in Beaumont close to noon, but the storm still raged, offering them a cover.

They pulled off the main road alongside the facility. The brief the team studied in training said that a patrol went out every half hour to check the tanks, but they had been watching from the Transit for two hours and hadn't seen a soul.

The tanks were huge, cylindrical beasts that held close to a million gallons each. The eight tanks were spread out over the property with dikes built up around each one just as the report explained.

"What do you think, Maestro?" Logan asked, as he took his eyes away from the binoculars. "We can get in and out under the cover of this storm. No one seems to be around."

Clifford nodded. "It looks like the storm interrupted a transfer on tank four. There's an abandoned transport that may have some fuel loaded up. Let's take that home with us. Parker, why don't you retrieve it first before we destroy the tanks."

Parker left the dry Transit to venture out into the storm. It was near impossible to see very far with the rain pelting the windows and the storm casting a dark shadow. Fifteen minutes later, Parker returned with the Transit. Not one inch of him had remained dry.

"OK, let's do this," Clifford said.

The explosive packs were doled out- two each to Parker, Simon and Logan and one each to Banner and Clifford. The team exited the Transit, while Della stayed behind without saying a word. All men were wet through in an instant. Clifford gave the men their stopwatches, yelling loudly to be heard over the storm.

All four sides of the wire fencing that surrounded the facility had cut-out openings that were fastened with metal clips. Parker had already unclipped the top and one side of the nearest cut-out, making it easy to swing the fencing open.

During the first tactical meeting of the team, Simon had suggested that the start-point for the attack be on the lowest elevation point of the facility. That way, if anything went wrong and gas flooded the area, the wave of fuel wouldn't have far to travel. It wasn't fail-safe, but it did eliminate one danger. He cited the bizarre molasses flood of 1919 in Boston that killed 21 and injured 150 to make his point.

The team, once through the gate, raised their stop watches over their heads. When Clifford lowered his, all the men pressed their buttons and took off. Parker was the fastest on the team, so he was assigned the farthest two tanks. It had been a bone of contention when Simon was given the number two spot, but Logan challenged Simon to foot races often and only beat him once. Banner was in the fourth position because he was indeed strong- not quick. Clifford may have possessed speed at one time, but it had disappeared with his youth so he was assigned the closest tank.

The moisture in the grass made it a slippery job getting to the tanks. The rain blasted the men while close lightning strikes threatened their safety. The only plus of the situation was the lack of patrols. The men could barely see their targets through the rain and darkness.

Parker arrived at his first tank, standing on the dike to assess the situation. The tanks were about 40 feet high and throwing the device up to the top had never been an issue in clear weather. The force of this rain, however, changed things. Torch, the guy who trained everyone on these "tank farms" and how they worked said a stairway was attached to the tank if they ran into any problems.

Parker found the stairway and ran half way up before setting the timer to 45 minutes on the device and throwing it on the top of the tank. Simon and Logan had successfully set their first bombs as well. Banner was halfway back from his tank because, even in the storm, he was strong enough to launch the device. Clifford had just gotten to the top of the tank to place his bomb on the top.

Clifford was too curious and wanted to see the top of the tank for himself. It was unremarkable, but he remembered Torch explaining everything with such excitement. He spoke of the ullage, which was the vapor space under the roof and how some tanks had floating roofs to keep the vapors to a minimum. These tanks had standard tops and that is how Torch chose what type of explosive to use. Torch's excitement about the subject must have interested Clifford for him to go all the way to the top of the tank in the rain.

A scream made it to Banner's ears before getting to the car. He looked at the Transit, knowing Della was probably getting worried. Never should one veer from the mission instructions, but Banner did just that when he turned around, moving toward the closest tank.

He found Clifford, hopping down the stairs. He had slipped, getting his foot caught under a rung. When he fell downward, the ankle snapped and he couldn't put any weight on it. Banner quickly grabbed Clifford by the back of his wet collar, placing him on the ground.

He removed his jacket and gave one sleeve to Clifford so the rest of the jacket could keep the rain off of his face. Banner grabbed the other sleeve and pulled Clifford as the wet grass made for a slick sledding-type experience. On the way to the gate opening, Banner saw shadows of his team running from different directions to return to the Transit.

When Banner got to the gate, he lifted Clifford over his shoulder. After opening the passenger door of the transit, he lowered Clifford into the vehicle. He glanced at Clifford's ankle, which wasn't facing in the right direction. He looked back at Della and smiled, attempting to ensure her that all was well.

"You guys had the shortest distance to go and you still couldn't get back here before us!" Logan bragged.

No one responded. Parker had already left in the Quadra fuel Transit. The unexpected acquisition would need to be de-bugged and stripped of any fuel-related markings before driving very far in it, at the risk of being traced. There were fuel stores in the van that would come in very handy for the resistance.

Banner climbed in the transit with the rest of the team and Della. They readied for a quick escape that didn't come because when Logan went to back up, the tires spun in the mud.

Chapter 27

Logan kept trying to back up, which only dug the tires deeper into the mud. Clifford put his hand on Logan's arm to stop him from making things worse.

"Rogers and Logan, get out and put leaves, branches, brush- whatever you can find behind the rear tires of the vehicle," Clifford said, through wincing pain. "When you're done, Banner can push the car out of the mud and we should get enough traction to get out of here. Banner and Rogers, you stay out of the car so the load will be lighter."

Everyone got out of the car, but Logan and Clifford. Even Della was searching for branches to help with the car's traction. The rain had not let up and when Simon saw how deep the tires were rutted in the mud, he wasn't convinced they'd be going anywhere.

When a short path had been made behind the tires, Banner told everyone to get out of the way. He went to the front of the car and nodded at Logan. Logan gassed the car while Banner pushed down on the front bumper, lifting the back tires up. They caught on the shrubbery and the car quickly sped backward. When the front tires hit the divots the back tires had made, the car jumped up and landed hard. Clifford's yelp could be heard through the noise of the storm.

Simon looked at his stopwatch, knowing that they were cutting everything too close. Only twenty-five minutes before the fireworks- if the lightning didn't hit the devices. There were metal safety rods to attract lightning all around the grounds, but Mother Nature rarely followed any man-made rules.

They took the same road out of Beaumont, but veered

left about ten miles out of town, heading northeast. A crooked sign, battered with age, announced they were traveling on Freeway 12. Soon, the storm started clearing, making it easier for Logan to drive at a higher speed.

The loud sound that rumbled through the air was different than the lightning they had heard all day. Clifford raised his stop watch, clicking the button…the others mimicked the action.

"Sixty-two minutes," Clifford reported.

"Yep. Within a minute," Simon said.

"Torch is good!" Banner said, smiling over at Della, who now got her own seat.

Simon watched the two of them, wondering what it was about Della that got her assigned to the escort hubs. There was a certain personality that got pulled for that post. Usually, the women had a lower self-esteem, which fed off male attention. The men escorts were the exact opposite, thinking they were a gift to all women. Simon imagined what might happen if Della were to flirt with another man at Angola or vice versa. If Banner ever caught wind of it, there'd be bloodshed.

The team met up with Parker in a deserted town, once known by the name Eunice. They gassed up, quickly sharing their stories. Luckily, the patrols or the potential of being pursued never entered into the equation, but they would have been ready.

The team changed into dry clothing, deciding to put the wet clothes in one bag for now. It was 5:30 and they planned to travel on a bit further, but wouldn't make it to Angola. A river crossing at night, with a wounded team member, wouldn't be wise.

Clifford had changed his clothes in the car. He turned around to calmly speak to Banner, "Della can't come with us."

Banner's expression read of disbelief.

"Parker is waiting in the fuel Transit to take Della back to Opelousas," Clifford said.

"You can't keep us apart!" Banner yelled.

"I know. You're free to go with her. Parker can take you both back," Clifford explained. "You made a choice a few years back to join our group and you know this isn't how we do things. You can't just take people in without the proper vetting or knowledge of their abilities." A couple moments passed as Clifford let the words marinate with Banner. "If this is what you want…go. No one will stop you."

Banner looked at Della and the whole car recognized his decision had been made. He got out of the Transit, walking Della to the waiting vehicle as she wailed. He begged her to understand, but she refused his explanations. Her crying turned to harsh obscenities and horrible insults, which raised eyebrows in both Transits. Parker finally drove away as she continued to yell out the window.

Banner returned to the Transit, where not one word transpired between them until their next stop. Logan knew where they were headed and Clifford was reeling in pain, while Simon awkwardly tried to avoid eye contact with Banner.

They made it to St. Landry right before dark. Clifford's injury would require a slight change in plans, making for a more northern route. There was only one bridge in the area that still stood and it went over the Atchafalaya River on highway 1. The roads that awaited them in the morning were not as straight forward as the ones they had traveled already.

Logan got out and made a fire by the vehicle, while Simon moved a couple stumps for seating. This looked like a place that had seen a few weary travelers before because the pit had stones built up around it.

"You made the right ch-," Logan started to say.

"Shut up," Banner demanded.

"I get it, too soon…too soon," Logan chirped, as he lifted his hands in the air as an act of surrender.

Clifford smiled while he sat sideways, still in the passenger seat of the vehicle.

Banner went to the back of the transit to retrieve a first aid kit. He took out a syringe and started tapping the sides, moving toward Clifford.

"Pain medicine will just make me groggy," Clifford said, "swatting at the needle."

"Listen, old man, if any of us are going to get any sleep tonight, you're taking this shot."

Banner didn't bother to roll Clifford's sleeve up, sticking him in the arm. He started to return the first aid kit, but spun around to address Clifford.

"I saved your life today and you couldn't do me one favor? Overlook one rule?" Banner complained. "I love her!"

"You didn't do me any favor, why should I do you a favor? I should've died on that field…blown to bits. Dead! No pain, but instead my ankle is killing me, look at it!"

"I'm not going to apologize for getting you out of there, you crazy, old bastard!"

Clifford softened. "I appreciate it, but you're never supposed to veer from the mission. Never."

Simon moved Clifford from the front seat to the larger passenger area of the transit so he could lie down when the medicine took effect. Within a half hour, Clifford was slurring his words and fighting to stay awake. Parker arrived shortly after Clifford started snoring and joined the men around the fire.

Parker distributed venison jerky, bell peppers and potato chips from his bag. It made for a strange meal, but all the items kept well and there were no complaints. Everyone seemed famished. The water jug in the transit was soon drained by the thirsty team. Parker made a makeshift clothes line out of some rope and branches, hanging up the wet clothes to dry by the fire.

Banner sighed when he saw Della's top. "So, do you think everything we're trying to do will make a difference?" Banner asked out loud, to no one in particular.

"I think so," Simon answered, staring into the fire. "We've never seen anything like them in our lifetime, but there used to be events called wars. Quadra banned the word a long time ago. But, countries would face off against each other, fighting to the death, if necessary. Sometimes there would be fighting within the same country."

The men listened intently to his words, but Simon continued to be mesmerized by the fire, while the other men looked at each other, confirming this wasn't the end of the thought.

"What's your point, Rogers!?" Logan asked, kicking Simon's stump.

Simon blinked, looking in Logan's direction. "I'm sorry. What I'm trying to say is that we won today. I don't know if we'll win tomorrow, but today- we experienced a victory. How I understood it, wars are these things made up of a hundred battles, smaller skirmishes that may or may not impact the larger picture. This year, Quadra won't have enough gas to cover their quadrants...do their searches…find the run-aways." Simon grinned, looking around the campfire at the men. "That's pretty amazing. That *will* make a difference."

The men nodded in response, feeling better about chipping away at Quadra's power. Parker brought out some oatmeal raisin cookies for desert. The kitchens at Angola, once again, didn't disappoint.

Banner took Simon's words into consideration. "Do you think being part of the resistance comes at too high a price? I mean, what about being able to make my own choices, like with Della?"

Logan scrunched his face up like he had just bit into a lemon. "Your own choices?! Quadra lets you make your own choices? Really?! Did they let you marry Della? No sir! And can she disappear off the face of the Earth? No sir! She lives too close to Lafayette and would be investigated. Besides, too many men are waiting for her escort graduation so they can order her hot, little ass up."

Logan knew he had said too much. Even though every word rang of truth, Banner didn't want to hear it. The last sentence cost Logan a broken nose and he took it like a man, knowing it was deserved and Banner could have done much worse.

Simon appreciated the swift justice, deciding their exchange garnered his respect.

Banner sat back down, with his head in his hands. His distress permeated the camp. When he lifted his head, he desperately questioned Parker to get his take during the ride back to Opelousas…if there was any hint that he still stood a shot with Della. Parker looked over at Logan with cotton up his nose and dark circles forming around his eyes.

"Well…," Parker said, trying to formulate the safest answer possible, but still be honest. Parker's leg started to bounce- a sure sign that nerves were getting the best of him. "No. She told me to tell you one thing when I saw you next. Destin Cooley."

Banner got up and disappeared in the woods.

"What does that name mean?" Parker asked Logan.

"It means you should have got punched in the face, too," Logan answered.

"You got hit because you knew exactly what you were saying. Parker had no clue," Simon said.

"Shut up, Rogers!" Logan yelled. "Well, we don't have to worry about Della anymore. Destin and Lance used to fight over her all the time. She's probably been seeing him all along."

Banner came out of the woods just in time to smack Logan on the back of the head.

"Ow, what did you do that for?"

"You used my real name."

"Oops! Why are you back so soon? I thought you left to brood over Della."

"No. I had to take a dump, if you must know." Banner announced. "I love Della and just want her to be happy."

"You don't love her," Clifford's voice weakly traveled through the darkness.

"What do you know, old man?" Banner challenged.

Clifford's voice was quiet, but all the men strained to hear. "If you loved her, you would have done anything to be with her." As if those words weren't enough, he added, "You don't let go of someone you love."

Chapter 28

The entire team was thankful to arrive back at Angola the next day. Clifford was taken to get medical attention and the rest of the team went to the dining hall for lunch. Even though the mission ended in success, the mood at the table was somber.

Simon enjoyed every morsel of the hot meal before excusing himself to take a shower upstairs. He grabbed a fresh set of clothes out of his room, which he now stocked with the same belongings he had at the museum. His $50 a week salary was used to purchase extra toothpaste, deodorant, clothing, etc. It had taken a while to get everything he needed in duplicate.

"Got room for one more in here?" Jen asked, startling Simon in the shower.

She had a towel wrapped around her and, before Simon could answer, had hung it up on a hook and entered the shower room. Simon decided he would play it cool, like this didn't bother him. He stole glances of Jen across the small room.

"So, I hear everything went as planned." Jen said, moving closer to Simon and soon washing his chest.

"Uh, ya," Simon said.

A knock on the door to the shower room broke the silence, but not their gaze.

"I've missed you. Have you missed me?" Jen asked.

Simon nodded. She leaned into him, sharing the suds between them, while reaching up and wrapping her hands behind his neck.

"A woman's on the floor!" Jen yelled at whoever knocked. Even though there were designated shower rooms for women, they were allowed to lock any of the rooms on the grounds.

And that's just what she did.

***

Earl drove Simon back to the museum before the rally, having gotten word that Quadra was settling in for their search month in Baton Rouge. Simon didn't have much to hide, but Earl hadn't expected this to be the week that the search commenced and he hadn't relocated all his contraband to Angola.

"After you throw your bag in your room and make sure Cass isn't around, come help me with a couple things in my gardening shack," Earl ordered.

The men placed miscellaneous belongings into small, green bags. Simon brought the batteries he had taken out of the listening devices. Once the small bags were packed up, the men climbed up a ladder under the largest tree and tied the bags in the leafy canopy. They returned to the shack.

Earl pulled out a bottle of hooch and told Simon to hide it poorly in the museum. Hopefully, it would be the only thing they discovered and because it would be found in what Quadra called a "general space," no one could be charged.

"Why do we want them to find this?" Simon asked.

"The trick with these searches is making them think they've found something, because if they're not impressed with themselves during the search, they'll look more diligently or even plant things to be discovered. So, the best scheme is to make sure whatever they find is not too incriminating. " Earl advised.

"Are you going to hide anything?" Simon asked.

Earl shrugged. "I don't need to hide anything." He looked over his garden. "This whole garden is contraband. We're supposed to rely solely on Quadra for sustenance.

They'll destroy it and be pleased with their accomplishment."

Simon had no idea. In Portland, no space existed for a garden even if he wanted to plant one, but this was yet another ridiculous power play and control tactic. A way to make sure the drugs in the food numbed the brain and encouraged compliance. Simon looked over the garden in disappointment as he enjoyed getting supplies for meals here.

"It's not too big of a deal. The Angola gardens are huge and will supply fresh offerings until I can start another garden. Oh, I almost forgot…"

Earl took out a small bag of Quadra fertilizer from the shack and put it right by the garden. The sight of it made Simon uneasy now that he was better informed, but any gardener worth his salt would use fertilizer. Although intended to be used for landscaping, Earl brilliantly chose to display it only as a prop. Odds were the men searching would have no idea that the fertilizer could possibly be filled with their ancestors, but they'd like to see that the Quadra name was represented.

Once they completed their manipulation tactics, the men joined Farrow in the kitchen for a meal. They ate any remaining items that were not Quadra-supplied. The items in the cupboards were manufactured at the food depots, making it appear that they were regularly used.

Farrow gave the men the bad news over their meal. "I was recently told that all the search crews are planning to come through the museum for a tour of the facility. At least one team a day."

The idea of Quadra searching the premises and being around all the time made everyone uneasy. Earl and Simon knew that a weekend get-a-way to Angola wouldn't be possible until Quadra left town. Otherwise, their absence might raise unwanted suspicion. With Quadra, everything raised suspicion.

"Cass is helping at the dorms again, so I went into the basement today to return the journals. My wife had been reading one at home, too, while taking notes," Farrow said.

"The notes are contraband," Earl mentioned.

"That's why I hid them in the basement."

"I don't think you understand, Farrow," Simon said. "If Quadra were to find the basement, it wouldn't be bad for us because we could play stupid- act like we didn't know a thing…even with all that metal on the ceiling. But, those notes would prove that someone was aware of its existence. It'd be a death sentence for you and your wife after they ran a handwriting sample."

The chair Farrow sat in screeched across the floor as he quickly stood, racing to the basement once he realized the error.

When he returned, he had the notes and a bottle of hooch that he hadn't mentioned hiding. The men made quick work of the alcohol and decided to burn the notes. She could always make new ones.

"Tell me, Farrow," Earl started, "what makes you fall in line with an organization like Quadra?"

Farrow's expression was that of surprise. "That's a deep question, but I've thought about it. Order…rules…known expectations- there is an attraction to those things. It almost comforts me."

"Even if those rules or expectations are shit?!" Simon barked.

"Apparently," Earl chimed in.

"In total, I don't find Quadra to be all that terrible," Farrow said.

"When you're seventy, they send you to a place where you either become fertilizer or food for sea life! There is no retirement!" Simon yelled in Farrow's direction. "People can't marry who they want! Travel! Work where they want!" He pounded the table and stood, pointing at Earl. The alcohol had obviously loosened his tongue. "Hell, Earl can't be given proper medical care for his cancer because it's too expensive!"

Farrow looked over at Earl and practically whispered, "You're sick?"

Earl nodded and then angrily stared at Simon.

"I'm so sorry," Farrow said, tears welling up in his eyes.

"Hello," Cass called from the side entrance. "Anyone around?"

The men straightened up. Farrow dabbed at his eyes and Earl smiled when Cass joined them in the kitchen.

"Did you guys hear the great news? Quadra is going to be coming to the museum all month!" Cass said, genuinely happy about the new development. "They said if I keep up the good work, I might join them in Lafayette!"

"That's great," Earl said, trying his best to mean it. "I'm very proud of you, Cass."

The men all wore fake smiles, but Cass didn't know any better in his current state of euphoria. He went off to take a shower after a long day.

Farrow looked at Simon. "What kind of foolishness are you spouting, now? Fertilizer or food! You're so full of …," Farrow stopped, seeing Earl shake his head.

"Every bit of it is true, Farrow," Earl affirmed. "You can't half-ass your allegiance anymore. Haven't you ever wondered why you couldn't speak to your maw-maw after she aged out?"

Earl knew this would hit Farrow hard. There wasn't a soul on this earth he thought more highly of than his grandmother.

"No one can contact people who age out," Farrow argued. "That doesn't mean they're killed by the government!"

"That's exactly what it means," Simon added. "If you don't believe us, you should ask Clifford."

Earl yelled at Simon, "You have got to shut your mouth, boy!"

Farrow looked at Earl, while pointing at Simon. "Are you trying to tell me Clifford is still around?! I was at his aging out ceremony! I waved at the bus as they drove off."

"Remember when you caught me and April talking in the basement?" Simon explained. "I kept talking about her grandpa. I was referring to Clifford! He's up at the hospital in Angola as we speak. He should be getting out any day now."

Earl once again couldn't believe Simon's big mouth.

"I just assumed she had another grandpa. Didn't think for a minute it was Clifford. He's been gone for so long. If this is true…" Farrow trailed off.

"It's true," Earl confirmed. "The question is- what are you finally going to do about it?"

Farrow pounded both fists on the table. It was the first time Simon had witnessed any kind of rage from Farrow. "I want to meet with Clifford as soon as possible," Farrow said, before storming off to his room.

Realizing that he had said too much, Simon apologized to Earl.

"No need for an apology. You may have secured an ally to the resistance with that incredibly huge mouth of yours. And Farrow is smarter than both of us put together. He doesn't have your memory or historical knowledge and he's not tactical like me, but no one understands human nature like that man. No one."

"Do you think he's trustworthy?" Simon asked.

"We're all trustworthy to a point," Earl resigned. "Like you…apparently you're trustworthy until plied with alcohol." Earl looked down, feeling sorry for Farrow. "This is hard for Farrow. He's learning that an organization he believed in may have killed his maw-maw. And the reason he's sad about my illness is because it reminds him of his wife, Lola. She had a small cyst in her uterus, but when they performed surgery, instead of just removing the cyst, they gave her a hysterectomy. No permissions, no warning…just took away their opportunity to have more kids in one fail swoop. They love their daughter, but they both wanted a big family. She was twenty-five."

"I think it may have something to do with those journals, too," Simon said. "Learning about history can fire a person up."

Earl smiled. "Sorry, kid. I don't think it has much to do with history. I've recently brought some of those journals to Angola to read and have enjoyed them, but I may know what Farrow is gleaning from them."

"What's that?" Simon wondered.

"He's coming to understand that what we're experiencing now is not as brutal or without hope, but it's a type of slavery, all the same."

Chapter 29

As though the Quadra presence wasn't bad enough with the tours, Cass had invited all the recruits and officers to come to the museum every Sunday night for an alligator cook-out. Cass failed at many attempts to cook the beast, which lead to him begging Simon to prepare the alligator on Sundays.

Any weekend getaways or trips might raise suspicion, so everyone stayed put during the search month and didn't travel to Angola or anywhere else.

Sunday dinner became quite a neighborhood shindig, with people bringing side dishes and joining in. Cass and Earl made some lovely tables and benches with reclaimed wood to accommodate all the guests. Earl got a kick out of the fact that Quadra was in such close proximity to the museum's basement that housed the largest amount of contraband most of them would ever see.

Simon ran most of the Quadra tours through the museum, with Farrow taking one every now and then. Farrow worked with the same conviction as before, but a fury had grown behind his eyes.

The weeks passed and the last Sunday dinner had arrived. Quadra would soon be moving out of Baton Rouge now that their search month was nearly complete. The museum had yet to be inspected, making nerves a little jittery.

Jen had been attending the dinners, but pretending not to know anyone. She cozied up to a couple of Quadra officers tonight, possibly to glean information or maybe in an attempt to make Simon jealous. She laughed and carried on, looking in Simon's direction.

Simon had returned to using the escort hubs a couple of weeks ago, deciding he only liked Jen with her clothes off and that being with her involved too much risk. He never had a conversation with Jen about his decision, but he was glad she had found some new friends.

When Simon finished cooking the last of the gator in the temporary outdoor kitchen, he saw that Bree sat at one of the tables. She looked at him and gave a head nod so he'd follow her. Jen saw the entire exchange, silently raging.

Bree and Simon met in front of the bench overlooking the river. They turned around to face the diners, ensuring they'd see anyone approaching.

"What do you have for me, Mr. Handler?"

Simon pretended to loosen his pants. "It's about time, Bree!"

Bree squinted, disgusted by the gesture. "It's officer Denton to you, Mr. Handler. You really do have a problem with authority."

"I really don't. You can even be on top." Simon smiled, much too proud of himself.

"When I get the go-ahead to kill you, I'm going to take pleasure in the act," Bree informed. Her words were measured and laced with anger.

Simon believed her.

"Your information thus far has led to nothing," Bree continued. "We didn't witness any river crossings at night and after questioning Cass, I'm convinced he would have shared any information to garner the approval of Quadra. So, if you don't remember anything out of the ordinary…"

This was a pivotal decision for Simon, still unsure if Quadra or the resistance deserved his help. If he told Bree everything he knew, he may be rewarded with a more comfortable life. But, the resistance gave him the adventure he longed for and an opportunity to fight for freedom. He needed more time. How could he be sure of anything Quadra promised after learning what happened at Cape Canaveral?

Simon looked to the side, pretending to search his memory. “A little over a month ago, there was a tour that came up from New Orleans. Had to be about fifty or sixty people trying to use up the last of their miles for the year.”

“That’s not unusual.”

Simon had baited the hook, getting ready to go fishing for information…to see how much Quadra knew about what happened in Beaumont.

“No, but a couple of them kept asking about the best way to get across the river. They asked citizens all over town, too, trying to pay for passage. Something about having to attend a big bang in…in… I’m not sure, but all the words started with the same letter. It sounded like a huge party or something. A big bang in Baker?”

“Was it Beaumont?” Bree asked, excitedly.

Bree’s amateur reaction disappointed him. He wondered how she got so high in the Quadra ranks without a cooler demeanor.

“Tell me everything you know,” Bree demanded.

“I just did.” Simon shrugged.

“I’m going to get the list from Farrow. This may be just the info we need!”

“I remember the chant,” Simon said.

Bree sidled up to Simon with a look of expectancy. He purposely spoke low, so she’d need to lean in.

“They kept repeating it over and over again: Going to a big bang in Beaumont. It’s gonna be a gas!”

The look of surprise on Bree’s face was priceless. Simon wanted to laugh at her response to the misinformation, but he tamped it down so it would retain its effectiveness. She marched off to find Farrow and get a list of the New Orleans tour group. That would keep Quadra busy for a while.

Simon returned to the outdoor eating area, helping Cass put away the tables as they became vacant. Cass thanked the recruits for coming, never faltering in his admiration for Quadra.

When Jen decided to leave, she side-kicked a table the two men were carrying. It almost toppled them both, but they were able to remain upright.

"What did you do to her?" Simon asked Cass, trying to redirect suspicion.

Cass didn't know Jen well, but wondered what he could have done. Earl came out of the shack and the three of them made quick work of cleaning up the entire area.

"Quadra leaves in a couple days," Earl said, with relief accompanying his words.

"It's sad," Cass added.

Simon merely nodded his head, thankful they'd be gone soon. Quadra must have been saving the museum for last on the search list. Two more tours were scheduled tomorrow so the inspection would either be late tomorrow afternoon or sometime the following day.

When morning arrived, Farrow greeted the first group to the museum. He asked one of the recruits when they had planned to search the museum under the guise that he wanted to make sure the schedule would be clear so Quadra could easily perform their search.

"There was nothing on the schedule about the museum, sir. I reckon we've been here all month for tours and if there were any irregularities, we'd have noticed," the recruit said. "And who'd invite us to Sunday dinners if they had something to hide?"

Simon approached the group. "This is Mr. Handler and he'll be your guide today. Enjoy," Farrow said.

Simon was caught off guard by Farrow's jovial tone, but understood when Farrow came to the kitchen later to announce the good news.

"Well, I'll be," Earl said. He laughed almost as much as when Simon got attacked by a swarm of mosquitos. He looked at Simon. "You better get that bottle of hooch you hid."

Farrow went back to his desk because the next and final tour started in 15 minutes. Simon finished up his snack and glass of water. He'd hid the bottle of alcohol inside a toilet tank in the public restroom and decided now was as good a time as any to retrieve it.

"The tour is going to start any minute," Farrow told Simon, pointing outside to the assembled group. "And I let someone in to use that restroom. He's still in there."

"I'll only be a second," Simon promised, heading in that very bathroom.

The door had just closed behind Simon when out of the stall came Parker in a Quadra uniform. Both men's eyes widened as they stood paralyzed with surprise. Simon was the first one to strike, but it didn't take long for a flurry of fists to land blows.

If Parker could have climbed his way out of this, he may have had the upper hand, but in the enclosed space, odds favored Simon. He got Parker into a guillotine choke hold and applied pressure until Parker passed out.

Simon peeked out of the bathroom and saw the tour assembled. "Farrow, can you take this one? I have a terrible nose bleed and want to keep the museum sterile."

Farrow nodded. "I'd be happy to. Let's all move to the staircase."

Simon knew he didn't have much time so he took Parker by the collar of his uniform and dragged him on his butt to his room.

"Keep your eyes focused on the glass ceiling for at least ten seconds! It's tradition." Farrow said, raising his voice.

Many of the recruits were tempted to look in Simon's direction because of the noise, but Farrow gave the instruction with such authority that they obeyed. After all, the ability to follow orders was one of the most important traits required in having anything to do with Quadra.

Simon grabbed the doorknob to his room, grateful to find it unlocked. A habit the south had encouraged. He flipped Parker over onto his belly and quickly tied his arms behind his back with a belt. He legs were bound with a shirt.

Simon mumbled that this wasn't what he signed up for and he heard April's warning about loyalty reverberate in his head. *There are only two sides…the resistance and Quadra. There is no in-between.* This seemed very much "in-between."

Parker gained consciousness slowly and Simon partially rolled him on his side. Simon grabbed a sock and shoved it in Parker's mouth, securing it with a bandana tied around his head. Parker once again stared at Simon with the surprise.

"I know. It's crazy, right? Just a month ago we were on a mission together!"

As Parker became more aware of his situation, he started to pound his feet on the floor, making quite a ruckus.

"Rookie mistake, recruit Jeffries," Simon said, looking at the nametag on the Quadra uniform. "You're showing your hand way too soon."

Simon removed Parker's boots and used the laces to secure the pillow to his feet. He also gave him a pat down to make sure he didn't have any weapons or a communication signal.

"Let's see. If this was me…" Simon said, looking around the room, "broken window, knock over the nightstand and maybe even bump the door so people could hear out in the hall." Simon bent down over Parker. "We can't have that!" Simon meant only to pat Parker's face, but the adrenaline levels swirling within made him slap the prisoner instead.

Simon knew Parker's strengths: nimble, amazing climber and very fast. He couldn't take any chances. Simon rolled Parker onto his stomach and pushed him under the bed. Parker barely fit which would better keep him incapacitated. Simon sat on the floor and pushed Parker further back with his legs.

Simon cleaned up the blood on his face, realizing that Parker got in a few good jabs before he was taken down. Simon needed to leave Parker just long enough to find Earl. He'd know how to handle this unusual situation.

If Simon wasn't sure where his loyalties rested, his actions this afternoon left no doubt. There would be no going back now.

Chapter 30

Simon ran outside to find Earl and Cass fishing down by the river.

"I need you to come help me, Earl," Simon said.

"Can't it wait until the last tour is done?" Cass asked. "If you need something, I can help." Cass started to put his rod down.

"Thank you, Cass, but this is really only something Earl can help me with." Simon smiled, acutely aware that this was not his best acting effort, but the longer this took, the higher probability that everything would come crashing down.

Earl looked in Simon's direction and cast his line into the water. Monday had become Earl's day off lately because he worked during all the Sunday Quadra dinners. He didn't like anyone to interrupt his fishing.

Simon got annoyed by Earl's lackadaisical attitude and decided to up the ante.

"There's a Quadra recruit I just met…was asking how to get to someplace called Angola," Simon said. "I figure you know these parts better than anyone."

Earl wasted no time handing his rod to Cass. "Here. Keep fishing and I'll be back to join you in a half hour or so. I mean it, stay here- I want lots of fish for dinner!"

Earl and Simon hurriedly walked toward the museum. Simon unlocked the door to his room, grabbing Parker who had almost gotten out from under the bed and drug him to the middle of the room. They both stood over him as he murmured.

"Well, I didn't see this coming," Earl said. "I'll contact a transit to bring him up to Angola and lock him up after the rest of his kind finish the tour. I have a mind to feed him to the alligators."

Parker wriggled on the floor and made inaudible sounds.

Earl bent down. "Shut up, you don't have a say in the matter."

Simon kept an eye on Parker while Earl returned to fishing and the tour continued. Farrow came storming into Simon's room once the tour had concluded.

"What have you done?!" Farrow yelled. "I thought we were supposed to be more of a defensive resistance. This, this is offensive…very offensive."

"I know this man as Parker, a member of the resistance," Simon explained. "As a matter of fact, he was my tour guide my first day."

"I don't understand."

Simon shrugged. "We don't either. A transit has been contacted to take him to the compound. I think we'll lock him up for a few days and see what he has to say for himself."

Parker moved violently on the floor until Simon gave him a little kick. Earl showed up and they tried to decide who was the best choice to accompany Parker to Angola.

"I'll take him," Farrow said. "I want to see Clifford and finally check out your operation. I'm hoping it's not the band of unrefined and unorganized outlaws I've envisioned in my head."

Farrow wasn't even a consideration, never having been to Angola, but Earl decided even though it was risky- it was the best choice. He wrote a note for Farrow to give to Banner or Logan. The two of them were in charge of guarding the entrance. If they weren't on duty- one of their men would be.

"Cass just went to take a shower, so now is the best

time to move him," Earl decided.

Earl took out a syringe from his pants pocket, tapping the side. When Parker began to writhe, Simon jumped in to keep him still.

"Hold him down, ass up," Earl instructed. "I'm not very good with these things."

When Simon got Parker in position, Earl stuck him with the needle, pressing the contents into his butt cheek. After a couple minutes, Parker passed out.

"Go ahead and take the gag out…untie him," Earl said. "He'll be out for hours."

Earl got a wheelbarrow and they rolled Parker to the transit, placing him in the cargo area. It was still daylight out, but they had to weigh the risks at this point. Farrow had packed a bag and joined the men on the street. They nodded at each other with a new-found trust.

Parker and Farrow were quickly on their way to Angola. Cass came out of the museum as the transit drove out of sight and put the wheelbarrow back for Earl. He was told that Farrow had to take emergency leave and wouldn't be back for a week.

"Since you did such a great job with Quadra," Simon said, "you should probably be in charge while he's away. And you'll be alone this weekend."

A transit pulled up on the street with a couple Quadra recruits inside.

"Is Farrow around?" the driver asked.

"I'm the man in charge this week. How can I help you?" Cass asked. His chest puffed with pride.

"We're looking for a recruit Jeffries. He wasn't at role call this afternoon and he attended a museum tour today," the passenger recruit said as he leaned over to look out the window.

"He's not here," Cass assured. "But, you're free to take a look around. Anything you need."

Both Earl and Simon held their breath, waiting for the next verbal exchange.

"I will say that alligator activity has been busier than usual," Cass continued. "If he went down by the river, they might have got him. Do you want to look for clues? Maybe a shoe or arm on the shore..."

Both Simon and Earl realized that they may need to engage these recruits. They stood ready, knowing the young men received training, but were still too green to be a threat.

The men looked horrified, probably not familiar with alligators. What Cass didn't understand is that Quadra recruits were relocated immediately after being accepted into the ranks. It served as a way to separate family or friend alliances so a strong bond would be made only with Quadra. This also meant the promise of a Lafayette assignment for Cass may not be a genuine offer.

Cass motioned for the men to follow him, but they didn't exit the vehicle. They'd never seen alligators before this location and they were terrified of the beasts.

"That's OK," the driver said. "He'll probably show up. We'll mark this area as searched."

The men sped off and Earl was the first one to break the silence with a short chuckle. He looked at Cass, grateful that he'd handled the situation with clueless wit and to the benefit of everyone.

"So, what did you catch for dinner tonight?" Simon asked.

"A big catfish, so I threw the Crappie back for another day," Cass answered. "You wanna show me again how to cook it? The seventh time might be the charm!"

"Sure, Cass," Simon said, putting his hand on Cass's

shoulder.

***

Farrow arrived at Angola, welcomed by armed guards. Arms were raised in the air as the guards aimed their weapons at the vehicle. Both guards came to the doors, told the men to get out of the vehicle and lay on the ground with their hands behind their heads. They obeyed. One guard went to check the cargo space, while keeping an eye on the driver.

"I have a note in my pocket from someone who belongs to your group," Farrow said.

The guard knelt down and retrieved the note addressed to "Banner or Logan."

"You need to see this," the guard said, looking in the back of the transit. The other guard came to the rear. "Isn't this Parker?"

"I think so. You better call for Banner or Logan, this letter is addressed to them."

The circumstances were so odd, that both Banner and Logan came down to the entrance checkpoint. They took the letter from the guard.

It read:

Banner or Logan-

Found Parker in a Quadra uniform. No idea what's going on. Please lock him up in Camp J until we have time to question him. Rogers and I will be up there this weekend.

Give him a change of clothes. If anyone sees him in that uniform, he may be in danger. Save the uniform with the others. Feed him, but do not let him out of that cell!

The man accompanying him is Farrow. He can be trusted. Give him a room and take him to Maestro.

For Freedom,

Rock

When the cousins finished reading the letter, they told Farrow and the driver they could get up. Logan pulled Parker out of the back of the vehicle with very little concern for the prisoner's welfare. Banner hoisted Parker up on his shoulder, carrying him to the golf cart that waited through the gates.

Logan paid the driver handsomely. He was the only driver in Baton Rouge that had ties to the resistance. He often got called in for emergencies. Farrow grabbed his bag out of the vehicle before the driver was instructed to leave.

"Weapons down," Logan said to the other guards. "Return to post." The two men lowered their weapons and went back to the small guard building.

Logan looked at Farrow. "My name is Logan, nice to meet you. Rock tells us you want to meet with Maestro, but that will have to wait until morning. Let's get you a warm meal and then I'll escort you to a room. It's only a short walk," Logan finished. "I need to search your bag before allowing it on the premises and because you are a guest here you're not allowed to be unattended at any time."

Farrow was confused about the use of strange names, but decided not to mention it.

The dining hall impressed Farrow, but the man who accompanied him remained quiet and guarded. Farrow didn't mind because he listened to the conversations at the neighboring tables.

People spoke about all manner of topics, which convinced him that the people here were more intelligent than the normal citizens Quadra produced. Two women argued over the ending of a book. A book! There must be books somewhere on the property and Farrow wanted to read every last one, even if it meant breaking the law.

Farrow could barely sleep, wondering what living a life

of true freedom would look like.

By the time morning light had come, Farrow had taken a shower and had a light breakfast from the lovely basket that he found in his room. A man he'd never met before came to pick him up in the morning, offering to escort him to the dining hall.

Farrow declined to dine, asking to go straight to the hospital to see his friend. When Farrow arrived at the hospital, he had to wait until a hospital representative came out of the building to collect him. When the woman arrived, she reminded him of his daughter.

They entered the hospital which also served as a type of "nursing home" for older members of the resistance, but that term was no longer used in society due to the lack of older generations. Farrow walked through, trying not to stare at some of the older occupants as he had never seen anyone over 70 in his lifetime.

"Your friend is down the hall on the left, room 142."

Farrow thanked the woman. When he reached the room, he got butterflies in his stomach. There were answers behind this door Farrow wasn't sure he was ready to hear.

Chapter 31

Farrow tapped on the door before pushing it open. The room was empty so Farrow walked back to the main desk and informed the woman that his friend was not in the room.

She rolled her eyes and shook her head. "I'll be glad when he's released on Friday. The way he chases women and doesn't follow rules has me at wits end." She pointed down another hallway. "Check the gym at the end of the hall. He's not supposed to be putting full weight on his ankle yet, so that's probably exactly what he's doing."

Farrow smiled because that kind of behavior was reminiscent of the Clifford he knew. Sure enough, at the end of the hall, he could be seen through the large glass windows, striking a heavy bag. He didn't look weak as he landed punch after punch.

Clifford glanced in Farrow's direction and did a double-take. He shouted and held his arms up before charging toward him to deliver a bear hug.

"Well, I'll be, Farrow James Freeman, as I live and breathe!"

Farrow fought back tears at the use of his full name because only his maw-maw used to call him that. After the greeting, they went to the hospital café to chat.

"I was at your aging out ceremony, Clifford. What happened?"

"Is this why you came to see me?"

Farrow nodded, feeling guilty that he didn't ease into the conversation or engage in more small talk.

"I need to hear what happened in your own words," Farrow explained.

Clifford understood his curiosity and the doubts that he

had. No one in their right mind would think such an atrocity existed in a supposed civilized time. Clifford took Farrow through the entire chain of events from when he arrived at Cape Canaveral to when he left.

Farrow believed every word, disgusted by the truth.

"When did your grandma get sent there?" Clifford asked.

"Eleven years ago, when I was about to turn thirty-four."

"She was a good woman," Clifford said. "I'm sorry for your loss."

"I remember the day she left. She couldn't wait to see her husband who aged out three years earlier." Farrow paused. "She used to tell me about how our people had risen up from low times. Did you know anything about slavery?"

"Sure. Learned all about it in school. You have to remember that I was twenty-three when Quadra took over," Clifford replied. "They came in real soft, like they had everyone's best interest at heart. And after most people had bought their rhetoric hook, line and sinker…they slowly ramped up the control. It was genius, really."

"I've learned a lot about slavery over the last few months," Farrow said. "What's the most surprising thing you remember learning about it?"

"Well, jus' owning another human being as property is deeply troubling all by itself, but that's not what gave me nightmares," Clifford began. "When the slave trade from Africa was cut off, you'd think that would be the end of it, but not so. People began breeding slaves like animals. For a time, slaves were Virginia's biggest export." Clifford shook his head in disgust. "That's one part of history I'm glad is being wiped out. Hell, when all us left-overs are gone, no one will know anything."

"It seems Quadra is attempting to breed us now," Farrow said. "Look at how April came to be married. Soon, my daughter will be expected to marry her perfect match, with no choice in the matter."

The men sat in silence, ruminating on their thoughts.

"Why didn't Quadra just kill all the adults when they took power?" Farrow pondered.

"Nah, they needed people to set everything in motion and from what I do remember from history, which isn't a whole hell of a lot…is that a surviving child of a slain parent is more deadly than just 'bout anything."

"And what purpose of ruling if you have no subjects?" Farrow asked, rhetorically. "Can you show me around this place? I think I'm ready to start supporting the cause."

"I'm not supposed to leave the hospital," Clifford said.

"Oh, OK, well perhaps someone else can show me around."

Clifford smiled. "Just because I'm not supposed to, don't mean I won't! That's your problem, Farrow, you gotta let go of the stupid rules. Lesson number one is to start making choices for yourself. C'mon, there's a hospital cart we can borrow." Clifford winked. "You're gonna like it here."

Farrow went by "X" the rest of the time he was in the compound as he met quite a few people. When the hospital realized that their cart and Clifford were gone, they reported the issue. Banner and Logan were responsible for policing the grounds, but didn't pay much mind to the complaint as Maestro was frequently "on the loose."

Clifford told Farrow about the history of Angola as they drove around and Farrow tried to imagine the place hundreds of years earlier. Perhaps he had relatives that tilled the very ground they traveled. He inhaled, filling his lungs with the spirit of the place.

After a long day of exploring, they planned to dine together. Clifford used the showers on Farrow's floor to clean up, afraid that if he returned to the hospital, he may not be able to leave again. He grabbed an extra outfit and put the one he had worn all day in the laundry chute.

They went down for dinner and the aromas of the place were not lost on Farrow. They had their pick of tables because many of them sat empty during the week days. Although there were fewer diners, the quality of the food always remained deliciously consistent.

"This place is very impressive," Farrow mentioned. "How do I join?"

"Well, the fact that you've been allowed to traipse around with me all day, not to mention you're even allowed on the property, is a pretty good indication that you're a shoe-in."

"I'm sure there's more to it than that! The fact that a hand-written note got me in here, leaves something to be desired in the way of security."

"What are you talking about? The only reason you weren't thrown into the alligator pit or buried on the property is because of who wrote that note."

Farrow looked confused, so Clifford leaned in and whispered, "Earl is in charge of this place. People here do whatever he tells them to."

***

Quadra was packing up and leaving Baton Rouge now that their search month was complete. Simon retrieved the contraband out of the trees while Cass, the consistent suck-up, helped Quadra move out of their dorms. Cass left Earl in charge of the museum while he was away for the day.

Both Earl and Simon had been itching to get back to

Angola for the weekend. They hoped to get some answers out of Parker and try to understand why he wore the Quadra uniform. Earl would also check in with Farrow to see if he was ready to make a commitment to the cause. Either way, Earl knew he had some hard decisions ahead.

"So, have you thought any more about leading the resistance, once I'm gone?" Earl asked Simon.

"Not really," Simon said. "I'm not sure how I'd pull it off because of my connection to Quadra."

Earl shrugged. "We'd have to stage your death."

The men were having their conversation at Farrow's office desk in the museum as Simon checked on the time of the one, scheduled tour.

"The decision you made yesterday eliminated any kind of choice in the matter. You can't just abduct a Quadra recruit and go about your day," Earl reminded. It was true. Merely touching a Quadra member carried strict penalties.

The men meandered through their day, not exchanging many words. A member of Simon's afternoon tour was a very beautiful woman. He made a mental note to call the escort hub for a delivery this week. After the tour, the woman asked to talk to Simon in private. The thought flashed through his mind that maybe he wouldn't have to call the hub.

"Hi, I was hoping you could tell me where Farrow is. I'm his daughter."

All the inappropriate thoughts came to a screeching halt. Simon had already made some less-than-ideal connections with Clifford's granddaughter and Earl's daughter- he wouldn't be attempting the relative trifecta. Thankfully, he could tell that her mind was otherwise occupied.

Simon didn't quite know how to answer that question.

"Earl is out back," Simon said. "I think he might have an idea where Farrow went."

She went off to find Earl, while Simon grabbed a glass of water. Earl came in the kitchen after a few minutes, pacing around. This is how he worked through issues. He went out to the shed, rummaging through the bags he'd hid in the tree and returned with a bright yellow walkie-talkie.

"Rock to bat cave, come in bat cave."

Simon had given up on a response until he finally heard a voice through the static. "This is bat cave. Go ahead, Rock."

"It's time for the guest to return home," Earl said, sweat dripping on his brow. "Tell Banner. And make sure he goes home. Now!"

"Will do. Bat cave out."

"Let's go, Simon. Lock up the museum and meet me at the clinic in five minutes," Earl instructed.

Simon did as he was told. When he arrived at the clinic, Jen was injecting her father with some medication. She called a transit under the name of Dr. Michon, since he rarely used his miles and got extra ones for house calls. The transit arrived and they hopped in.

"Quadra is waiting for Farrow at his house," Earl said. "His daughter said they needed to talk to him about a tour from New Orleans. When they didn't find him at home, they started a search of the premises."

The drive to South Baton Rouge seemed longer than the ten mile trip. Stopping a short distance from Farrow's house, they witnessed the Quadra presence milling around like ants. Simon recognized Bree's silhouette on the front yard. He let out a sigh, opening the car door, but Earl grabbed his arm.

"You need to trust me. I'll take care of it," Simon said.

Simon walked down the small pathway to the house,

hoping that his strategy would work. His plan would require that Bree had some semblance of humanity and Simon had no evidence that she did. Bree watched him approach, her officer embroidery glinting in the sun.

"May I speak to you?" Simon asked. He used his manners, but refrained from calling her by name, as "Bree" would show his normal lack of disrespect and "Officer Denton" would show too much respect, making her immediately suspicious. A man flanked each side of her. "Alone?" He added.

She nodded and they walked into the middle of the street.

"Your boss, Farrow, is in trouble. He's not here or at his scheduled post. Now, we're searching his house for some clue to his affiliations or where he spends his spare time."

"He's on his way here." Simon did some quick math in his head. "He should be here in less than an hour. You're not going to find anything in his home. I've been trying to get something on him the whole time I've been at that museum because he's a pain in the ass, but he's a Quadra loyalist, through and through."

"If that's the case, you'd think someone would be able to locate him." Bree squinted, still suspicious of his absence.

"Can I trust you?" Simon asked. He looked down into Bree's eyes, knowing that he'd never trust her.

And, in fairness, knowing she'd be a fool to ever trust him.

Chapter 32

Bree crossed her arms while tapping her foot. Both actions were signs of a guarded, impatient approach to the conversation. He couldn't blame her because he'd been precocious in the past.

"O.K., I'll take your silence to mean that I can't trust you and go about my day," Simon said. He turned to leave and was half-way to the transit when he heard Bree yell for him to come back.

"You work *for me*, Mr. Handler. Any information you have belongs *to me*."

"I work for you within the parameters of my assignment," Simon corrected. "This information is of a personal nature and has no direct correlation with my duties."

They stared each other down for a few seconds before Bree dropped her arms.

"Fine," Bree conceded. "If the information is of no interest or harm to Quadra, I will not speak of it."

Simon rolled the dice and hoped he was betting on the right storyline to appease Bree's bloodlust for traitors.

"Farrow is sick," Simon started. "He doesn't want to worry his family, but he has the early stages of cancer. If his treatment doesn't take and he's deemed too expensive to treat, he'll be euthanized." Simon shook his head, while mustering up a tear or two. "That's where he is right now…receiving a treatment."

Bree closely watched Simon as he spoke, sure she could identify a lie if one was offered. But, Bree's eyes were also misty, thinking of her sister who died of cancer. She snapped around 180 degrees and headed for the Farrow home. She didn't want Simon to see her pain.

"Wrap it up, recruits!" Bree yelled, at the top of her lungs to tamp down her emotions. "Let's go. Back to Lafayette. The man's been found."

Earl watched with curiosity from the transit as all the recruits left Farrow's house at Bree's command and marched down the road. Before she got into a transit, Earl heard Simon thank her, addressing her as officer Denton.

"How did you manage that?!" Earl asked when Simon returned to the transit.

"She's the officer that assigned me here to find resistance factions," Simon explained. "Apparently, she has a weakness."

"What's that?"

"She's human," Simon said, shrugging his shoulders. "Who knew?"

The transit drove them back to the museum where Cass waited on the steps near the side door. Understandably, he was upset that he had been put in charge of the museum, but was never given any keys or other symbol of authority. He pouted about the situation all afternoon.

Earl and Simon went up to make sure the room was ready for the aging out ceremony that would take place on Sunday. There weren't many buses left in Quadra, but they were mostly used for recruits and the elderly.

After hearing Clifford's story, Simon wanted to save every last one, but that wouldn't be feasible. Until the resistance could make a bigger dent in Quadra's power, they had to watch the men and women ride away. What made it even harder is that the elderly looked forward to traveling to what had been described as "paradise."

There were easels set up around the room with a large poster board representing the life of each person aging out.

Family members displayed pictures, put down favorite quotes, or shared stories of their loved ones.

Simon and Earl walked around the room.

"How come you don't let everyone at Angola know about what happens after these people age out?"

Earl shook his head. "No, that would cause a lot of problems. Heck, even the people going away would never believe it. It's kinda like savin' a swimmer in trouble. They splash and fight when you're tryin' to rescue 'em."

"We have to get someone on the inside at Cape Canaveral to rescue a few people. Let them see just enough of the horror so they can help spread the word."

"That's a really good idea," Earl agreed. "And older people are more apt to trust people their same age. Thoughts like that are exactly why you need to promise to lead Angola one day."

***

Simon and Earl thought of little else during the rest of the week besides questioning Parker, wishing they could go see him early. They ran the best and worst case scenarios around in their heads, with no concrete hypothesis about why he wore the uniform of Quadra.

The fear that haunted them was that Parker had told Quadra about Angola, leaving the community in danger. But the fact that Parker eagerly trained and participated in the missions contradicted that thinking. If he was loyal to Quadra, why didn't he warn them about Beaumont?

After Simon's last tour on Friday afternoon, he walked into Farrow's office to find him looking at the wall, deep in concentration. Pieces of paper scribbled with notes were hung all over, resembling a type of wall paper. It reminded Simon of the pictures he had seen of crime scenes with all manner of newspaper clippings or other pictures on their walls.

Simon informed Farrow that he and Earl were leaving for the weekend, which garnered a grunt of acknowledgement.

Once they got on the road to Angola, Simon asked Earl, "What's going on with Farrow back there?"

"Well, he's makin' some big plans and I'm gonna leave him be because he's like his own little resistance faction," Earl said as he steered the transit. "His wife is responsible for the baked goods at the local food factory and they are planning to switch the drugged foods that are normally shipped to the citizens and ship those to Quadra."

"No shit!" Simon slapped his knee.

"Oh, ya. He's fired up. I told him we'd help out however he needed. Now that he's seen our operation, he's more confident about carrying out his plans. He thinks the drugs that Quadra's been putting in the food is why his wife couldn't have any more babies and got that cyst."

Hearing about Farrow's plans encouraged Simon. He always thought Farrow an intelligent man and the more brain power lined up against Quadra meant more chance of true freedom.

The transit pulled up outside Angola around 4:30pm. Logan greeted both men, but saw they were not interested in small talk- only Parker's location. Logan gave them the keys to the cart, directing them to Camp J.

It was the furthermost cell block, about a mile from anything else. While most remote cell blocks were leveled or repurposed, Camp J remained for this exact type of situation. A place to isolate and house prisoners accused of crimes against the resistance.

When the cart stopped outside Camp J, Earl took a minute to gather himself before going in. No guards stood watch anywhere and Simon realized why when they entered…no one could escape from the place.

The steel door that opened once Earl entered his passcode had to be six inches thick. Inside the facility, the cells had bars with such a large diameter, that a hand couldn't grasp it all the way around. Simon tested that theory when passing the first cell.

There was a line of cells on the left and one large cell at the end of the row that went from one wall to the next. Parker sat in the third cell. Although Earl had put Parker here just as much as a form of protection than to detain him, it was obvious Parker had been beaten.

A cement bench jutted out of the wall opposite the cells. Simon followed Earl's lead, taking a seat. Parker just watched his visitors as a dog would, guilty and awaiting the pain of their disapproval. He grabbed some water, slugging it down. Earl remained silent, studying Parker intently.

A noise at the end of the hall got Simon to peer down to the large cell where a man now stood. Neither Parker nor Earl felt the need for a glance because they were most likely aware of the strange character. Simon would alternate looking at Parker and then down at the large cell.

"This is your chance to tell me your story, Parker," Earl said. "I wouldn't let it go to waste."

A short pause hung in the air before Parker started to speak.

"I lived in Marksville, across the river and I was a scout and map-maker for the bayou system. My job was simple. Scout the area for possible resources…make maps of the terrain, record weather trends and monitor water levels."

"I was mostly out in the forests or bayous and would camp with my horse, Jacques. If my supplies got low, I'd often rummage or hunt for food so I could stay out in the wilderness. That's when I met Inez."

Earl shifted in his seat. "You knew her?"

"Yep, met her almost five years ago. Easily the most beautiful woman I had ever seen. She introduced me to the resistance and brought me here to check things out." Parker smiled, lost in the memory of her. "I'd have followed her anywhere, but this place got under my skin…became a part of me. I believe in what we're doing here."

The half-forgotten man at the end of the hall shuffled around until he disappeared from view.

"Then why the Quadra uniform?" Simon asked, his curiosity bursting at the seams.

Parker lowered his head. "I didn't have a choice. I was re-assigned to a new post on my twentieth birthday as a Quadra representative in Marksville. I stayed there as a recruit and spy of sorts, but often got pulled into Lafayette for special assignments. That's why you saw me at the museum. It's a new program that Quadra instituted a while back. A local is less suspicious."

"That's smart," Earl commented. "Are you loyal to the resistance?"

"Yes."

"Do you want to continue being a part of this movement?"

"Yes."

"Who beat on you?"

All of Parker's previous responses were confidently delivered, but this one already had a shaky beginning. He didn't answer right away, realizing his error.

"Uh, no one. This is all from the struggle with Rogers," Parker lied, pointing to Simon.

"O.K., Parker," Earl started, "give us 'til tomorrow to make a final decision on this."

Before they got up to leave, Earl glanced down the corridor at the last cell. When the men got into the cart for the ride back to the barracks, they were both embroiled in thought. They knew every word that Parker spoke bore truth, except about the beating.

"Parker's still keeping a little sumthin' hidden," Earl mumbled to himself. "Not lying, but holdin' back."

"You know," Simon started, "if you were to pardon Parker's actions and let him stay here- you'd never find a more loyal follower."

Earl nodded and grunted. "Maybe, but if we're doing our job right, we make him a good leader."

Chapter 33

After leaving Camp J, Simon assumed they were headed toward the dining hall. Not a moment too soon, either, as Simon's stomach began to make unfortunate noises. Instead, the men pulled the cart up to the entrance of Angola. Simon assumed to return the cart, but Earl sprang from the cart and quickly had Logan underneath him, and on the other end of some devastating blows.

Logan didn't resist the beating. Earl got to his feet, while Logan remained on the ground. Banner stood by the guard shack, witnessing the brawl, but never coming to the rescue of his cousin.

Winded, Earl pointed at Logan on the ground and yelled, "Why?"

"Because he's a little weasel," Logan answered, with a glare in his eye. He got to a sitting position to spit blood onto the ground. "I deserved this, but I can't believe he told you. What a little…," Logan started.

He never got the full sentence out of his mouth because Earl dealt him one last round-house punch to his mouth.

"He didn't say a word, you asshole! As a matter of fact he lied to protect you," Earl said. "You're the only man on this whole compound foolish enough to go against my orders, so I knew exactly where to go. Banner, lock him up for a couple of days."

To Logan's credit, he didn't argue or struggle when Banner handcuffed him to the cart, knowing he deserved the punishment. The irony that Logan would be in close proximity to Parker, in one of the neighboring cells, wasn't lost on anyone. When Banner drove off, Earl stumbled a bit and Simon helped him balance.

“Get me to the hospital,” Earl told Simon.

They took the last cart at the guard shack, assuring the remaining guards that Banner would be back shortly in case they needed to take turns eating at the dining hall. Earl showed Simon where to park the cart at the rear of the hospital. No one knew that Earl was sick and he hoped to keep it that way.

Earl used an entry passcode to get into a stairwell at the back of the hospital. Simon cautiously entered, looking around all the while.

“It’s OK,” Earl said. “I’m the only one who uses this.”

Earl grabbed the handrail while holding on to Simon at the same time. He was weak, but made it up two flights of stairs until exiting through the door marked with a three. Simon deposited Earl in a recliner that sat near a window before he opened it and a couple others across the room.

Earl grinned, inhaling the fresh air now circulating the once stuffy area. “Nothin’ like a breeze off the Mississippi to make everything better.”

Earl picked up a walkie-talkie and said he’d be in need of two meals, instead of one. The room was the entire width of the hospital and must have served as a kind of apartment for Earl when he was not well or needed a place to lay low. It had many amenities to include a kitchenette and full bathroom. But, the hospital bed in the corner of the room made it an eerie residence.

Simon couldn’t understand why Earl would go after Logan on his own, in his weakened state. He noticed that Cass had started covering for Earl at the museum when he needed things done requiring great strength or stamina. Why couldn’t someone besides Earl beat on Logan? There had to be no limit to the men that would happily volunteer for the opportunity.

A red light near the door came on and Earl sent Simon down to retrieve the delivery. Before Simon left he looked at the other side of the room and noticed that Earl's room was walled in and not accessible from the hospital side.

Banner delivered the meal, looking upset. Simon wondered if he and Logan had an argument, but his hunger overrode the curiosity. He thanked Banner, quickly delivering the lovely meal upstairs.

The delivery included an IV fluid bag that Simon placed on the wire post attached to Earl's bed. After putting a table between them, Simon moved a chair over and set things out. After all the fuss, Earl didn't eat much. Simon ate every last morsel of his meal, but wrapped up Earl's, hoping he may want some later.

"What are you going to do about, Parker?" Simon asked.

"You know what I'm going to do. He told the truth…he's loyal. Logan will respect him because he wouldn't talk. You respect him because he almost bested you at the museum. He's valuable and he's one of us," Earl finished. "Maybe he can even spy on Quadra for us."

Earl coughed, while struggling to get out of his chair. He retrieved a leather-bound notebook from a kitchen cabinet and handed it to Simon as he passed by him to sit on the edge of the hospital bed, unlacing his shoes. When Earl removed his shirt, Simon gasped at the sight of his gaunt frame, wondering where he got the energy to beat on Logan.

A port for medicine was on the inside of his right wrist. It made sense now why Earl was never dressed in anything but a long sleeved shirt, even in hot, humid weather. Simon's cheeks blushed when Earl caught him looking concerned.

"Oh, I know, friend. I know," Earl said.

Earl lay back on the inclined bed, adjusting the pillow

and covering his body with a light blanket.

"It's still early," Earl said. "Let's talk before I take my medicine. It makes me so loopy. Ask anything you'd like."

"How long have you been resisting Quadra?"

"Well, in this capacity, about twenty years, but I dare say my whole life. When they told us we couldn't hunt or fish anymore and only eat Quadra food, we thought they were plum crazy!"

Simon had mastered all the facts, figures, and motivations of the resistance over the last couple of months. There wasn't much he didn't know. Simon feared talking about Earl's personal life or feelings may bring him down, so he asked what seemed an innocent question.

"How long has the other man been at Camp J?" Earl tensed at the question. "You know, the one in the last cell, with the haunting eyes."

"I know who you mean," Earl said. "He's been there for a little over four years."

Normally, Earl would elaborate on an answer or further explain, but he seemed less than eager to talk about the man. This reaction only made Simon more curious.

"What did he do?"

"He killed a girl. I know for certain of one and suspect that he is guilty of two more."

"Why don't you kill him and be done with it?"

"Because I made a promise," Earl admitted. "It's the last and most regrettable promise I ever made."

He was visibly upset by the conversation and hooked the IV fluid into his port. It didn't take long for the medicine to take effect, which made him emotional, tears filling his eyes.

"He's my brother. No one knows that," Earl said, looking off into nothingness. "The girl that Parker spoke about, Inez…he killed her."

Simon's eyes grew wide as he tried to decipher Earl's slurred speech.

"Made my mom a promise to protect and look after him." Earl turned his head toward Simon, squinting in anger. "Before I knew he was a sick bastard. A rapist. A murderer. He even touched my Jen years ago! His own flesh and blood!"

Simon went over to his bedside, touching Earl's hand in an attempt to comfort him as he faded to sleep. When he became quiet, Simon turned around. Earl grabbed Simon's arm and pulled him closer, giving Simon the fright of his life.

"Your first order of business," Earl instructed, "is to kill that som'a'bitch."

Simon merely nodded, not sure of a proper response to such an instruction, but Earl quickly went back to sleep. Simon sat in the recliner, deciding to rummage through the notebook recently given to him because he wasn't the least bit tired.

The notebook contained all the codes around the compound, special talents of each member of the resistance, and intel regarding future missions. A list titled "the fallen" had dates and names of those who gave their life for the cause. He saw the relationships between many resistance members. On one of the older pages, he spotted the name Inez. It was listed by Tarzan, explaining her relationship to him as "younger sister."

Simon poured over the pages, committing everything to memory. He didn't understand why Earl would keep such a log with so much information. What if someone were to find it?

Near the end of the notebook, Earl had written an entry

when he found out he was sick. He listed Jen and Banner as the only two people that were aware of the illness. The notes said 'Jen must know because of the treatments/pain relief at the clinic and Banner needs to know because Jen would not do the hard thing.'

Simon didn't have to wonder what that meant for long. A small notation by Banner's name explained. If Earl ever called in from the hospital room and said that he needed two meals, instead of one- that was code to deliver the IV bag that contained the pain meds and pentobarbital. Simon recognized the name of that drug because there was a huge debate in his history lessons about the right to euthanasia.

He held his breath as he looked over at Earl, lying in the bed. The early sun's light had begun shining into the room- proof that Simon had lost all track of time as he poured over the notebook. Earl's chest did not rise and fall. Simon walked over to the bed, checking for a pulse, but the body had long been cold. He looked at the bag that was clearly marked with its contents. How could he not have noticed?

The red light near the door illuminated. It could only be Banner, who knew the outcome of ordering more than one meal. Simon tucked the notebook in the back of his pants and easily lifted Earl up, cradling him across his arms. A haunting siren sounded across the compound as Simon carried his leader down the stairs.

He opened the door to a teary-eyed Banner who gently took possession of the body. He laid him in the back of the cart, covering his body with a sheet. Banner and Simon rode toward Lake Killarney in silence. When they got close to the stadium, Banner stopped the cart.

"Everyone is coming to the stadium for an important announcement," Banner said. "You must be the one to inform the resistance. Bring everyone to the lake for the send-off."

Simon stepped out of the cart and walked toward the stadium, feeling as though his legs wouldn't make it one more step. He'd never been here for an important announcement that required the siren. Judging by the looks on everyone's face, it usually meant bad news. People continued to arrive on horseback, by foot, and other odd means of transportation. The kitchen was emptied, a representative from the hospital came and the neighborhoods were cleared out to attend.

When the stadium was at capacity, people started congregating outside the structure. The murmurs were at a minimum in the early morning hours, but a hush came over the crowd as Simon stepped onto the platform.

Chapter 34

The microphone that had been already set up on the platform crackled before Simon spoke a word. The expectant throngs stared at him, knowing the sirens never sounded for trivial matters. Faces in the crowd, he had never seen, blinked at him expectantly.

"Good morning," Simon's voice rang out.

Hearing his own voice bounce back to him was unsettling, so he took a couple steps backwards from the microphone. Seeing Earl's lifeless body and having to speak about the loss was one thing, but he couldn't bear hearing the news…even from his own lips.

"I'm sorry, but Rock has passed on in his sleep last night," Simon said quietly. "He's been sick for a long time, but wanted to serve you until the very end. He now has the freedom we've all been striving for."

Simon lifted both his hands and made the sign for 'respect.' The people followed suit and filed out of the stadium toward the lake. The only sounds were that of mourning. Earl had been laid on a wooden raft and as the crowd lined the shore, a wail of grief rang out. Jen splashed into the waist-deep water, kissing her father on the forehead. When she made no movement to leave his side, Curry fetched her out of the lake.

After a few moments, Clark, the owner of the Angola lands, came to stand by the body.

"Rock was a good man, a true friend and the best leader I've had the pleasure to serve," Clark yelled. "We shall mourn his passing, while respecting the foundation he has built. There are great things to accomplish…hope to restore."

Clark paused to light the torch he carried. "Rock has left us in the capable hands of Rogers, here, who will lead us further in the direction of our goals." Clark nodded at Simon. "So, with that, I pass this torch to symbolize Rock's fire and passion for the cause and that it now burns within Rogers."

He walked up to Simon, ceremoniously handing him the torch and nodding at the body. He had read about different types of burials around the world and this mimicked a Norse burial for someone held in high regard. His mind wandered briefly with amazement realizing that no one here could possibly know this, but they were repeating history.

Banner, Curry, Tarzan and Clark each grabbed the corner of the raft. Simon walked into the shallows and dropped the torch onto the raft. It quickly engulfed in flames and the men gave it a good thrust out onto the water

Simon couldn't stop staring at the fire and sat there for hours. Every now and then a pat on his shoulder was felt or a morsel of food left as he kept vigil. Words were spoken in his vicinity, but he concentrated on the raft.

As nightfall came, the flames dwindled, but Simon looked on, unchanging in his countenance until no firelight shone off the lake. He rose from his spot, traveling back to the hospital. His usual cell would not give him the peace he desired.

He keyed in the pin from memory and climbed the stairs, throwing the notebook onto a table. After a shower and some of Earl's left-over meal, Simon nestled into the recliner with a blanket. He radioed Banner to pick him up at 7am the next morning from the hospital.

His time by the lake today cleared his head, gave him direction and strengthened his resolve. He would move forward in a way that honored Earl. He would be a strong leader, happily accepting responsibility for the people in the resistance and doing all he could to thwart Quadra.

The day had exhausted him physically, mentally and emotionally. It seemed the only functioning part of his body were his tear ducts.

He quietly cried himself to sleep.

***

When Simon awoke, he viewed the hospital bed and resolved that it must be taken away. Although he'd been given a house in the neighborhood, he rather liked the idea of this apartment being a hide-a-way of sorts.

Banner would have waited for as long as necessary, but Simon finished his morning routine right when the red light flashed on. He greeted Banner and they headed toward the packed dining hall. Weekends would always garner more patrons, but the real attraction was their new leader. People stared and whispered as Simon made his way through the line.

Banner elbowed Simon. "C'mon, let's go eat in the private room."

Banner brought Simon to a beautiful room and shut the door behind them. There were four tables in the room with large windows to an outside atrium, full of greenery and birds. Banner excused himself and came back with a carafe of hot coffee. Simon wanted to hug him, but decided that was not the best course of action.

"My name is Simon Handler." A small pause came as Banner lifted his head. "I know Earl trusted you and for that very reason, I plan to do the same."

During breakfast, Simon shared with Banner his relationship with Quadra and why he was sent to Baton Rouge. He told Banner all he knew about the euthanasia depots, shared some history and divulged what lay in the basement of the museum. The men talked for hours.

"You're not going to understand everything that happens today, but will you trust me?" Simon asked.

Banner stuck out his hand, so they could shake on it. It was the first time that Simon didn't think anything of it, reaching his hand out to reciprocate. The men exited the room into an empty dining hall.

"Our first stop is Camp J," Simon said.

When they came through the door, Logan yelled, "It's about time!"

Parker turned around. "Earl said he was going to come here yesterday with a decision, but I heard the sirens blare. Is everything OK?"

Simon was pleased that the news hadn't made it to the prisoners. Even though they were to be cut off from all communication, he believed the news may have been too tempting to spread during the food deliveries. But, once again, the kitchen staff proved remarkable.

"You still have one day left, Logan," Simon informed. "That is, if I feel like letting you out."

"Who the hell do you thi…," Logan started, but saw Banner give him the sign for silence.

Banner stepped forward and cleared his throat. "Rogers is our new leader here at Angola," Banner explained. "Earl passed away last night in his sleep."

A sob came from the last cell. Simon looked at Parker, only one of them understanding the prisoner's response.

"Banner is going to be my number one and I'd like you to be my number two, Parker," Simon offered. "Is that agreeable? Quadra has marked you as missing and presumed dead. You will live here and become important to the cause."

Parker nodded his head, while Logan looked like he was about to have a coronary in the adjoining cell. Simon entered the passcode for Parker's cell and it clicked open. He took a step into the cell and put his hand on Parker's shoulder, looking him in the eye. He trusted Parker completely.

"We'll talk about specifics later, but for now I need to feed a prisoner to the gators," Simon said, making a way for Parker to leave the cell.

Logan back-peddled in his cell, begging for forgiveness until he watched Simon pass by, heading toward the last prisoner remaining.

There was a family resemblance to Earl, but his eyes were void of anything. He was skinny, pale and broken. His hair had been cut by someone who had no clue how to do it. No words were exchanged, almost as though Earl had previously narrated this scene to the prisoner. Simon led him to the cart and the four men headed toward the gator pit.

Simon asked Banner to stop at the gym before making their way to the pit, to which Banner complied. Simon jumped out of the cart, walking through the gym and was met with handshakes, condolences and congratulations. When asked what he was doing, he said he was getting ready to feed a prisoner to the gators.

The men scoffed, but Simon's expression remained serious. When some of the younger men heard, they started running to the pit in anticipation. He bid everyone a nice day and saw Jen's face in the crowd as he departed.

Tarzan came out of the small shack when they pulled up to the pit and pleasant greetings were exchanged. The prisoner remained in the golf cart, while the other men visited. A small crowd started to gather and Simon found the number of witnesses perfect for his purposes.

"What's going on?" Tarzan asked.

"Well, we're here to feed a prisoner to your friends," Simon said, pointing at the alligators.

Tarzan looked surprised. "Rock would just threaten that. We've never actually fed someone to the gators before."

"Well, today is a good day to start new traditions." Simon spoke loud enough for the small crowd to hear.

Tarzan scanned the faces of the three men, trying to discern the humor, but Banner and Parker's expressions were solemn. Parker fidgeted, but followed Banner's lead in supporting their new leader. Banner retrieved the prisoner from the cart.

Simon took the man behind the fencing, while Tarzan made a path, hissing at the gators in the way. Tarzan stood between the two men and the wild beasts.

"This isn't right," Tarzan pleaded. "Has this man been proven guilty?"

"He has," Simon spoke. "Prisoner, have you committed heinous and unspeakable crimes?"

The prisoner nodded his head. "But a promise was made," he whispered.

Simon whispered back, "That promise was not made with me. You don't deserve to fill your lungs with breath when you've deprived another their right to do so."

Tarzan tried a different angle, explaining how he didn't want his gators to get a taste for human flesh as it might prove dangerous for him.

Simon let go of the prisoner, who stood frozen in fear. He grabbed Tarzan by the arm and took a couple steps away from the front of the pen, where everyone stood. In the next few seconds, Simon explained the prisoner's crimes to Tarzan and walked out of the enclosure.

"I am nothing, if not a man of reason," Simon declared. "So, if Tarzan deems this man can be set free, I will allow it."

Some of the men, knowing Tarzan's care for all creatures, let out disappointed moans. But, ever so slowly, Tarzan's face twisted in a rage. He had wanted justice for Inez for so long, not knowing where his anger belonged. It had now found a home.

He went to the prisoner, picking him up over his head. The crowd held their collective breath as Tarzan took one step after another, closer to the small swamp in the enclosure.

He hurled his sister's killer into the middle of the water, letting out a blood-curdling scream. The gators that weren't already in the swamp, slid in the water quietly from the sides, to angle for scraps. The man never surfaced, only gators splashed where the body had gone down as air bubbles rose from the depths.

Tarzan came out of the pit and fell, sobbing into Simon's arms. Simon held him, not able to fathom his pain, but hoped today would bring some closure and healing.

Simon had to get back to the museum as soon as possible, even though it meant missing the rally. Cass would be beside himself when Earl didn't come home.

Chapter 35

When Simon arrived at the museum, he found left-over food in the kitchen from the aging out ceremony, deciding to eat an early dinner. Before taking a seat, he peered out the tall windows, noticing that Cass was down by the river fishing.

"I need to tell you something," Simon said to Farrow, as Farrow arrived to make a pot of tea.

"We know. Earl left letters for us. It was inevitable, given his illness, but it doesn't sting any less." Farrow walked to the window, looking down at the river. "Cass has been inconsolable all weekend." Farrow looked back at Simon. "Sounds like he had everything planned for a while."

"I think so," Simon said, softly.

After Farrow's tea was made, he joined Simon at the table.

"How have all your plans been going?" Simon wondered, trying to change the subject.

"I've had to reevaluate some things but, all in all, very well." Farrow sipped on his tea. "I wanted to add poison to the baked goods going to Quadra in Lafayette, but my wife talked me out of it. Said that too many innocent people could die…family members, children, even the people who deliver the goods sometime will help themselves to a roll or cookie."

Farrow spoke with little or no emotion in his voice as he looked out the window, obviously pondering if the correct decision was made. The devious nature of his plans concerned Simon, but given Simon had been party to some distasteful acts himself, he kept his mouth shut.

"I forgot to tell you," Farrow said. "Earl left you a note, too. I imagine so it wouldn't look conspicuous. He could plan things to the letter!" Farrow giggled at his own double entendre like a bit of a madman. "Cass read it. I tried to stop him, but he's a rather large man-child."

Simon went to his room to find the letter. Cass didn't bother to hide the fact that the letter had been opened as the envelope lay on the pillow, while the note rested on the bedside table.

Dear Simon,

Losing me is going to be hard for Cass. Please be there for him when he needs someone.

It's been a pleasure working with you,

Earl

"I don't need you to be here for me. I'm a grown man," Cass said from the doorway of Simon's room.

By the looks of Cass, he'd obviously had a couple emotional days under his belt, with very little sleep. Simon didn't understand his pain, but he remembered similar emotions of leaving Dr. Michon and, more recently, feeling the loss of April.

"You wanna go out to his garden shack and have a drink to honor his memory?" Simon asked.

Simon was surprised by Cass's nod. They went out to the garden shack and toasted to Earl. Cass moved around the shack, brushing his hand over many of Earl's belongings.

"Quadra will be here next week to finalize all his business and close his accounts," Cass remarked. "Did you know that people used to will their belongings when they died? Give their stuff to whoever they wanted?"

Even though Simon knew all about that, he shot Cass a quizzical look.

"It's true," Cass said. "My granddad told me about it

when I was a kid. He gave me a ring when he aged out and retired."

Thunder rung out after Cass finished his sentence, rain splashing down on Baton Rouge. They watched as nature watered Earl's garden. Cass drained the rest of the small bottle of hooch, becoming increasingly talkative.

"You're never going to believe this one!" Cass grabbed the collar of Simon's shirt, telling him that Earl wrote in his letter than Jen was his daughter. He bandied about his choice of marriage vs. escort hub, wondered if Quadra would accept him, and questioned the cruelty of the universe.

At this point, a surprised expression or feigning interest wasn't necessary because Cass wouldn't remember much in the morning. Simon's only goal was to maneuver Cass to his room so he could plop him into bed for the night. It took quite a bit of cajoling, but Simon was finally walking backward out of Cass's room as the snoring from within escaped into the hallway.

Still soaked to the bone, he visited Farrow's office to find all trace of dastardly plans had been removed from the walls.

"Can I help you, Simon?" Farrow asked, without lifting his head.

"The contents of the basement will be moved to Angola. Some will travel direct, while others will go to Clifford's place until they can be moved. If you wanted to borrow anything, you can, but it will eventually need to be returned."

"Are you telling me what will happen in my museum?" Farrow asked, looking over his glasses.

It was obvious to Simon that Farrow was angry, but Simon had taken his place of authority, killed a man and watched a man die in very short order. There was no going back to pretending Farrow was his manager.

Without skipping a beat, Simon answered, “I am.” He hoped Farrow would understand, but couldn’t be swayed from the objectives.

He walked down the hall toward his bedroom, wanting to rid himself of his wet clothes. A light tap sounded on the outside door. Once past the kitchen, he opened the door to find a young lady, umbrella in hand, smiling up at him.

“May I help you?” Simon asked.

“I believe so, sir; did you order an escort for the evening?” She inquired.

He closed his eyes at his forgetfulness. “I did. My apologies, it’s been a hectic couple of days. Won’t you come in?”

She smiled and walked past him. As Simon stood in the doorway, he saw Jen near Earl’s shack, standing in the rain, watching him let in the escort. She needed to be with someone tonight and of all the men she could choose from, she came to find comfort with Simon.

“Let’s get you out of those wet clothes and warm you up, shall we?” The escort purred from behind Simon.

He slowly shut the door. “Yes. That sounds like a marvelous idea.”

***

The storm still raged the next day. Any tours scheduled for that Monday were cancelled in order to keep the museum in the best condition. People could take the tour during lighter rains, but were not allowed to trample water through the building when the area got hit by larger storms.

It’s a good thing Cass had no pressing responsibilities because his headache rendered him useless. He spent most of the day in bed, with the covers over his head to keep out the sunlight.

Farrow and Simon completed his only chore, which was straightening out the ballroom upstairs now that the aging out had been completed. Simon thought of the men and women that would never see Christmas this year.

Farrow threw a chair, turning to Simon in frustration. "We have got to figure out a way to circumvent these ceremonies where innocent citizens are being sent to their death!"

"We will, Farrow. There are some things we need to get done before that, but we should be ready. When is the next aging out ceremony…in April?"

Farrow nodded. "How are you going to convince these people? My maw-maw was thrilled to be going off. They think paradise awaits."

Simon continued folding up the easels and storing them in the closets. "I don't know yet. Clifford will need to be involved somehow and he's not going to like it."

"That old coot doesn't like much," Farrow said.

Both men shared a laugh, finding solace in the moment.

"We need to promise to be honest with each other at all times," Farrow remarked.

"I've recently learned not to make promises," Simon said, remembering Earl's experience. "But, I'll do my best."

"That's fair. Listen, I'm sorry about how I reacted last night when you told me you were going to move things out of the basement. I should have asked why."

"No apologies necessary. Things have been tense. Next month, I expect to get a visit from Bree Denton, the P.O.L. officer who stationed me here. That will mark a six month period of service and it's time to give her something concrete."

"I don't understand," Farrow admitted.

"When the time is right, you will. How are your

operations going?" Simon asked.

"We've moved ahead with the food swaps. Area citizens are getting the clean foods, while Quadra receives the drugged batches. I'm not sure how much that will help, but it might make things easier for both of us, dealing with recruits that are not working with full brain capacity. If the drugs take about three weeks to evacuate the body, we figure it probably takes the same amount of time to dull the senses."

"Sounds like progress, Farrow, very encouraging."

"There's one thing I wanted to ask you," Farrow mentioned. "We're trying to provide treatment for people that Quadra deem too expensive to care for. Can we use the hospital at Angola?"

"No. Sorry, Farrow, but that's not a place we want anyone knowing about unless they're properly vetted."

"How can you possibly know if everyone at Angola is truly trustworthy?" Farrow scoffed.

After the hiccup with Parker, he had a point.

"We have Jen sort through full medical records, looking for potential candidates or if we have a possible pledge. The records include their coming-of-age test results, but it also lists their demeanor, IQ, personality traits, level of discontent with Quadra, health and mental issues…you name it."

Farrow looked impressed, wondering if he should ask Jen about viewing profiles when he starts working with people outside his family.

"That's O.K.," Farrow decided. "We really should find somewhere closer anyway. The bigger issue is finding people that can treat citizen's maladies. If the cure isn't simple, doctors and nurses simply choose to euthanize or butcher people…like they did my Lola."

Cass came into the ballroom, squinting. "I'm going up

to the clinic to see if I can get some medicine for my head."

Cass headed out of the room, but turned, remembering something else. "Earl's got a lot of tools and belongings that I'd like to keep. We might get a new groundskeeper soon, so could you help me gather his things and move them to my room later?" Cass asked Simon.

"Sure, but won't the new post need those tools to care for the grounds?"

"That's all I have left of him," Cass said, his eyes getting misty, while his demeanor remained serious. "The hours he spent using those tools…they were his most prized possessions and I want to take care of them."

Cass left for the clinic. The two remaining men shot each other concerned glances.

"Poor boy," Farrow said. "Maybe when your friend from the P.O.L. comes here, you can put in a good word for Cass. I'm not sure staying here will be very beneficial for him."

"I'll see what I can do," Simon agreed.

He believed Cass would be better off elsewhere, but selfish reasons also existed to rid the museum of his presence. Simon had a few unknowns amid his plans and one big mystery would be the replacement for Earl. He needed to get the artifacts from the basement moved as soon as he could.

Farrow interrupted Simon's thoughts. "Earl was my oldest and dearest friend, but he obviously trusted you more than anyone he knew."

"I don't know about that," Simon disagreed.

"I do. He trusts you with his most prized possession."

Simon looked at Farrow, confused. "What do you mean?"

"The resistance…Angola…his people."

Chapter 36

The weeks after Earl's death were busy ones. Moving the museum's basement contents proved easier than expected as Cass had taken to using pain medication that Jen supplied to ease his grief. Logan and Parker became fixtures at the museum during the week, sleeping in April and Earl's old rooms. Cass barely noticed as he only had vague recollections of his surroundings.

The entrance to the basement from the fireplace was treated with oil and lifted up on the hinges so the metal wouldn't scrape the stone floor. Down below, Chance was left unmoved, regularly freaking Logan out. The door that lead to the basement from Chance's room was sealed off to look like it didn't exist. So, if anyone went downstairs from the toolbox closet, the other entrance would be unseen.

Simon visited Jen up at the clinic one day, asking her to stop giving Cass the medication. Cass needed to be stable if there was a chance Quadra would consider him. Jen would follow her new leader's orders, replacing his pills with placebos.

"You know, I always thought I'd be the one to take over the resistance one day," Jen stated. "My dad taught me a great deal over the years."

With the most assuring tone he could muster, Simon said, "Earl did make his wishes clear."

Jen still roiled from her father's loss and, out of respect for her, he would keep to himself that Earl barely mentioned her. She had been wounded enough. They smiled at each other, knowing the closeness they once shared no longer existed.

Farrow eventually received notice that a small Quadra

unit would be in Baton Rouge by the end of the week and all the final preparations were made. Parker and Logan removed the last of the metal on the ceiling of the basement and hauled away everything meant to be taken. The two rooms they left vacant were made up for Bree and another officer, if needed.

The fog lifted from Cass's head over the next few days, which got him functioning again and excited for another opportunity to charm Quadra. He went out to a friend's greenhouse and got some crocus flowers to put in the rooms.

Quadra, being predictable, arrived when they said they would- right before the dinner hour. An elaborate dinner was presented and Farrow warned Simon to avoid eating any of the baked goods. The Quadra unit consisted of five recruits and officer Denton.

"Good to see you, Bree," Simon said from the kitchen as people mingled in the hall. "Dinner will be ready in fifteen minutes."

She gave a curt smile, annoyed by the disrespect Simon continued to show her by using her first name.

"Officer Denton," Farrow explained, "we have two rooms available for you and one other recruit."

"We'll only need one for me. A new post arrives tomorrow to replace Earl," Bree said.

Farrow, surprised he hadn't been informed earlier, smiled and nodded. Simon identified the contempt on his face, but the expression was not easily discerned by others. The rest of the unit was led to the upstairs ballroom to arrange their sleeping bags. Judging by the packs and supplies they brought with them, this would be a short stay.

The unit washed up in the museum bathroom before meandering into the kitchen. Simon wasn't surprised that Bree traveled with an all-male unit. She seemed to prefer that.

Everyone enjoyed the meal. Simon and Farrow took baked goods, but spread them around on their plate, not eating them. Farrow felt guilty that he couldn't tell Cass about the situation, but it would raise suspicion. Simon must have had the same idea, telling Cass after dinner to stick more to protein and produce in case he had to run or train to get into Quadra.

"Mr. Handler, can I see you outside, please," Bree said.

"Of course. Let me grab a jacket."

Bree grabbed a jacket as well. The weather in Baton Rouge in the middle of January hovered around 50 degrees this time of night. They walked out to the bench where a light now stood on one end, Earl's last job as groundskeeper. Bree sat on one end, while Simon occupied the other, keeping everything above board.

"I think I'm going to need to pull you from this post."

"You could just leave me here," Simon suggested. "This job is better than reading food labels all day."

Bree grimaced. "It's not up to me, Handler. You're a liability. You know that."

They watched the Mississippi run past on its way to New Orleans. After a while, their breath became visible.

"Whatever happens to me, you should see the basement before you go." Simon pointed back to the museum, seeing the men still hanging out in the kitchen.

"What are you talking about?"

"There's a basement that has some historical artifacts. It seems that the groundskeeper was up to no good." Simon turned toward the river once again.

Bree didn't get overly excited like Simon expected. He thought that Farrow's drugging of Quadra must have been working quite well.

"I'd like to look at it in the morning," Bree said, yawning. "It's been a long day and I need to get some rest."

Bree got up and went back to the museum. Simon sat outside on the bench, enjoying the peace until Farrow joined him.

"I told her about the basement to include the artifacts and she said she'd take a look in the morning," Simon told Farrow. "I don't get it."

"That's my fault," Farrow admitted. "We're trying different drugs in the bakery items and apparently the ones tonight make them tired."

"You can't just treat them like guinea pigs, Farrow!" Simon whispered.

Farrow turned to walk back toward the museum. "Of course I can."

The next morning, Simon found himself being shaken awake by a very determined Quadra recruit. When his eyes focused, he saw that Bree and the rest of the recruits were also in attendance. They were fully dressed with eager expressions.

"Simon, show us the basement you told me about last night!" Simon gave Bree a confused look. "Let's go. Mr. Handler!"

"You didn't even seem like you gave a damn when I mentioned it, but now you're rousing me from my bed?" Simon said, confused.

Bree looked ashamed in front of her unit. "It was a long trip here. We were all tired last night," she said, offering an excuse.

"Can I please have some privacy so I can put some clothes on?"

Given her enthusiasm to see the basement, she didn't even consider that he was bare-ass under the sheets. Her cheeks flushed with color.

"Of course!" She evacuated the room as though a fire alarm was rung. The unit followed.

When Simon came out of his room, they all stood in the hallway. Not just the unit, but Farrow and Cass as well.

"What's this about a basement?" Cass asked.

Simon led the group to the closet that housed the tool box. He pushed the toolbox aside and clicked the secret panel open on the back wall of the closet like he had so many times before. The witnesses released gasps of excitement. He led them down to the basement, turned on the overhead lights and let them investigate the area.

One of the men in the unit rifled through an armoire. It housed artifacts with a journal describing the items and their historical significance. Farrow did a great job feigning amazement as Cass offered more of an authentic awe.

The items were mostly duplicates of things previously stored there or items that were found in Angola. Bree grabbed the journal from the recruit, flipping through some of the pages and then slamming the tome shut.

"How did you discover this?" Bree asked Simon.

"I couldn't sleep one night because of a terrible storm. So, I got a glass of milk from the kitchen and climbed up the stairway to watch the lightning through the glass ceiling. Next thing I knew, Earl came out of the closet, moved the tool box to the left and went to his room carrying something. It took a couple of tries before I figured it out."

Bree seemed annoyed. "How long have you known?!" She squawked.

Simon shrugged. "Since the beginning of December, right after the search month."

"Why on Earth wouldn't you contact me?"

"I don't have any way to get ahold of you," Simon

answered, attempting to keep his voice down.

Simon cleared his throat, trying to alert Bree that she was blowing his cover. Cass had no idea that Simon worked for Quadra, nor was Farrow supposed to know. When she glanced in his direction, Simon gave her a stern look, furrowing his brows. She realized her error.

"Did you know anything about this, Mr. Freeman?" Bree asked Farrow, trying to correct her misstep.

"Earl never said a thing about this place to me," Farrow answered, looking around to really convince them of his shock.

The answer given was true, but surely Bree would press further as Farrow didn't actually answer her question. That's when it dawned on Simon that the drugs they'd been ingesting at Quadra must be dulling their minds…making them more accepting of whatever rubbish is offered. He wondered to himself how much easier citizens must be able to control and why a lot of city-dwellers were scared of rural citizens because they were "emotionally charged."

Bree had the men in the unit box up everything found in the armoire and seal it. Before going upstairs, Simon noticed her walking around the basement, looking at the floor. It was the exact reason that Simon had Logan and Parker collect dirt and sweep it around the basement. She was smart, looking for dust marks…to see if anything else had been here, but Simon remained a step ahead.

"Why don't we all go up and enjoy breakfast, it should have been delivered by now," Farrow suggested, eager for his next science experiment.

When they got to the kitchen, the breakfast had been delivered on the counter and a woman rifled through the bag, eventually plucking out a piece of bacon.

"Thank you, Miss, I think we can handle it from here,"

Farrow said. "Cass, why don't you wash up and get the plates out."

There were small pieces of colored paper on the kitchen table. A man in Bree's unit picked one up and the color drained from his face.

"This can't really be what happens!" He shrieked.

Bree walked over, snatching the paper from his hand. Her eyes grew wide. "Where did these come from?!"

The woman eating bacon said, "There were all kinds of these flying around outside. I never did learn to read, but I was hopin' someone else could read it to me."

Bree gathered all the small fliers on the table and saw out the window that brightly colored pieces of paper dotted the grounds.

"I need my unit to go out and gather all the pieces of paper they can," Bree ordered. "As a matter of fact, Simon and Cass, you join us!" They all bolted out the doors and began their chore.

Farrow went out on the lawn and picked a piece of paper up.

Quadra sends people to their death after aging out. No retirement. No paradise. Euthanized by gas. Why can we never speak to them again? Visit?

Don't go. Don't be fooled. – The Resistance

Farrow smiled. Not many would believe this truth at first, but it was a start. He watched as the paper rolled through the town like tumbleweed. Never had litter made him so pleased.

Chapter 37

Everyone returned to the museum with armfuls of fliers. The wheelbarrow was rolled toward the museum's side door, the papers placed in the wheelbarrow and the contents lit on fire. A little girl skipped by with a couple in her hand and Bree practically wrestled them away from her.

After the impromptu, morning bonfire, they went to retrieve their breakfast. The meal delivery included beignets and Cass didn't possess the will power to forego the treat, eating quite a few. Farrow and Simon, hoping to keep their wits about them, dipped the beignets in the jelly, licking it off. They also employed the trick of taking a bite only to deposit the uneaten beignet into their napkin.

Laughter broke out in spurts. People started slurring their words. Farrow motioned to Simon to follow him. They convened at the sink.

"This drug reaction should mimic consuming alcohol," Farrow informed.

"Nicely done," Simon said, impressed. He looked back at the loopy crowd. "This should help us accomplish many things this morning."

Farrow nodded, "It's supposed to stay in the system for three hours and their memories will be muddled."

"Perfect."

One of the recruits in the unit pounded the table and asked no one in particular, "So, could those papers be true?" His mouth stayed open in wonder. "I mean, did the government just kill my granddad?"

The mood in the room grew solemn. Simon didn't take his eyes off Bree. She stood up clumsily, instructing that there would be no more talk of those papers. Her mistake was further mentioning that she had recently visited her mother there. This meant the officers of Quadra knew about Cape Canaveral…or at least Bree did. You can't visit the dead.

Farrow removed all the beignets off the table, realizing the dosage was far too high. He would make note that the outcome of this dosage was slurred speech and a number of heads resting on the table.

Simon went to sit next to Bree and asked, "So, given the discovery in the basement and this group called the resistance, it looks like I should stay here, continuing my assignment."

Bree nodded.

"You will need a local to join forces with you, too. Maybe Cass can return to Lafayette as a Baton Rouge specialist," Simon added.

Bree nodded again, letting out a chuckle as a burp escaped her. After a couple of hours passed, personalities started returning to normal, but many were hampered by a pounding headache. Once everyone had recovered, Bree gathered her unit in the ballroom, trying to piece together the events of the morning. No one could recall anything after the bonfire.

"Maybe something was placed onto the paper that soaked into our skin," one of the recruits suggested.

"Breakfast could have been mixed up with regular citizen food," another chimed in.

"No," Bree said. "I placed the order for the meals myself." She paused. "And putting something on the paper makes no sense. Those notes weren't meant for us."

Bree sent the unit out to question the townspeople…see if they saw where the notes had come from and to collect any fliers they may have missed. Simon went upstairs as the unit descended the stairway. He found Bree looking out a window in the ballroom.

"I just wanted to thank you for letting me stay at the museum and also taking Cass with you to Lafayette," Simon told Bree. "You're right, it makes sense."

Bree couldn't remember talking about these topics, but was too proud to admit it.

"So, what other fascinating things happened after breakfast?" Bree fished.

"I don't know. I got such a terrible headache that I had to go rest for a while. Don't you remember?"

"Oh, yes," Bree lied, "such a busy day." She smiled uncomfortably and excused herself.

Simon went to the museum desk because a tour had been scheduled for the afternoon. Weekend tours were highly unusual, but Simon accepted this one, hoping to free himself from Quadra's presence for part of the weekend.

Simon went through the tour, but found the crowd busy gossiping about the colored pieces of paper they had read this morning. Once Simon got up to the second floor, a woman on the tour, clearly upset by what she had read, raised her hand.

"Yes, ma'am, a question about the ceiling?" Simon asked as he pointed toward her.

"Uh, no," she said, "Although it's very beautiful." She looked up. "What do you make of those little colored papers?"

Simon grew pleased that she would even ask such a potentially dangerous question. The fliers were working. Simon wanted to tell her how hard his organization had worked on printing those over the last few weeks...that men and women risked their lives distributing them in the dead of night.

"I heard someone from Baton Rouge escaped from Cape Canaveral and wants everyone to know their story," Simon answered in hushed tones. "He may be behind the papers."

"It's just so unbelievable," a man added.

"I think so, too," Simon lied. "I wish we could, at the very least, receive pictures or the date our loved ones pass away. That doesn't seem like much to ask."

The tour completed smoothly and all the guests left with the intended seeds of doubt the fliers were meant to induce. Farrow smirked in Simon's direction after he thanked the guests for coming.

"I think I'm going to substitute the drugged foods for regular servings at dinner," Farrow said. "Officer Denton seemed suspicious. It was too much, but now I know."

"That's a good call," Simon agreed. "What did you have in store for tonight?"

"A drug that makes one feel amorous."

Simon grinned as he started walking down the hall. The door to Earl's room opened and Simon jumped to the side of the door jamb, ready to pounce. The figure barely darkened the door frame when Simon grabbed the person by the shoulders.

The figure emitted a high pitch scream and when he saw that he held a woman, Simon loosened his grip. She looked at him with irritation.

"I'm sorry," Simon said as he quickly put his arms to his side. He looked at her, quizzically. "Aren't you the woman that was eating bacon in the kitchen this morning?"

She nodded her head.

"Why are you still here?" Simon asked.

"Excuse me?!" She squawked.

Farrow made his way down the hall as fast as he could

when he noticed things did not look like they were going well. He reached the two of them, breathing heavy.

"Simon, this is Dani, she's the new grounds keeper," Farrow explained.

"Oh! I'm sorry, I thought you delivered the food this morning," Simon said, smiling and putting out his hand as a proper southerner would. "I also assumed Earl's replacement would be a man."

At this, Dani's eyebrows shot up and she quickly withdrew her hand. Once again, his first impression was lacking. He shut his eyes, realizing the mistake, while Dani walked away.

"That went well," Farrow said, sarcastically.

Simon figured he might be able to smooth things over later and went to the kitchen to deliver some good news.

"You better pack up your things," Simon told Cass. "You're going to Lafayette with the unit when they leave."

Cass was overjoyed. "This is the best news! Well, this and I'm getting married in a couple weeks," Cass said. "I decided to marry and they found a match for me."

Losing Earl must have made a bigger impact on Cass than originally thought. Cass still had a few months before he needed to make a decision to marry or use the hubs.

"You know," Simon mentioned, "some wise person once said that no big life decisions should be made a year after you lose someone close to you."

"I wonder if that person had ever been alone," Cass said, barely audible.

When Cass got up to go, Simon offered his hand, congratulating Cass on all the good things that were happening for him. He told Cass that Earl would be very proud of him.

Bree and the men in her unit entered through the side

door of the museum. "Cass, be ready to go in fifteen minutes," she barked. "Go get your packs and sleeping gear," she instructed the rest of her team.

"What's going on?" Simon asked as the men all rushed past him to carry out their orders.

"It appears those fliers are up and down the entire area. From here to New Orleans and from New Orleans to Lafayette. Can you believe they would have the balls to scatter those in Lafayette?!"

Simon didn't answer, as the question seemed rhetorical, but he did believe it and took great pride in the fact. It was originally suspected that the recruits had no idea what awaited their loved ones at Cape Canaveral because Parker didn't receive training on the matter during his time at Quadra. Bree unknowingly confirmed the recruit's lack of knowledge. This would cause a stir.

For Clifford's part, he spoke openly about his time of "retirement" during a rally. The resistance, in their collective outrage, spent weeks printing the fliers and working on a plan to disperse them.

Two transits pulled up outside the museum and the team, plus Cass, made a quick exit. As they traveled toward Lafayette, Bree's face got hot, turning red in anger. Pieces of colored paper were posted on buildings and trees. Some were rolling along the ground. Quadra recruits could be seen, attempting to collect them, but Bree understood the effort would not be enough.

The damage had already been done.

Chapter 38

Quadra did as they always had, which included not feeling the need to refute the allegations of the fliers. However, this only fueled the doubt. Citizens begged to get a photo or written note from their loved ones that had aged out. All requests were denied.

In the following weeks, Cass married without much fanfare. All marriages started quietly, unless it was a chancellor family marriage or high-officer relation. He settled in Lafayette, quickly acclimating to life as a Quadra recruit.

Dani excelled at her job, even handling all the chores left behind by Cass. Simon and Farrow grew to appreciate her, both as a person and co-post. She made it possible to keep Cass's position unfilled, which gave them more freedom.

Her family lived close by in an apartment complex where she still kept a small apartment. She'd travel the two miles home every night, barring the evenings she had an escort appointment. Dani never came to like Simon much, but she managed to be civil.

The museum would regularly be locked up on the weekends because everyone had their own interests to pursue. The resistance had upped their game when it came to informing the public about aging out, telling those in Baton Rouge they didn't have to go. No other information was distributed as it would be even more dangerous for the resistance.

There were twenty people in the area scheduled to age out in less than a month. They were told to attend the ceremony, where they'd be given a choice. No other specifics could be shared. These were dangerous times.

***

"It's good to have you going up with me, Farrow," Simon said as the two men traveled to Angola on a Friday afternoon. "It's been a while."

"Yes, indeed, but if I can offer any help, I'd like to."

"There's a lot of work to be done," Simon admitted, sounding a bit overwhelmed.

Once the two men arrived at the guard building in front of Angola, Banner approached the transit, looking upset. And although Simon couldn't wait to dig into the dining hall cuisine, Banner told Simon that he was needed at an important meeting.

Farrow made his way to his room on foot, while Banner and Logan whisked Simon away. As far as Simon knew, no one was currently housed in Camp J, so he grew concerned as the cart stopped in front of the prison.

After the code was keyed in, the men entered the cell block. No one was in the first few cells, but a still shadow fell on the floor from the last cell. Simon slowly walked to the end of the row, stopping a few feet in front of the bars.

"Hello," Simon greeted. "Come out, please."

A shuffle of feet soon produced a prisoner and Simon's heart sank in his stomach. He had no pre-conceived notions of what to expect, but seeing Jen in front of him was not as shocking as it should have been.

Simon looked back at Banner and Logan and then at Jen. "Well, is anyone going to explain?!"

"I've got nothing to say," Jen decided, disappearing back into the corner of her cell.

Simon left the building to go sit in the cart. Banner and Parker joined him shortly afterwards. They all sat in the vehicle, waiting for Simon to give direction. He had no clue what the offence could be that got Jen locked in the cell, but history had no shortage of betrayal to those closest to their leaders.

"Why is she locked up?" Simon asked.

"We were hoping she'd tell you herself, but we'll take you to the people that reported the issues," Banner said. "Logan and I would just be giving you second-hand information."

Simon grabbed the steering wheel. "I'd like some of that second-hand info right now."

Logan sat in the back and piped up, "She's been flirting and sleeping with certain men in an attempt to sway them to her side."

"What side is that?" Simon asked.

Banner drove toward the dining hall, as he replied, "She made her intentions clear. She wants to be the leader of the resistance and throw you out. She's been telling people that you work for Quadra and you can't be trusted. She's also hinted around that you had something to do with Earl's death."

Rumors like these would never be believed by those close to Simon, but the harm they could do, if left unchecked, could cripple the resistance. After the men piled their plates high, Logan led the way to the private room in the back of the dining hall. The sun had begun its decent for the day, but shone brightly into the room, which was a direct contradiction to Simon's mood.

All four tables were filled, but the plates had long been removed. Simon recognized most of those in attendance, but not all. He nodded his head as a greeting. Banner shut the door behind him and took a seat at a small table that needed to be added for the occasion.

"Help me understand what's going on," Simon said.

Only two women were present, but one of them shot straight out of her seat and accused Quinn (Jen) of many things, to include seducing her husband. It wasn't a far stretch to believe that the man sitting next to her, with his head lowered, was indeed the husband.

Everyone went around the room, giving an account of their experiences with Jen and offensive claims she made against Simon. Tarzan and Parker had been the two men to come forward and report her behavior. Many of the other men were ashamed that they were duped by her.

"I'll address all these claims at the rally on Sunday," Simon said. "I assure you that I never had any part in Earl's death and I'm working with Quadra, but only for the benefit of the resistance."

Parker raised his hand and Simon nodded. "Quinn claimed that you had been her lover in the past. Is that true?"

Simon wished more than anything that Parker would have asked that question in private, but here they were. The room went silent, Simon wishing to be anywhere else, but here.

"Quinn and I work in the same town and I met her on my first day," Simon explained. "We did have a physical entanglement for a brief period, but haven't been together in quite some time. I returned to the escort hubs and have been happy with the decision."

Parker wasn't done. "And did you know she was Earl's daughter when you started seeing her?"

"I had no idea. I was shocked when I found out about their bond. They didn't advertise the fact they were related." Simon looked over the crowd. "Are there any other questions?" No one replied. "O.K., well we're going to continue to review the evidence and speak to witnesses. We'll decide what needs to be done. Tarzan, Parker, Logan and Banner- please stay behind."

The small crowd filed out of the room. Those that remained discussed the serious accusations against the prisoner. Tarzan shared that while they were in an intimate embrace, she asked him to kill "Rogers."

Parker, now part of the resistance's inner circle, had been privy to sexual favors in hopes she could gain important information. She never received information and Simon couldn't fault Parker for what he received.

Banner told the men that Quinn had promised to let Della come here and stay at the compound. That no more vetting would be necessary when she became the leader. She never attempted to seduce Banner, but made him enticing promises instead.

"Why did you ask me those questions?" Simon asked Parker.

"The rumors are all over Angola. Quinn probably was the source of them because I never suspected the two of you," Parker explained. "The only way to squash the talk was to admit to it. You played it perfectly."

Logan quietly took it all in which gave Simon an uneasy feeling because he trusted Logan the least.

"You've been quiet, Logan. Anything to add?"

Banner elbowed Logan as though encouraging him to speak.

"Just a hunch," Logan said. "I've got no real proof."

"Well, throw it out there. Let's see what you got," Tarzan encouraged.

"The first woman that spoke…I think her husband is in love with Quinn and would do anything for her, to include rescuing her from the prison."

"I didn't recognize the man sitting next to her," Simon said.

"The man sitting next to her was some other, poor sucker. Her husband is Torch, our pyro guy. He would know how to blast a hole into the cell and get Quinn out," Logan finished.

That's why Jen had nothing to say. She wouldn't need to say a word if she wasn't expecting to stay much longer.

"Let's go!" Simon yelled. He jumped into a cart when they got outside.

Simon willed the cart to move faster, but the five men weighed it down. Simon told Banner and Tarzan, the two largest men, to jump off and go back to their posts. The cart immediately sped up toward their destination. Half-way to Camp J, a loud boom sounded, raising birds of all sizes and species to flight.

The men's hearts raced at the anticipation of what they would find when they arrived. Simon squinted, trying to see the building ahead, but only a small plume of smoke was visible.

"There," Parker pointed. "The corner of the building is missing."

"She's escaped!" Logan shouted.

Simon turned off the motor before the cart came to a stop and the men jumped out. They stood near the gaping hole, looking in all directions. Small pieces of stone still dropped from the explosion, while others moaned in place. A sob from the other side of the hole was heard by all three men.

They peeked in to find Torch sitting on the ground, cradling Jen in his arms. The sob was his. They approached respectfully, realizing that Torch had lost someone he loved, even if the circumstances were of their own making.

"She's gone," Torch said. "The stones were much less dense than I figured. So, when the charges went off, she was riddled with fragments." Torch rocked back and forth. "This is my fault!" he screamed.

Logan put his hand on Torch's shoulder. "Go home," he said. "Let us handle this."

The explosion had kicked up dust so there were trails of Torch's tears down his cheeks. Parker bent down, lifting Jen off the floor. One of her arms fell toward the ground. He put Jen in the cart and covered her with a blanket from her cell.

"Logan, please accompany Torch to the lake house. Get him cleaned up and fed," Simon suggested. "You may want to sleep there for the night. It'll be dark soon. We'll let Torch's wife know where he is so he doesn't get in any more trouble."

Logan and Torch set off towards the lake on foot. A cool breeze carried patches of fog that dotted Angola's fields.

"Let's go bury her up at the cemetery," Simon said.

The cemetery's white headstones almost shone by the light of the cart. The only sound that cut through the air was that of the shovels slicing into the dirt. Jen's body was carefully laid in the grave and mere seconds after the last bit of dirt was patted down, the battery died on the cart and the lights went out. They put the shovels in the back of the cart before walking down the hill in silence.

Parker remembered Quinn's laugh and how infatuated he used to be with her…how her eyes would light up with mischievous intent. He flashed back to their time in the cave when they shared a mission, speaking of deep subjects and secrets that forever bonded them as friends.

Simon, on the other hand, felt like he had let Earl down by allowing harm to come to his only daughter. He wondered what he'd say at the rally on Sunday and how her disappearance would affect Dr. Michon. Jen's death meant the resistance would no longer have access to Quadra records.

All things considered, a pang of guilt shot through Simon as he grew thankful. Relieved that, in the end, he didn't have to be the one responsible for Jen's fate. Torch's mistake had freed him momentarily from the harsh burden of leadership.

Both men shed tears that evening, but for vastly different reasons.

Chapter 39

Farrow assisted the resistance all weekend with their plans for the upcoming aging out ceremony. There were twenty people aging out and the resistance figured that a maximum of fifty percent, or ten people, would possibly choose not to go to Cape Canaveral.

Since Quadra would no longer care for these citizens, it was important to have a support system and living quarters set up. Angola needed to keep space available for more pledges, not begin a home for the aged, so Clifford's plot of land was selected to start the community. In the future, if the idea caught on, there was plenty unclaimed land in the vicinity.

Farrow, Clifford and a couple sisters, named Zan and Jayna, were handling the specifics. They had support from quite a few other resistance members and Rosa, Clifford's girlfriend, also joined the efforts. The trickiest part of the mission would be the extraction of the men and women on the day of the ceremony, but Farrow, in his wisdom, came up with a solution.

Other considerations were clothing, food reserves, medical needs, chores and so on. They tackled each concern one by one. Because these men and women would no longer be under Quadra care, they would need to contribute to either the resistance or life at Benton Oasis. Rosa compiled a questionnaire for the aged to help figure out each person's talents, contacts or abilities.

Small homes had been erected on Clifford's land to supplement the containers. Nothing fancy, but small, individual living spaces. In the upcoming weeks, there would be more homes built. Simon would forego next weekend at Angola to labor at Benton Oasis, eager to compare the changes from his first visit.

Despite the talk of Jen's death, spirits were high around Angola. People of the resistance had an excitement around the upcoming mission, involving the aging out ceremony. Odds were that most people had their lives touched by the Quadra practice of "retirement."

Bets were placed between resistance members as to how many aged they thought would ultimately decide to go to the Oasis instead of Cape Canaveral. Many believed that even one life should count as a victory.

When Sunday arrived, Simon ate a large breakfast, put on a jacket, and went out to Lake Killarney. According to all the talk Simon had heard around Baton Rouge and Angola, the area was experiencing a cooler March than most. He never understood why the weather in the south was a constant topic of conversation.

Not many people were out. Simon sat close to the lake, listening to the small ripples of the water come ashore. He had found this spot a safe place to think and reflect. Curry came to visit him during the lunch hour, bringing him some water.

"You're troubled about the rally tonight?" Curry asked, taking a seat beside Simon on the sand. "Parker told me parts of it when he and Torch were here. Gotta say that I don't envy your position."

"Any suggestions?" Simon asked.

"Yep. Never ask me for suggestions. I'm only an expert on water related-things and ya have better advisors," Curry said. He raised his eyebrows. "But, ye gotta be honest and true to who ya are. They're either gonna respect ya or not. Ya may think gaining respect has a lot to do with you, but it don't. Mostly has to do with whatever else is up their arse."

"You don't think I can garner their respect?"

Curry shrugged, "Maybe, but my pops told me that an old leader once said that if he walked on water in the morning, the afternoon headlines would read: president can't swim. People are weird creatures, likely to enjoy a bit of gossip over truth. Go figure. Important thing is that when all is said and done, ya respect yaself."

Simon smiled. "I haven't thought about that quote for a long time. You're a smart man, Curry. Thank you for the water and the chat," Simon said, handing him the empty glass.

Curry got up to leave, turning around to offer one more piece of advice. "Oh, and don't be long-winded. No one wants to hear ya rattle on and on." He turned and walked toward his house.

Simon laughed and said to himself, "A smart man, indeed."

Before the dinner hour approached, a cool breeze traveled over the lake, disturbing Simon's concentration. His hands and face grew cold, so he decided to get out of the weather and warm himself up with a bite to eat or a warm beverage. He chose on both.

He sat in the main room, next to the buffet line and smiled or greeted people as they walked past with their trays. The importance of getting to know everyone better was not lost on him. The focus of his resistance work had been intensely focused. He had laid a strong foundation with those close to him, but needed to start making himself more available to others in the resistance.

Farrow sat down with him and asked if he was ready for the rally tonight. The time spent at the lake helped clear his head so he nodded. Others slowly joined them at the table, turning the conversation more jovial. Simon became incredibly appreciative to hear what he considered "regular conversation." It caught him off guard, but in the best way.

As time passed, people filed out of the dining hall, toward the stadium. For a short time Simon had a reprieve from thinking about the rally. Farrow put his hand over Simon's before leaving.

"My family's been praying for you."

Simon had no clue Farrow was a believer, wondering why he wasn't in a GIL town, with others like him. But he had no time to ponder the notion. He had a rally to start and announcements to make. Simon made his way toward the stadium, looking forward to when he could return to the museum.

He decided to go up and begin the rally himself. "I pledge…" he started.

"I pledge to resist the," they yelled, signing the word for lies. "I honor this," signing the word army. "And I'll die for my…," they finished, signing "freedom."

"It's been a whirlwind of change, has it not?" Simon asked the crowd.

They answered with nods, shouts of "yes," and guttural responses. He looked over the crowd with so much appreciation.

"So, I never had designs of being a leader of the resistance. It's what Earl wanted…insisted upon, really," Simon started. "Seemed like a lot of responsibility and pressure."

The crowd shifted, wondering where he was headed.

"A lot of untrue information has been circling Angola and I want to set it straight. I didn't have anything to do with Earl's death. I'm still mourning his passing. He was a good man, but illness riddled his body. I think he kicked Logan's ass right before he died just to see if he could."

Laughter.

"I don't technically work for Quadra, but my posting in the area is, ironically enough, to gather information about this group and others, while working undercover. My allegiance is to the resistance…never doubt that."

Some gasps of surprise peppered the stadium, which was understandable.

"Furthermore, I did have a brief entanglement with Quinn months ago, but learned only recently that she wished to overthrow my authority, including possibly having me killed. Quinn was detained for her betrayal and died in an effort to escape. She will be sorely missed." Simon lowered his head, truly sad to make that announcement.

Simon raised his hand to stop the chattering running through the stadium.

"A very long time ago, this country, when it was called America, had something called elections. There is a lot to it, but the gist is that every four years, two people would be nominated and each citizen had an opportunity to vote."

People squinted or looked around at others, trying to understand.

"A vote would be your choice for the person you wanted to see run the country or sometimes just a decision about who you didn't want to see run the country. I suggest that we pick a few people in the resistance and everyone has the opportunity to pick from the group who they would like to see be in charge of Angola. That way it's not Earl's decision, but yours as well."

Banner walked up on stage, pointing at Simon. "This man is a hard-worker. He's fair and honest. He's smart. He recognizes the importance of every one of you and what you mean to this cause."

Tarzan came up to the stage next. "He is a good man,

who gave my sister justice and I trust him with my life."

As Tarzan spoke, Parker, Logan, Curry and other leaders of the resistance went on the platform. Simon stood still, visibly humbled. Once the others voiced their support for Simon to lead, Curry came to the head of the platform.

"I'm not going to lie," Curry started. "When I first met Rogers, I thought him a bit of an arse. But, I've watched as the weight of leadership weighed heavy on him, sitting at the edge of Lake Killarney. On so many occasions, thinking on what's best for the people at Angola. Thinking on what's best for the people out there," Curry pointed high, over the heads of the crowd. "Cause, let's face it, he's taken on a responsibility that no one here probably wants. And the fact that he doesn't much yearn to be leader, tells me he's probably the best one for the job."

Cheers rung out.

Curry raised his hand. "I tell ye what. Anyone out there who wants to be in charge, raise yer hand."

Everyone looked around, while not one hand went in the air. Anyone who could possibly lead the resistance stood on the stage, backing Simon.

"I guess it's settled," Curry said to the crowd and they all cheered. He looked back at Simon, smiling. "Now let's hear some music."

The rest of the night, the air was filled with beautiful music and song. Simon stayed until the end of the rally, socializing. Farrow finally came to retrieve Simon from his frivolity and asked if they could head back.

On the way back to Baton Rouge, Simon had a feeling he hadn't yet experienced. A longing to stay at Angola because it was slowly becoming home.

Chapter 40

Spring was in the air and the aging-out ceremony was only two weeks away. After a forgettable week of tours at the museum, everyone set off for their weekend destinations.

Farrow went home to continue experimenting with a special concoction for Quadra's menu to be served days before the ceremony. Because the fliers had garnered so much attention, the resistance didn't know how many recruits would be called in, so they were betting on Farrow's baked goods to ensure a less-than-effective Quadra force.

Simon headed toward Benton Oasis, Clifford's land, to help with the home-building. He had collected a cache of small household goods to bring to the new homes. Wooden spoons, toiletries, hand towels, a few bowls…things that the aged wouldn't have in their suitcases for their trip to Cape Canaveral.

He drove a transit that used to be Earl's vehicle. The resistance had started limiting their fuel consumption as much as possible because their supply had dwindled, mostly because of the high fuel-usage on the missions to distribute the flyers. When he arrived at what he thought to be the entrance to Clifford's place, Simon questioned himself.

He drove down the road, finding the supports for the gate, ensuring he was in the right place. The gate had to be removed to haul building supplies, if needed. Simon flashed back to when he and April walked this path. Coming here had risks associated with memories of her, but Simon invited them.

Before arriving at the gate that announced "Benton Oasis," a few cars were parked at the side of the road so Simon followed suit and parked. He made his way down the path to the entrance gate, hard-pressed to believe his eyes at the sight of a burgeoning little town. Dilapidated buildings were the norm under Quadra rule, but this little village of newness truly inspired Simon.

Rosa was the first to greet him, calling him by his Angola name of Rogers. She carried flower pots full of spring's bounty. The colors around the camp made the efforts that much more beautiful. The small houses boasted flower beds and small garden patches ready to be landscaped by the new owners. Potted flowers sat on the landing of each home as a bright welcome.

Most of the helpers would arrive tomorrow so the area was peaceful. Simon dropped his bag and the household items off in container number 5, where he swore he could still smell April's scent on the pillow.

Simon went to the fire pit to start a blaze for the night as the sunlight started fading. Additional people would arrive as the evening continued. An unfamiliar, but tantalizing smell wafted by the fire. Simon followed the smell to the barn where a small buffet table stood, filled with foods he had never eaten.

Tamales and tacos overflowed in the serving dishes. A large pot of beans simmered on the end of the table. Rosa invited him in to grab a plate. She informed him that all the food offerings tonight were made with wild boar. Simon got a plate, taking a seat at one of the makeshift tables before devouring the food like a starving man.

He watched as others straggled in, enjoying the meal as much as he did. While sitting at the table, he spotted cows in the field that weren't there during his last couple of visits. His ears caught noises of chickens and other farm animals that were not visible in the shroud of night.

Simon went back to the fire, staring into the flames, lost

in thought.

"You look like the burdens of the world rest on your shoulders," a man said.

Simon looked up to see many sitting around the fire pit. He smiled; shocked by the accuracy of the statement and that he now had an audience.

"This place looks amazing. We've all worked so hard and risked so much on this mission." Everyone nodded. "But, it's not up to us if people come. And I worry if any of the aged will make the right choice."

"You're not alone," the man said, patting Simon on the shoulder. Heads nodded around the fire.

The two sisters, Zan and Jayna, rose out of their seats, asking everyone to set up their tents for the weekend and get some rest. Everyone departed. The irony wasn't lost on Simon. He was, in fact, now very much alone.

Morning came quickly, with noises of progress permeating the air at Benton Oasis. The early-risers had already eaten and launched into productive fits. Simon still struggled to get up for the day. A knock on the container, inviting him to breakfast, would be all the incentive he needed.

He answered the door to find both Clifford and Farrow. The men headed off to breakfast. Although the one main dish hardly compared to the selections at the Angola dining hall, Rosa proved to be an amazing cook. Huevos rancheros, another meal Simon had never eaten, pleased his taste buds and fueled him for the day.

"I thought you were spending the weekend at home." Simon mentioned to Farrow.

Farrow explained he'd be leaving once he harvested an ingredient he needed for a concoction. He invited Simon to go with him and after walking a quarter mile along a field,

Farrow showed Simon a huge patch of what he called pokeweed.

"Haven't I seen some of this on the Angola farm?" Simon asked.

"Most likely. It grows all over the area. I learned about it in maw-maw's gardening journal. The leaves are poisonous to most humans, but slaves ate them with mixed results."

"Why would slaves eat poisonous plants?!"

"It's a survival food. The first offering of spring," Farrow explained. "The leaves need to be boiled two or three times to remove the poison and make them edible."

Simon snipped off the leaves close to the ground, placing them in his sack. "What are you going to do with these?"

"Boil them and save the second pot of boiled water to use in our baked goods," Farrow shared.

"Is that safe?"

"For the most part, especially used in small doses," Farrow admitted. "No one will die, but they will have symptoms of the flu…cleaned out from tip to tail…vomiting and diarrhea mostly. The water may be of use medicinally, too. There is tale that the pokeweed can help cure certain cancers or illnesses. We're going to experiment with that as well."

"How do you know that?"

Farrow smiled, pleased to share his information. "Apparently, long ago, when people ran around barefoot, worms were a common ailment. The worms came from animal feces which, in itself, is disturbing. But, when the leaves of the pokeweed were boiled and eaten, the worms would die and leave the body through excrement. Fascinating, really."

Simon shook his head, with a disgusted look on his face.

"Not fascinating?" Farrow asked.

"Not really. Kind of disgusting, if I'm picking my own adjective."

Farrow looked over the bags and decided they had picked enough for his purposes so they started walking back toward the barn. After retrieving some water in the barn, they took a break before Farrow left and Simon started a new chore.

"How'd you come upon your maw-maw's journals?" Simon wondered.

"That's the sad thing. They've always been at my home," Farrow said, ashamed. "She gave them to my wife when we were married as a gift and neither of us ever cracked the covers."

"You can't beat yourself up over such things," Simon said.

"Maybe not, but I wish I would have sat with her more often, listened better…learned more. She used to call me her little king and I never asked her why."

Simon shot Farrow a puzzled look. "A king was a supreme ruler over a country or area. It was one of the highest titles that could be bestowed on a man. When Quadra took over, children were no longer able to be named anything that symbolized royalty or power."

"I didn't know that, but I don't understand why she called me King. I have no power or position and she named me!"

She called you king *because* of your name," Simon shared.

"What? I've always hated my name. It literally means a litter of pigs! Kids teased me constantly."

"That's because they didn't have the same understanding that your maw-maw did. The word farrow is a homonym for another word, spelled p-h-a-r-a-o-h…pharaoh. It means an Egyptian King. Your maw-maw would have known about the history because she had pre-Quadra knowledge."

The information rattled around in Farrow's head, but Simon had more to share.

"I've always liked your name," Simon admitted. "Often times, slaves would take on their master's last names, but many freed slaves wanted to shed everything about their time in bondage. One of the first things they'd do is pick a new name for themselves. There were many that chose the last name Freeman, to symbolize that they were a free man."

Simon got up from his seat, patted Farrow on the shoulder and said he needed to get to work.

"Your maw-maw has given you a lot to live up to. It's like you're king of the free man." Simon chuckled, walking away. "No pressure! See you Sunday night."

Farrow sat there stunned, but grateful to Simon for sharing his knowledge. He would go home and tell his wife and daughter everything he learned today. Opposing Quadra had a great deal to do with what he had learned from his ancestors over the last few months.

It made sense why Quadra hoped to stifle history. It proved anything is possible.

Chapter 41

When Simon returned to the museum on Sunday afternoon, he was utterly exhausted. Every muscle ached from two days of manual labor on Clifford's land. The last time he remembered being this tired involved an involuntary trip down the Mississippi.

That evening, the regularly-scheduled escort arrived, but it was she who had to do most of the work before he passed out asleep. Although Simon, since becoming leader of the resistance, had many women interested, he preferred to stick to the escort hubs. He knew his position carried a certain mystique. A leader always garnered special attention. He remembered his history well.

Simon woke to a rustling in the kitchen, across the hall from his room. The escort, a new woman for Simon, must have let herself out. He moved to get out of bed, his tight muscles reminiscent of the weekend tasks.

He found Farrow in the kitchen, warming up a kettle of water.

"Why are you up in the middle of the night?" Simon asked.

Farrow raised his eyebrows, grinning, "It's nine-thirty."

"Oh," Simon said, surprised and a bit embarrassed. "So, how did your experimentation with the pokeweed go?"

"Really well. It produced flu-like symptoms in varying degrees. Quadra won't know what hit them."

"That's great. Everything seems to be in place." Simon yawned and rubbed his eyes. "The homes are ninety-nine percent done and all mission plans are completed. But, I'm still nervous to see how many people, if any, decide to forego Canaveral."

"Short of kidnapping people from their homes and removing their choice in the matter, we've done all we can," Farrow encouraged. "Would you like some tea?"

"Sure. Thank you."

Farrow grabbed another cup from the cabinet and put it by his own. He placed a few freshly baked tea cakes on a plate to accompany the tea. Once the water boiled, Farrow seeped the tea and delivered a steaming cup to Simon.

"These are good," Simon said, holding up a tea cake, "but I've been craving another oatmeal cookie."

"Must have been a while since you ate one of those," Farrow remarked.

"Not really. I ate one on my first mission, when we were returning to Angola."

Farrow looked puzzled. "Oats don't grow in this quadrant. Each quadrant gets flour, but oats are grown way north of here and are not a distributed good. My wife told me they used oats in her kitchens a long time ago, but not for many years."

"But, the cooks at Angola made them."

Farrow shook his head. "I doubt it... doesn't sound right."

"I'm probably confused. Must have been some other kind of cookie," Simon lied. "Thanks for the tea. I'm going to bed."

"G'night," Farrow called after him.

Simon went to his room, confused by the conversation. Oatmeal cookies were one of his favorites as a boy and he knew that's what he ate that night, coming back from Beaumont. Farrow was married to a baker and likely right about oats not being available in the SE.

Simon lifted up a small floorboard in his closet. He hid things under it when Quadra wasn't in the vicinity. A small walkie-talkie sat on top of the pile of contraband. He tuned the dial to 5 and turned it on, hearing only static. He pressed the button on the side to communicate.

"Banner, come in, Banner," Simon said.

"Banner here," said the familiar voice through the radio.

Simon pressed the button. "This is going to seem like a strange request," Simon admitted, "but I need you to ask all the kitchen staff the last time they baked oatmeal raisin cookies."

The static lasted longer than usual. "Will do," Banner responded.

"No rush. It's a low priority, but within 48 hours seems reasonable. Thanks, Banner. And don't let anyone know what you're up to."

Simon turned the device off, returning it to its hiding spot. He knew that Banner would get in touch in 48 hours, so Simon would turn it on Tuesday night around 10pm. They did this to conserve Simon's batteries so the walkie-talkie didn't have to be on constantly or wouldn't make unwanted sounds, giving away its location.

Simon soon succumbed to exhaustion, sleeping restlessly. The only saving grace being that he found the bed at the museum more comfortable than his other sleeping spots.

There were quite a few tours scheduled on Monday and Tuesday. People came and went while Simon attempted to interject a little enthusiasm on the tours, but found the boredom hard to escape. By Tuesday afternoon, suspicions monopolized his thinking. He couldn't wait to hear back from Banner.

Simon went for a run through Baton Rouge to rid himself of excess anxiety. As much time as he'd spent at the museum, he knew more of Angola and Clifford's place then the town he lived in. Between the beautiful weather and the stillness, he felt as though he could run forever.

When he returned to the museum, a strange man stood outside the side door, knocking.

"The museum is closed," Simon said, irritated he needed to speak.

Just then, Dani opened the door, smiling at her escort while inviting him in. She glared at Simon because she must have heard him being a little sharp with her guest.

"Can you wait for me in the kitchen?" Dani asked her escort. "I need to shower."

"Of course."

Simon couldn't pass up the opportunity to chat with the man. He'd never met a male escort. The closest he had come was Tarzan, but it wasn't his job- he just naturally had women fawning all over him. Simon followed the escort to the kitchen and offered him a glass of water. He declined.

Simon studied the man. He was about the same height as Simon with a dark head of hair and blue or maybe green eyes. As men go, he was attractive. He caught Simon looking at him and smiled. Nice smile…good teeth. The escort took a seat and Simon sat across from him.

"So tell me, man to man," Simon started. "What the hell is it like to be a male escort?! I have to know."

"Well, you have quite a bit of meaningless sex with a variety of different women. It's not the best way to make a living."

"Really?" Simon said, shocked by his answer.

The escort busted out laughing, "No, it's the best job in the world," he admitted. "I feel like I should be paying someone for the privilege!"

Both men were still laughing when Dani's door cracked, shutting them both up. She stuck her head out. "I'm ready."

The escort disappeared into Dani's room, but not before turning back to Simon and winking in his direction. Simon didn't have any love for Quadra, but they had posted that man correctly. He clearly loved his job.

Simon devoured some dinner then took a shower. He tried to pretend he couldn't hear the ruckus in the next room, but both of them were quite vocal lovers. He wondered if Farrow was privy to the noise as well.

Time seemed to stand still as Simon waited for the ten o'clock hour. He removed the closet floorboard to retrieve the walkie-talkie. Right before ten, the noises from the other room started up again, to which Simon rolled his eyes. He turned the device on at a very low volume. Static.

After a few minutes, Banner could be heard through the device.

"What did you find out?" Simon asked.

"No one in the kitchens has ever made an oatmeal raisin cookie," Banner shared.

"You asked everyone?"

"Yes. I was thorough."

"O.K. Lock Parker up again in Camp J and I'll explain when I see you Friday night. I'm not taking any chances with the upcoming aging out ceremony. If you can keep his whereabouts a secret…do that," Simon finished.

"Will do," Banner agreed.

"Thank you."

Simon shut off the walkie-talkie and put it back. He didn't want to jump to conclusions, but Parker would need to explain a couple things before he'd be released from the cell. And if his answers didn't satisfy Simon's lingering doubts, he'd let Logan do whatever he wanted with him. Logan enjoyed hurting people- he was overdue for a simple beat-down sacrifice.

It upset Simon how much he had come to trust Parker, letting him in his small, but important circle of influence at Angola. They were like brothers to one another. Simon believed Parker to be honest, but no one really understood the depth of Simon's gift. He didn't forget things and easily called up behaviors or conversations in his memory.

Simon couldn't shake some of Earl's last words…that Parker was still keeping something to himself.

Chapter 42

Simon wasted no time when he arrived at Angola, making his way straight to Parker. He told Banner that he'd go alone.

"This is probably nothing," Simon told Banner with a smile, trying to assure himself as well.

When he drove to Camp J, the wind whipped around as rain started to fall. Simon caught a glimpse of the hole in the side of the cell where Jen stayed. It had yet to be repaired. The pang of guilt quietly landed on his shoulders, thinking of Earl more than anyone.

He stopped the cart as a picture of Jen in the shower materialized. He shook off all the unhelpful emotions and memories before making a run for it. The rain pelted down, soaking through his clothes before he arrived at the building.

The sound of the door momentarily interrupted Parker's push-ups. When he glanced at his guest, he continued his exercises. It was a sign of disrespect, but Simon understood being locked up could garner some anger. He'd wait for Parker to engage.

After finishing the set of push-ups, Parker popped up to his feet, shaking his head.

"I don't understand," Parker said. "What the hell is wrong with you? I've done everything you've asked and I pledged my allegiance to this cause!"

Parker spat when he spoke, resentful about his location behind bars. He went on to list things all he had done for Simon, to include the recent work involving the aging out ceremony. Simon didn't doubt Parker's words. He searched his memory, which backed up all of Parker's recent claims. When the aggravation calmed, Parker took a seat in his cell, with his head in his hands.

“I only need to understand a couple things that don’t add up,” Simon quietly remarked. Parker lifted his head, waiting for what came next. “Tell me about the oatmeal cookies the night we left Beaumont.”

Just for a second, a look flashed across Parker’s face that gave him away. Nerves fluttered around in Simon’s stomach because he knew this conversation would either mark a fresh start or a tragic end for the two men. The decision rested with Parker.

Shame quickly replaced the indignant attitude as the prisoner cast his eyes downward. Parker inhaled deeply before letting out a long sigh, and then raising his head to meet Simon’s gaze.

“The cookies were laced with high doses of sleeping medication,” Parker admitted. “Enough to knock someone out even Banner’s size.”

Simon took a seat on the cement bench, positive this would involve further explanation.

Parker snorted. “What happens when I tell you the truth and you don’t like it?”

“I don’t know,” Simon admitted. “But there’s a chance I might like the truth. There’s no chance I’ll like a lie.”

Parker nodded. “When we were on our Beaumont mission, do you remember when I drove Della to Opelousas?”

“Yes. Assume I remember. It’s my thing.”

“Well, I drove fast, barely slowing down when I let her out. I needed to get to Quadra in Lafayette. I had squirreled away some oatmeal cookies in my room.”

Simon squinted, not quite understanding.

“Quadra recruits see a lot of things or are asked to perform tasks that make it hard to sleep. The oatmeal cookies are Quadra's answer to that. Recruits can request a cookie sleeping pill and I had asked for one every night before we went to Beaumont."

"Because you wanted to drug us?" Simon asked.

"Yes," Parker answered easily, shrugging. "My plan was simple. After everyone at the camp was passed out, I'd drive to Lafayette and report that I found the crew that destroyed Beaumont. It wasn't far-fetched because I live up that way. I'd let Quadra also know about Angola and be a hero for years to come."

"You'd been a part of the resistance for so long. Why would you do that?" Simon wondered, heart-broken to hear his intentions.

"I've always loved nature. The beauty is never more captivating as when it's untouched by man. Quadra has helped bring that back."

Simon smiled. "When we stood on the edge of the Mississippi and talked about the wild miles and how the water ran so much fresher than it had in years past. I recognized your love for nature then."

Parker nodded. Simon rose from the bench and grabbed ahold of the bars to Parkers cell.

"I couldn't live two lives anymore," Parker added. "I needed to pick a side…decide which master to serve. And, for a couple months, I thought that would be Quadra." He stood up, pacing. "They get inside your head. They make you believe that they have the citizen's best interest at heart."

"What am I missing?" Simon asked. "All you had to do was alert Quadra and they would have detached our heads from our bodies. As people like to say around here, it would be like shooting fish in a barrel."

"It was Maestro," Parker answered. "Someone must

have given him some sort drug for his pain. I couldn't get him to eat the cookie. He kept spitting it out. I didn't know how much of the drug he had. You guys would be out for at least eight hours, but I had no guarantee how long the meds would stay in his system."

"C'mon, Parker, you could have taken him with you or tied him up. He wasn't going far on a bum ankle."

"It's not that. Clifford started saying that I couldn't kill him…telling me he wouldn't give up without a fight. Then, he launched in to the string of events that he experienced at Cape Canaveral." Parker shook his head, not wanting to repeat the story. "It was hard to believe. But, as much as I wanted it all to be the ranting of a crazy man, he told the tale with such clarity and answered all my questions. If what he said was true, I could never pick Quadra."

"You said "if" what he said was true. Sounds like you weren't convinced."

Parker continued to pace like a caged animal. "No. Not totally. Only because it was such a wild tale, completely foreign to any ideologies I'd experienced before."

"So, then how did you decide? Why haven't you told Quadra about Angola?"

"I let you guys sleep it off and reported back to Lafayette on Monday until I could confirm Maestro's claims."

"How on earth would you be able to do that?"

"When I had a free moment, I went to a local clinic. No patients were around, which made it easier. I wore my Quadra uniform and asked the nurse at reception if I could perform a standard workspace inspection."

"She agreed so I went to her desk, while she took a seat in a chair close by. When I first came into the clinic, I'd dropped a bag of Quadra fertilizer in the entranceway. The monitor at the nurse's desk scanned the bag, just as it does patients. Lo and behold, the bag was riddled with cells identified as human. Small, blue lights glowed on the screen." Parker paused. "I've never been so angry."

Simon didn't doubt Parker's words for a moment. He, himself, had wrestled with which side to choose, so he wouldn't fault him for that…not without proving to be a hypocrite. Simon still held onto the bars, watching Parker contemplate his past choices.

"That's the day I decided to dedicate myself to the resistance. To hell with Quadra!" Parker finished.

Parker shed silent tears, while Simon studied the man before him.

"Thank you, Parker. I know what you said bore truth. You're a smart man and testing the fertilizer was a brilliant move," Simon said, letting go of the bars and taking a couple steps back to sit on the concrete bench. He locked eyes with Parker. "I know you. You wouldn't be shedding a tear unless something else burdened you. Quadra has its hand in various evil deeds, so why did this have such a profound impact?"

Emotionally exhausted, Parker sighed and looked up to the ceiling as though some answers could be found there. He continued to cry.

"My love of nature and all things wild comes from my grandfather," Parker sniffled, before smiling at the thought of the man. "He used to take me out in the woods on camping trips and show me the ropes. It was heaven. His aging out ceremony is next week in Alexandria. I can't let him go, knowing the fate that awaits him."

Simon unlocked the cell. "You go get your grandfather and bring him to Benton Oasis. You can use Angola resources, but I don't want the two of you coming through Angola. If you can find a way to get him there, and I know you can, he's welcome."

Parker enveloped Simon in a hug. "Thank you!"

Parker then grabbed a couple of belongings from the cell and darted past Simon.

"Parker," Simon called.

Parker turned.

"What we spoke of here today…it's never to be repeated."

He nodded before exiting the infamous Camp J.

Parker had never been so thrilled about a mission, a romance or any other life event. He was about to embark on the most meaningful undertaking of his life.

Chapter 43

That weekend at Angola, final plans were solidified for operation "Oasis" as it had come to be known. A replacement driver was selected in Parker's absence and the mission was practiced twice in a full run-through. The only unknown variable would be what kind of Quadra presence they would have to contend with.

Farrow had readied the pokeweed-laced muffin batter and they only needed to be baked and delivered three days before the ceremony. Some muffins would be glazed with additional pokeweed and others would have a normal glaze. This would ensure a variable in the flu-like symptoms. There would even be a few muffins that would be sent with no pokeweed at all.

At the rally on Sunday, Simon extended the Oasis offer to family members of those in the resistance. When the family members were about to age out, they could register to become an Oasis resident. It only seemed fair, given that Parker planned to bring his grandfather there.

The announcement was received with excitement, bolstering Simon's popularity. He also announced that although the cover names had served their purpose, given names could now be used, especially for the residents at Angola that were full time. He introduced himself as Simon and said he'd answer to Rogers or Simon, whichever they preferred.

The drive back to Baton Rouge resembled his time at the banks of Killarney Lake. While he drove, his mind was at peace, helping him to clearly ponder serious matters. He hoped Parker would successfully retrieve his grandfather, that mission Oasis would produce at least one aged, and that

Quadra would find him just useful enough to let him remain at the museum.

He arrived in Baton Rouge a half hour before his escort appointment. After taking a shower, he went to the kitchen to grab a snack. Dani was sipping tea by the window, looking down on the river. He let her enjoy the view in silence, keenly aware that she'd rather not talk to him, given a choice.

Simon kept peeking out of the kitchen, checking the side door for the escort, but she was over a half hour late. The last time he went to check, returning to the kitchen, Dani faced him.

"If you're waiting for your escort, I wouldn't hold your breath," Dani advised.

Simon froze, deciding not to respond. It did nothing but get him in trouble where she was concerned. He blinked, still looking in Dani's direction.

"I tried to schedule one tonight, too. I pay extra for the once a week service, like you do," she explained. "They said that fuel stores are low and it's now required to travel to the hub for any upcoming appointments. I don't know how I'm going to manage that."

Dani seemed stressed over the thought of no more escorts coming to the museum. The fuel shortages were directly related to Simon's actions, but he'd never divulge that information. He also didn't pay extra, but scheduled some appointments as Cass, now that he'd reached legal age. They hadn't caught on, for whatever reason, that Cass had a wife. Simon wasn't going to share that either.

Simon sat down after pouring a glass of water, still silent. Dani sat opposite him.

"You know, there is a reasonable solution to this. Why don't you and I be each other's escorts?" Dani suggested.

Simon's eyebrows shot up at the ludicrous proposition, but he kept his mouth shut. The last time a woman offered herself up in such a way, he had to deal with unwanted drama.

"It's a perfect solution. No strings, no expectations…just sex. At least until the deliveries resume," Dani said, excited about the idea. She pointed to their rooms across from the kitchen. "And the proximity to one another doesn't get any better than that!"

Her smile made Simon smile, but he still wasn't talking or agreeing to her idea.

"Are you not attracted to me? Is that it?"

Simon shook his head no.

Dani walked around the table. "Maybe we won't work well together. Can I try a kiss to see if there's anything there?"

Simon nodded. Dani motioned for Simon to stand and she ran her fingers through his hair, looking into his eyes. Her dark eyes seemed an easy place to get lost. She lightly pressed her lips to his before applying more pressure and barely opening her mouth to lick his lips. Simon's eyes closed, enjoying the unexpected kiss.

He tried to weigh the pros and cons of this situation, but blood slowly left his brain for other regions. He knew this was a seduction…that this may mean trouble for him later. He wrapped his arms around Dani, giving in to the urge to have her. It made sense to be with each other until the escorts could be delivered again. Simon, knowing full well, that day was a long way off.

Dani stepped back from Simon. "Farrow won't be in until tomorrow morning," Dani mentioned, breathing heavy.

She removed her top and shook out of her pants once they were unfastened. Simon finally decided this was a really good idea. Together, they watched the river flow by the museum, while they were pressed against the window. The glass ceiling was observed from different angles of the stairway and the welcome desk had never seen that kind of hospitality.

Dani smacked Simon's behind before disappearing into her room. He realized it was the first time he'd ever been with a woman and never said a word. Before going to sleep, he accepted that this situation would bode well for him instead of spending time going to the hubs or having a woman at Angola. But, like any relationship, only time would tell.

When Simon had gotten up the next morning, Dani was already working on the grounds. Farrow sat in the kitchen, sipping his tea. Simon poured himself a glass and joined him.

"How many tours do we have today, Farrow?"

"Two, but we need to set up for the aging out ceremony soon. No need to wait until the last minute." Farrow got up to leave, pointing at the plate glass window in the kitchen. "Hopefully, someone will clean that window before then."

Simon looked behind him to see the sun lighting up four handprints on the glass, with a body-sized smudge below them. He smiled and grabbed something to clean off the window.

Over the next couple of days, life at the museum carried on as usual. Dani would leave every night and return for the work day. They didn't speak during the day other than a quick hello. If it wasn't for the markings on the window, Simon would wonder if he'd imagined the events of Sunday night.

Quadra sent word that they'd arrive on Friday night for the aging out ceremony on Saturday. This went against typical protocol, but given the attention the fliers garnered, Quadra may have planned extra measures.

Farrow and Simon went over the plans to see if Quadra's early arrival would cause problems. They both thought it wise to have the ceremony set-up early and send Dani home Thursday night for a long weekend.

After the ballroom had the easels, chairs, and buffet tables in place, Dani got ready to leave. She wouldn't argue about an extra day off.

"I'll see you Sunday night, right?" Dani asked Simon before she left.

The question caught him off guard. So much would happen in the following two days. For all he knew, Quadra could have him in custody by Sunday.

"That's the plan," he answered.

Nerves were getting to Simon, wondering if he missed anything, hoping the resistance was one step ahead of Quadra and not the other way around. Momentary fits of sleep dotted his evening until he finally woke in the morning, covered in sweat.

The smell of Farrow's specialty tea wafted into his room. Simon discovered he had overslept, but Quadra wasn't expected until noon, the ceremony had been set up and all tours were cancelled. The fact that it was ten didn't bother Simon because he'd finally calmed. All the bases were covered for this to be a successful mission.

He got out of bed, showering like any other day. He joined Farrow in the kitchen, whose chipper mood was contagious. They clinked tea mugs, toasting to the next forty-eight hours. They hoped to complete many other missions and affect additional change in the area, but this would prove a great first step.

All stress had evolved into a giddy excitement and

anticipation. As time passed and noon came and went, Simon couldn't believe he was frustrated by Quadra's tardiness. He desired to be in their presence which, on any other day, was an unfathomable concept.

The vehicles started to roll into town around 3pm. The sound of the brakes on the bus that would travel to Cape Canaveral let out a loud whoosh when it parked. It gave Farrow butterflies in his stomach. Farrow attended or helped organize so many of these ceremonies, but this weekend he planned to make a real difference. Today would mark the day that the Canaveral tragedy didn't continue unopposed.

The Quadra forces kept coming…twice as many recruits for a typical ceremony. However, when Simon and Farrow saw the shape they were in, they had little to worry about. Between racing to the bathroom, vomiting in the bushes and merely trying to stay upright, they were a sorry sight, indeed. Out of the thirty men and women, roughly five seemed unaffected.

Simon stood between the museum and the garden shack, when he saw Bree exit a transit. She had no symptoms of any illness. Simon didn't understand why she was there because these types of functions aren't attended by the P.O.L.

He could hear her barking orders at the men walking beside her. Before getting inside, she retrieved a muffin from her bag.

Chapter 44

The day of the "Farewell Ceremony" had finally arrived. Quadra always preferred "farewell" in the title opposed to "aging out" because it was more positive and sounded like a celebration.

Simon woke early, teeming with excitement. He went to the loose floorboard in his closet, removing a piece of paper. It was the last thing Jen had done for the resistance- provide a list of attendees and their pick up addresses from the medical records that she gave Quadra.

After a quick shower, Simon went to the kitchen where he found a few struggling recruits and Farrow, enjoying a nice breakfast. Simon got a plate, filling it with eggs and sausage, but his hand hovered over the French toast, concerned it could be tainted.

Farrow saw Simon pause from a nearby table and said, "The French toast is especially good, Simon. Try some."

Simon grinned, stabbing the food with his fork and piled a couple pieces on his plate. His meal was half-eaten when he saw Bree barely able to exit April's old room. She opened the door, but leaned her entire body weight on the casing.

Simon went to see if she needed help. As he got closer, he noticed her complexion had taken on a greenish hue and she'd fallen quite ill. He grabbed her, returning her to bed. She wouldn't want anyone in the unit to see her weak. As soon as she laid down, she wretched in a garbage can she'd placed by the bed. The can appeared to be well-used through the evening.

"I can't stay in bed," Bree whispered. "So much to do…"

Simon admired her drive, but wished she used it for something other than Quadra. "I don't think you're going anywhere today." He placed another pillow under her head.

The sweat soaked through her clothing and there were no empty glasses by her bedside that hinted she was hydrated. Vomiting combined with the sweat had hollowed out her eyes, worrying Simon that she could die from this poisoning.

"You need to drink and I'm going to bring you some plain French toast to soak up the acid that must be in your stomach." Simon got up to leave.

"I've been trying to soak up the acid all night with a muffin someone in my unit gave me. I liked the one I ate yesterday so much, that he gave me his on the ride over."

Simon froze. Two muffins. He didn't turn around, afraid that his expression would betray him. He left the room and searched for Farrow, finally finding him on the bench outside. He sat down beside him.

"She ate two muffins," Simon whispered. "What would happen if she ate two highly-laced muffins?"

With little emotion, Farrow replied, "She'd die."

A couple of recruits came out to ask Farrow about the ballroom and some security concerns. He followed them back into the museum, while Simon stared at the river. He decided to do anything he could to help Bree survive. The mission would soon be underway and Simon had every confidence that his team would pull it off in amazing fashion.

Simon went to his room, retrieving the walkie-talkie. He got Banner on the airwaves and asked him to come by the museum before his first pick-up. Banner delivered the first aid bag that included the pain medicine Simon needed.

A couple recruits asked about Bree when Simon entered

the kitchen to retrieve a large glass of water. He said she didn't want to be disturbed because she couldn't keep anything down. The men understood, having experienced the same illness. Even now, they weren't in top form.

Simon joined Bree in her room, sitting on the edge of her bed. "If you can drink this entire glass of water, I'll give you pain medicine so you can sleep and stop throwing up. You've got to drink it slow."

He handed her the glass as she sat up, leaning against the wall. A half hour passed before the water was gone. She demanded the pain meds to which Simon obliged. Soon, she rested peacefully on the bed. Simon felt as though he'd done all he could.

***

The transits arrived at the homes of the aged between 11-11:30am, before the ceremony started at one. Five transits, manned by members of the resistance, were responsible for four pick-ups each. Twenty aged was a large number, as the ceremonies normally aged out no more than eight or ten people.

Banner met the first passenger on his list, named Anna. She went on and on about how excited she was to finally retire. She awaited the sandy beaches as a welcome respite.

"You haven't seen the fliers about Cape Canaveral all over town?" Banner asked, giving her a chance to voice any concerns.

"Utter hogwash," she insisted.

Banner drove her straight to the museum. He teared up after dropping her off, understanding that her long life would end shortly. But, if people continued to put their faith in Quadra's false promises, they would cease to live, one way or another.

Zan, one of the sisters that headed the mission, picked

up a man named Arnold. He murmured to himself when entering the transit.

"And are you looking forward to retirement?" Zan asked.

"Hell no," Arnold answered. "I'm opting out!"

Zan smiled and drove Arnold to the meeting place, where the aged would soon be transported to Benton Oasis. Heading east on Government Street, the street name changed to Independence Boulevard, where Independence Park was located. The irony was lost on no one. Rosa waited at the park in a transit.

Logan picked up a man named Gordon and asked him if he was looking forward to retirement. It was the standard question they all had been trained to ask.

"What do you think I should do?" Gordon asked.

Logan looked at the man in the rear view mirror, intently staring back. It occurred to him that this man could be a plant for Quadra. Not only did he not answer Logan's question, but he asked a question out of the conversation's context.

Maybe he was a doddering old fool or maybe he was trying to trick Logan, in an attempt to discover his allegiance.

"I haven't thought about it," Logan countered. "I'm not old."

It pained Logan to drop him off, but Gordon didn't clearly communicate a choice. When the passenger's intentions were unclear, they were to be dropped off at the museum.

That morning would see four more people choose to forego Cape Canaveral. A total of five lives saved was reason to celebrate. By the time anyone realized they were missing, the transit already shuttled them safely to Clifford's place.

The other men and women dutifully registered their medical records, food preferences, belongings, allergies, etc. The only information used would be the medical records to determine a final purpose…food for the sea life or the flower beds. After completing registrations, the family members started to show up for the ceremony, some realizing their elderly relative was missing.

Simon and Farrow had figured correctly. Quadra expected the resistance to make a move at the museum, not before the ceremony. Recruits that were well enough, guarded the bus and the drop-offs outside, but they weren't counting the number of aged. If they had, the oversight would have been caught much earlier.

But, they were ill and the unusually warm day made it that much harder to perform their duties well. The recruits scattered around the museum like rats, having no solid plan. When Simon was returning to check on Bree, one of the men in her unit asked to see her. He needed orders.

Simon unlocked the door, but Bree's unresponsive state didn't aid the recruit. He left to join the other rats. Simon got a wash cloth, rinsing it in cool water and placing it on Bree's forehead. Her eyes slowly opened.

"Danny, I've got to get up," Bree slurred, trying to rise off the pillow.

"It's Simon," he corrected, easily pressing her shoulders back toward the bed.

Her eyes grew wide. "Don't worry about Simon. He doesn't even know why we're here."

Simon remembered the story Parker had told him about Clifford on these same drugs and that Clifford shared his darkest memories. Simon suddenly decided to see if Bree would be willing to share some of her honest thoughts or motives.

"Why are we here, again?"

"To take Simon back to Lafayette. But, we've got to be tricky because he's dangerous. Knows a lot of martial arts and stuff. Smart, too, I kinda hate him." Bree rolled over and started a low-volume snore.

Simon gently shook her awake.

"Danny, why aren't you kissing me? We're alone. No one will find out."

Simon found the mere suggestion repulsive, given her current condition. He wasn't sure how long she'd be coherent, so he wanted to make the next few minutes count.

"Simon has done a lot for Quadra while he's been in Baton Rouge," Simon probed.

"Ha! The only thing he's done is find those historical artifacts, I'll give him that. Everything else," she slurred, "full of shit!"

Bree yelled so loud that Simon had to shush her. She mimicked his shush, apologizing.

"What do you think will happen to Simon when he goes to Lafayette?"

"The little prick is gonna get his due. He'll probably be executed. So disrespectful. I'd like to do it myself." She moved her hands around a little. "Probably won't let me."

The light snore returned, but Simon didn't disturb her this time. He went to his room where he gathered a few things, knowing anything left behind could be easily retrieved by Farrow. Out in the hallway, recruits were still in a panic over the missing aged. Searches were being performed in the museum and on the grounds.

Simon radioed Banner, asking how soon he could pick him up. Banner gave him an ETA of twenty minutes. In the chaos, Simon walked out of the museum, heading north.

Banner picked him up a couple blocks away.

After shutting the door to the vehicle, Simon looked over at Banner.

"Let's go home."

Chapter 45

When Bree woke up from her near-death experience a couple days later, Simon was long gone. Farrow still can't keep a straight face when he relays the story, to anyone in the resistance, of the day Bree asked after Simon. Farrow took pleasure when informing Bree that Simon left, having no plans to return. He'd always say, "She got madder than a wet hen!"

Bree discovered a note in her bag, while traveling back to Lafayette. It read:

I took care of you when you were ill. In your delirium, you spoke about many interesting topics.

You came to the ceremony to bring me back to Lafayette, hoping to kill me. You were obviously screwing a subordinate (I'm 100% sure his name is Danny) and there were other juicy tidbits that Quadra might appreciate knowing...

If you look for me, I'll ruin you.

Have the life you deserve,

S

Bree didn't divulge additional information, but human nature guaranteed she had more dark secrets. Just to be sure she didn't go unscathed, Simon sent an anonymous letter to Quadra, thanking officer Denton for warning him that Quadra wanted him pulled from the post. That would keep her busy for a while.

Simon settled into Angola, happy to no longer commute back and forth to Baton Rouge. The fields yielded so much bounty during spring and summer that the entire Angola community pitched in to assist with harvesting the crops. Now that there would be more mouths to feed at the Benton Oasis, every little bit helped.

Parker safely got his grandfather, Ollie, to Clifford's the day after the aging out ceremony. It took some doing because Ollie insisted on bringing his bee hives with him. Parker got stung no less than a dozen times during the trip.

When the six new residents of the Oasis had settled in, Clifford gathered them around the fire pit one night, briefing them about his time at Cape Canaveral. Many of the aged were motivated to go into town, bringing friends and family back, well before they aged out. They spread the word.

Other than the constant bickering between Arnold and Clifford, the community grew over time and remained peaceful. A couple of the aged worked on journaling history, with Simon visiting once a month to confirm the records.

Simon would visit his good friend Farrow during his trips, but they'd meet away from the museum. Between the tours and Dani, he couldn't be seen. Simon's absence merely inconvenienced Dani because she had to start traveling to the hubs. Other than that, he wasn't missed.

In Baton Rouge, the resistance had managed to get someone posted in the clinic that had worked at the Angola hospital. The qualifications were that they would funnel patient information back to the resistance and be willing to sleep with Dr. Michon, if needed. Surprisingly, three women initially volunteered.

The new post at Dr. Michon's identified people close to aging out and they would be contacted at differing times to get a read on their retirement intentions. This plan proved less dangerous than shuttling aged around the day of the ceremony. Quadra's lack of effectiveness couldn't be guaranteed every time with tainted muffins.

The next goal for the resistance was to destroy the factories making drugs that went into the food for citizens. The locations had yet to be identified, but Farrow's wife had intercepted some recipe drug additions at her factory with varying success.

Banner and Logan were still in charge of Angola security and did a fabulous job. They were dating two sisters, but no one could talk about it because they were the daughters of the man who owned the Angola property. Simon, Parker and others were convinced things would end badly, but both men claimed to be in love so they were not accepting any solid, common sense advice.

Simon, on one of his many trips to the Oasis, went to drop his overnight bag into the container. He recognized the brunette hair immediately even though she wasn't facing toward him. She placed folded clothes in a suitcase.

"April?" he questioned, hoping to be right.

When April turned around, they both smiled, hugging one another- the bump between them evident. Simon loosened his grip, looking down at her stomach.

"Congratulations!" Simon said.

The enthusiasm was forced and uncomfortable. Seeing her again made him long for impossible things.

"Thanks. I've got four more months to go," she said. "Listen, I'm so sorry I don't have all my stuff packed up. Grandpa said that you were coming this weekend and I planned to be gone before you got here." She continued to pack the suitcase.

"Is your husband here?"

"God, no. He can't ever know about this place."

Simon lightly touched April's hands to stop her from packing.

"You mean you didn't even want to say hello?" Simon

asked, pained by the notion.

"What good would that do?" She answered, barely in a whisper. "I really need to get back to packing."

Simon took a step in front of her, standing within inches. He didn't want the feelings to be real, but his heart beat loudly. He touched her arm, waiting for April to look at him...even for a moment. But when she finally met his gaze, Simon caught flashes of fear. He understood why she felt the need to hurry off. Had Simon known she was there, he would have avoided this, too.

"What you've helped to accomplish here is so amazing, Simon," April complemented.

Hearing his name from her lips made his stomach flip. Simon leaned toward April, his head by hers. Looking at her proved difficult.

"Are you happy?" He whispered.

"I am."

Her answer brought a small grin to Simon's lips.

"I better let you get back to your packing," he said, kissing her cheek for much too long.

He went to leave the container, but when he got to the door, he turned for one last look because something told him this was goodbye.

"I just want you to know that you are the first and only woman I've ever loved."

No response came. He didn't need one. He'd done his best to let her know what she meant to him. April never faced Simon, but continued packing as she hushed her sobs.

Simon went out to the barn to grab some breakfast. A little boy held Rosa's finger as they walked around the tables. Simon filled his plate, taking a seat.

"Can you hold him while I get some food?" Rosa asked.

Simon didn't have much choice in the matter because

Rosa plopped the tyke in Simon's lap. The little boy smiled up at Simon, as he stole bits of food off his plate. Simon awkwardly gave the boy just enough support so he didn't fall to the ground.

When Rosa came back, Simon quickly handed the boy back, making Rosa giggle. She took a seat opposite Simon. The boy continued to steal off her plate. Maybe he'd grow up to be a thief, Simon thought, but he needed a little work on his sleight-of-hand. Simon stole a piece of bacon off Rosa's plate, making the young boy giggle.

Clifford walked over, retrieving the boy off Rosa's lap.

"It's time for this little one to get back home," Clifford said.

The boy wrapped his arms around Clifford's neck and it was evident that his heart melted at the gesture.

"That boy has reduced Clifford to quite the softy," Rosa said.

"He's a cutie. The boy, not Clifford, just to be clear," Simon said, smiling. "Whose son is he?"

Rosa looked up at Simon, pausing before answering his question. "That's Clifford's great-grandson."

It didn't take Simon long to figure out that he must be April's son. Cass and his wife were unable to conceive. He stared across the table at Rosa. She looked back, willing him to ask more questions.

"How old is he?"

"About 14 months." Rosa kept her gaze in Simon's direction, while Simon ate a few more bites of breakfast.

Simon slowly did the math. April probably conceived on her wedding night. Simon remembered the face of the boy…so familiar. He didn't understand why April wouldn't mention her son or introduce the two. There could be only one reason for that.

Simon posed a final question to Rosa, "What's the little boy's name?"

Rosa grinned. "His name is Benton. Benton Simon Wallace."

Simon leapt from the table, running toward the property's entrance. Clifford stood by the gate, waving, as a car disappeared from sight. Only the plume of dirt that rose from the tires was still visible. Simon went to unlatch the gate, but Clifford stopped him.

"No, son, this is for the best," Clifford assured.

Simon had run so fast to the gate that he couldn't call up words to counter Clifford's argument. Simon bent over, trying to catch his breath. Clifford put his hand on Simon's shoulder until his breathing slowed and he could stand upright again. Simon screamed to the heavens, tormented by this new knowledge.

Simon pointed down the road. "Was that my son?"

"Yep," Clifford calmly answered, noticing Simon's pained expression. "I'm glad you got to meet 'im."

"Let me go after them," Simon said, going toward the gate again.

"Your place is here and at Angola. Benton has a family…he has what he needs."

"But…" Simon trailed off, unable to finish the thought.

Clifford put his arm around Simon, leading him away from the gate.

"If you want to make a difference in that boy's life, you keep opposing Quadra…continue forging a path for him to be free of their tyranny, control and lies. Give him hope and history," Clifford encouraged. "He'll never have any of that without you."

Simon nodded, knowing what Clifford said to be true. This little light of a child would surely motivate him to accomplish great things. He had the best reason of all to strive for a better future.

Both men walked on, misty-eyed.

"He's a handsome little guy," Simon said, swallowing hard to fight back tears.

"Just beautiful…"

Other titles by TL Harty:

The Line of Enya series:

Behold Ellowee
Danu
Scotia's Grave
(Book Four Coming Soon)

Ass in a Ditch

Made in the USA
Monee, IL
02 July 2021

71908232R00184